Anna's Courage

By Kristin Noel Fischer

Dear Reader,

If you read my previous book *A Mother's Choice*, you know I'm a romantic at heart. While the journey may be painful, I guarantee love will prevail, and there will always be a happy ending.

Anna's Courage is a love story between two people who meet during a difficult time in their lives. Anna and Nick's story first came to me when my husband deployed with the army. At that time, we had six children under the age of 10. Needless, to say, it was one of the most difficult times in our lives. Even though I prayed all the time, I woke up every morning sick to my stomach with worry.

While this book is not about deployment, it does touch on the sacrifices of military life. Most importantly, however, it emphasizes the truth that family, friendship, and faith can sustain and uphold you when life knocks you down.

For this reason, I dedicate *Anna's Courage* to military wives everywhere, but especially the women on Hano Court at Ft. Hood, Texas. Your love, strength, fidelity, and outstanding margarita-making skills strengthened me more than you can ever imagine.

All my love,

Kristin Noel Fischer

The best way to stay in touch is to subscribe to my New Books Newsletter. Go to www.KristinNoel.com and subscribe.

Acknowledgements

Thank you to everyone who helped with this book! My editors Valerie Walker, Chrissy Wolfe, and Liza Tice. My beta readers Cerrissa Kim, Kari Trumbo, Joe Fischer, Beth Roberts, and Jeanne Smith.

Special thanks to helicopter pilot Chuck Tully, Jr. You're more helpful than a YouTube video!

The Killion group created my beautiful cover and Paul Salvette formatted the book.

Thank you to my brother-in-law Dick Fischer, the best Santa I ever met. The Santa scene is for you!

Thank you Alice Liu Cook who read an earlier version of the book and fell in love with Nick all those years ago. Your question about whatever happened to that hot military guy gave me the inspiration to finish this book!

Thanks to Mindy Miller who talked to me about a difficult decision regarding this manuscript.

Thanks to my agent, the wonderful Emily Sylvan Kim, who boosted my confidence by believing in Nick and Anna's story.

As always, love and hugs to my husband and our six gorgeous children. And thanks, Mom and Dad!

Anna's Courage

Rose Island Book 1

Chapter 1

Nick

New Year's Eve – Rose Island, Texas

WANTING TO ESCAPE the loud New Year's Eve party, I stepped outside and strode across the wooden deck of my brother's beach house. Ocean waves crashed against the Texas Gulf Coast as I leaned against the railing and inhaled the warm, salty air.

Tomorrow at this time, I'd fly back to my army post in Germany. Back to the life I knew and loved. The life I'd always wanted.

Yet, for the first time, I found myself envying my older brother Ethan. What would it be like to live on this peaceful island and work a stable civilian job? To have a wife and kids?

Shaking my head, I pushed the thought far away. Domestic life on Rose Island, or anywhere else, had never been part of my career plan. Never been something I'd wanted.

Startled by a noise behind me, I turned to see Anna

Morgan sitting on a bench against the house. Had she been here the whole time, watching me contemplate the meaning of my life?

Even though she had no way of reading my thoughts, I was embarrassed and scrambled for something clever to say but went with the lame, "Are you enjoying the party?"

She wiped away a tear, making me want to kick myself. I should've commented on the beautiful night. On the full moon. On the deafening music. Of course she wasn't enjoying the party. She was sitting alone on a bench, crying.

"Your brother and his wife really know how to entertain, don't they?" she said, putting on a brave smile.

I glanced inside at the conga line weaving around the living room furniture and elaborately decorated tables laden with appetizers and desserts. Over the music, the DJ's boisterous voice shouted, "Forty-five minutes until midnight, y'all!"

The crowd raised their drinks and shrieked so loudly I feared the wall of glass windows would shatter. Tired of the commotion, I turned back to Anna. We'd met earlier tonight, and without a doubt, she had the warmest smile and softest blue eyes.

Unfortunately, she fell into the category of women I avoided at all costs—single mothers.

"Is everything okay?" I asked, stepping closer.

She waved a dismissive hand. "Don't worry about

me. Apparently, I'm being overly sentimental."

"Oh?"

She held up her phone. "I just talked to my son. We have a silly New Year's Eve tradition, but he'd rather stay at his friend's house than humor his mother for thirty seconds."

Curious, I stepped closer. "What's the tradition?"

"Nothing, really." She gave a soft, self-deprecating laugh. "Just something we've been doing since he was three."

I liked the gentle sound of her laughter and how she didn't take herself too seriously despite being upset. "Tell me about your tradition."

She studied me carefully. Was I worthy of such knowledge? Apparently, I passed the test because she nodded and said, "Okay. We stand on the couch and hold hands. At exactly midnight, we jump into the air and shout, 'Into the garbage chute, flyboy!' It's his favorite line from—"

"Star Wars," I finished, taken aback by the eagerness in my voice. "I know. I can quote every line of that movie."

"So can Travis." She smiled again, giving my stomach that fluttering feeling of anticipation similar to what I experienced every time I jumped out of an airplane. If I were a wise man, I'd politely excuse myself and return to the safety of the party, because as much as I enjoyed this exchange with Anna, it didn't change the fact she had a kid.

That probably sounded harsh, but I'd never felt comfortable around kids. My niece was fun, but most kids scared me. A single woman with kids? Now, that type of woman downright terrified me.

I'd never admitted this aloud, but long ago, I'd vowed *never* to become a parent. Growing up, I'd been abandoned by my mother and ignored by my father. Not that I wanted anyone to feel sorry for me. My mother left when I was a baby, so I didn't even remember her, and my father hadn't been abusive, just highly focused on his career, proving you shouldn't mix family with ambition.

No, children and their single mothers would only complicate my military aspirations. Besides, I felt sorry for those kids who were dragged around the world, forced to change schools and leave their old friends behind. It didn't seem fair to them.

"Don't let me keep you from the party," Anna said, bringing me out of my reverie.

"You're not." I smiled, then, against my better judgment, I sat beside her and did the one thing I knew I shouldn't.

I asked more about her life with her son.

Her face brightened at the question, and she told me all about nine-year-old Travis, the smartest, most talented, greatest kid to walk the face of the earth. Anna lived next door with her son in the little turquoise beach cottage called The Blue Crab. And yes, the cottage was as *adorable* as it sounded—black shutters, colorful flowers in pots, and a porch swing with comfy pillows. The Blue Crab was as cozy and charming as my brother's nameless house was sleek and modern.

"Have you enjoyed being back in the states for the holidays?" she asked. "Ethan said you'll take command when you return."

"That's right. Being here has been fantastic, but I'm excited to begin the new challenge." I sat back and gazed up at the stars in order to keep from wondering if Anna's shoulder-length blond hair felt as silky as it looked. I'd never been intimidated by beautiful women, but there was a sweetness to her that made me nervous.

She continued asking about my job, where I'd received my training, and my past deployments. Because her father was active duty and she'd grown up as a military dependent, she knew a lot about the army.

Without even trying, we fell into an easy, relaxed discussion about the military and our experiences on different posts. When she admitted her disdain of eating eel in Japan, I grinned. "It actually tastes good, but I imagine a kid might find it disgusting."

She nodded. "I used to have vivid nightmares about eel replacing all my favorite foods . . . eel burgers, eel pizza, eel enchiladas."

I laughed, completely understanding the power of nightmares. "Why do some dreams feel so real?"

"I don't know, but after you wake up, does it ever take you a minute to convince yourself it was only a dream?"

"Yes," I answered, feeling an instant connection with her. "When I first became an officer, I had a dream that I lined up for formation only to realize I'd forgotten my boots. The whole time I was praying nobody would notice my bare feet."

She gave an amused smile. "That sounds like the military equivalent of going to school in your under-wear."

We both laughed and something inside me shifted. A sort of loosening and tightening all at the same time. An uncomfortable sensation, but not necessarily a bad one.

Over the music came the DJ's rowdy voice. "Ladies and gentlemen, it's almost midnight, so grab someone you love and help me count it down. Ten, nine, eight, seven, six . . ."

An awkward silence passed between us. I stared down at my hands, wanting to take Anna in my arms and kiss her. Instead, I came to my feet and climbed onto the bench. She gave me an odd look, but I held out my hand. "Come on. I think this will make a good launch pad for your New Year's tradition."

A sly smile grazed her lips, and she hesitated a second before kicking off her sandals, clasping my hand, and joining me on the bench. All across the island, alarms blared, announcing the midnight hour. I squeezed Anna's hand, and together, we leapt into the air, shouting, "Into the garbage chute, flyboy!"

We landed on our feet, both of us cracking up.

Her blue eyes danced as they locked on mine. "Happy New Year, Nick."

A sizzle of excitement knocked the wind out of me, and I swallowed the unexpected lump in my throat. "Happy New Year, Anna."

For a moment, neither one of us moved. Then, without forethought or caution, I leaned forward and brushed my lips across hers.

She gave a sharp inhale, and I expected her to move away, but she surprised me by leaning closer to kiss me again. Her arms wrapped around my waist, igniting a fire deep inside me. I ran my hands through her hair to discover it was even softer and smoother than I'd imagined.

You've been waiting for this woman your whole life.

Before I could analyze or freak out about that absurd thought, Anna pushed me away. "I'm sorry," she said, stepping back to distance herself. Her eyes were wide, and she shook her head. "I didn't mean for that to happen."

"It's okay." I smiled, mostly because I couldn't help it, but I also wanted her to know it wasn't a big deal. I wasn't looking for anything. Whatever she wanted from me was okay. I just wanted her to stay. Just wanted to continue our conversation and enjoy this evening together.

"I have to go."

"What?" My head spun. "Why? Don't leave. I'm sorry I kissed you, but—"

"Good-bye, Nick." She turned and strode down the steps that led to the beach.

"*Anna.*"

Without a backward glance, she raced along the seashell path toward her cottage. A strong ocean wind whipped through the dunes, practically knocking over her slim body, but she kept running. When she reached her home, she bolted up the porch steps, flung open the door, and disappeared inside.

I clenched my fist and pounded the railing in slow motion. *Way to go, Casanova. You really have a way with the ladies.*

Loud music poured from my brother's house, and I glanced over my shoulder to see Ethan and Ivana step onto the porch. My brother placed his hand on the small of his pregnant wife's back and guided her across the deck.

"Happy New Year," Ivana said, standing on tiptoes to kiss my cheek.

I forced a smile. "Yeah. Happy New Year."

My brother grinned. "You weren't scaring away the neighbors were you?"

I glanced at Anna's house and shook my head. "Of

course not."

"That wasn't you putting the moves on Anna Morgan?" Ethan's eyes twinkled with mischief.

I shrugged, pretending I had no idea what he was talking about. "No."

My sister-in-law's face scrunched into that pitiful *Oh, Nick* look. Sighing, she patted my arm. "I can understand why you like Anna Morgan. She's very sweet and pretty, but she's an army widow. Her husband was killed in action several years ago, so she doesn't date soldiers."

"She doesn't date *anybody*," Ethan said, sounding put off. "We tried to set her up, but she wasn't interested."

Ivana rubbed her round baby belly. "She's still in love with her husband."

I glanced over at Anna's cottage, empathizing with her loss. Despite my desire to stay unattached and focused on my career, I'd felt an intense emotional connection to her. And when we kissed . . . well, as corny as it sounded, it'd been a long time since I'd felt an attraction like that.

Ethan nudged his wife. "How long would you mourn for me if I died?"

"Don't talk like that," she scolded. "Don't even go there!"

My brother tossed an arm over his wife's shoulder. "I'm sorry, sweetheart. I shouldn't mess with a pregnant woman like that. How about I bring you another slice of your renowned caramel turtle cheesecake?"

Suppressing a smile, Ivana jabbed Ethan in the ribs and rolled her eyes. "You're only offering because you want a piece for yourself."

"Hey, the baby's hungry." He placed a hand over his own belly, which had expanded alongside his wife's pregnancy. Yesterday, I'd asked when he was due, and he'd tackled me to the floor like we were kids instead of grown men with successful careers.

"I'll get the cheesecake," I said, heading back inside in order to distance myself from my brother's happy marriage, this peaceful island, and the woman who'd captured my heart tonight.

Chapter 2

Anna

Eleven Months Later

HOLDING MY MORNING cup of coffee in one hand and my son's stubborn tabby cat in the other, I stepped onto the sand-covered back deck of my beach house. I placed Felix on the ground, only to have him mock me by darting back inside. Defeated, I took a sip of my coffee and looked up at the gray sky. Such depressing weather for such a depressing day.

Rain wasn't predicted for Rose Island today, but the smell of rain hung in the air. Besides, didn't funerals require miserable weather to match the mourners' somber moods? Closing my eyes, I offered a quick prayer asking God to comfort the Peterson family on this difficult day.

My son wandered onto the porch and snuggled next to me. I pulled him close and kissed the top of his reddish-brown hair, still mussed from sleep. I loved the innocent smell of Travis in the morning. Loved how

Pert shampoo and Dove soap from his evening bath clung to him. Later, he would reek of elementary school pizza, dodge balls, and wet sneakers, but right now, he smelled delicious.

"Hey, isn't that Hailey's Uncle Nick?" Travis asked, pointing down the beach.

I followed his direction to see Nick Peterson running along the shore in shorts and a West Point T-shirt. My breath involuntarily hitched at the sight of him.

Travis looked up and crinkled his brow. "What's wrong, Mom? Indigestion?"

Embarrassed, I tousled his hair. "No, nothing like that. Let's go back inside for breakfast, okay?" Clamping down on my emotions, I turned away before Nick came close enough that I'd be forced to say hello. I'd have to face him soon enough at the funeral.

Inside, Travis and I sat at the sturdy, wooden kitchen table my husband and I had bought from a garage sale shortly before he died. The surface was now marked with gouges and cup rings. Recently, my sister-in-law Bianca suggested sanding down the table and re-staining it, but I wasn't ready yet. Maybe next year. Maybe never.

Despite the unease in my stomach, I sprinkled walnuts over my oatmeal and forced myself to eat.

It'd been nearly a year since I'd last spoken to Nick. He'd called before returning to Germany, asking if we could write, but I told him no. Honestly, I liked him a lot and that tender kiss we'd shared at midnight had been wonderful, but Nick was a soldier. And I would *never* get involved with another soldier. *Never.* I couldn't do that to Travis, and I definitely couldn't do that to myself.

Seven years had passed since I stood on my in-law's front porch, listening to the army's casualty notification officers explain how my husband had bravely made the ultimate sacrifice for our country.

I should've been somewhat healed by now, but losing Marcus had broken me. Destroyed me. His death had left an enormous hole in my life, making me feel years older than twenty-nine.

Travis took a sip of his orange juice. "I guess Hailey's Uncle Nick came back for the funeral."

"I guess so." My gut twisted. My next door neighbors, Ethan and Ivana Peterson, had died in a horrible car accident last week, leaving behind two daughters: ten-year-old Hailey and her baby sister Gabby. My heart broke for the Peterson family, but it also broke for myself as the memories of losing Marcus inundated me.

A loud drop of rain smacked against the window. I pulled my bathrobe tight, wishing Travis and I could stay home today drinking hot chocolate and watching old movies. This weather was perfect for a *Star Wars* marathon. Or endless episodes of *House Hunters*. I had an unnatural obsession with *House Hunters* and felt a personal interest in making sure each family found their perfect three-bedroom, two-bath dream home.

"Can we turn on the heater?" Travis asked, shivering dramatically. "I'm freezing."

"Good idea." I walked over to the thermostat and flipped the switch from cool to heat. It was early November, but yesterday, we ran the air-conditioning all afternoon. Today would be the first time I turned on the heat this fall. That was Texas for you. Hot one day and cold the next.

Feeling warm air flow from the vent, I snuck a quick glance out the kitchen window just in time to see Nick disappear through the dunes toward his brother's house. *Still good-looking as ever,* I noted, finding it impossible to ignore the broad shoulders, narrow waist, and muscular thighs. Was there a reason he had to be so good-looking?

The cat wound his way through my legs, and I gently nudged him aside before rejoining my son at the kitchen table.

Frowning, Travis pushed up his thick glasses, smudged with all sorts of boy gunk. "What's that smell?" he asked, panic lacing his voice.

"Just my coffee."

His face grew serious, and he shook his head. "No, that *fire* smell. Is the house on fire?"

My pulse quickened. Was that smoke I smelled? Gripping my mug tighter, I imagined an old wire burning in the attic and the ancient beach house bursting into flames.

Forcing myself to remain calm, I exhaled slowly. While the cottage had been built years ago and didn't meet today's standards for new construction, the fire inspector had assured me running the heater was safe. Besides, my in-laws owned the house, and they would never allow us to live here if it was unsafe.

Reaching out, I patted my son's hand. "Hey, everything's fine. That smell is just dust in the vent. It will burn off eventually. This happens every year when we run the heater for the first time, remember?"

His face grew pale with a fear that'd exploded since the Petersons' accident. He started coming into my bedroom in the middle of the night, refusing to sleep in his own room. And last night, he wet the bed. Something he hadn't done in years.

"Turn it off," he demanded.

"Travis—"

"No! I'd rather be cold than die in a fire."

Giving in to his fear, I returned to the thermostat and shut it off. Guilt overwhelmed me because I'd been the one to make him fearful and neurotic.

I tried to hide my own anxiety, but underneath my calm demeanor, I was a complete basket case. I didn't want to live in fear, and I certainly didn't want to pass on my anxiety issues to Travis. Marcus wouldn't have wanted that.

Before my husband's death, I'd worked as a part-time helicopter pilot, ferrying tourists all over the island. I'd loved the challenge of flying and interacting with new people. I'd also enjoyed the flexible hours, not to mention the decent income.

Losing Marcus, however, changed that. Since his death, I hadn't been able to drive through the gates of the airfield, let alone think about flying again. Constant unease dominated my thoughts. I worried about everything from Travis getting hit by the garbage truck to running out of money. The recent deaths of my neighbors only exacerbated matters, reminding me of life's fragility.

I knew my reaction to stressful situations had a profound impact on Travis, and for that reason, I'd sought help for my anxiety via therapy, acupuncture, prayer, and medication. But nothing worked.

Several times a week, I'd awake in the middle of the night, my heart pounding and impending doom coursing through my veins. I'd turn on my light, read my Bible, and pray to God for healing. While that helped, the struggle continued.

For Travis's sake, I needed to relax. I needed to cling to my faith and believe God would not abandon me. But knowing what to do and doing it were two separate tasks I seemed incapable of accomplishing.

Swallowing, I started to tell Travis that everything would be fine, but fear stopped me. Things weren't always fine. People died. The world was a dangerous place. Death unexpectedly swooped in and took away the people you loved. And sometimes, no matter how much you begged, prayed, or cried, there was nothing you could do to prevent disaster.

"What time are you picking me up for the funeral?" Travis asked, returning to his breakfast now that the threat of fire had passed.

I rubbed my bare foot across the braided rug underneath the kitchen table. My mother and I had made the rug while I was pregnant with Travis, and it always comforted me. "I'll pick you up after lunch, but are you sure you want to go to school today? You could come and hang out at the salon with me this morning."

He shook his head. "No, thanks."

Wanting to keep him close to me today, I resorted to bribery. "I bet Aunt Bianca will snag a donut for you from Vicki's Bakery. Maybe the chocolate one with sprinkles you like so much?"

The donut comment caused him to pause, but he pressed his lips together and shook his head again. "Don't make fun of me, okay? But I *need* to go to school today."

I studied him carefully. "Why would I tease you for going to school? I think that's very admirable."

He tapped his spoon against the edge of his bowl and bit his bottom lip. Nervous lip biting was another bad habit he'd learned from me. "Hailey's missed a lot of school, and when she finally comes back, she's going to need my help getting caught up with her homework. Fifth grade is hard, and if I don't go to school, I won't be able to help her."

I melted at my son's explanation. "Honey, that's so sweet. Why would you think I'd make fun of you for something like that?"

He groaned and buried his face in his hands. "Because everyone says that I like her. But I don't. She's my friend, and I want to help her, but I don't *like* her."

I smiled, finally understanding the problem. "All that matters is you're a good friend, and she needs a friend like you right now."

"Who's going to take care of her and Gabby now that their parents are gone?" he asked, tossing a grape into the air and catching it in his mouth without choking.

I promptly covered his hand with mine. "Don't. That's dangerous."

"*Mom.*"

I gave him my sternest look. "Kids choke on grapes all the time. I was just reading on Yahoo News—"

He moaned. "Grandpa says the news isn't always true."

Ignoring his comment, I shifted the conversation back to Hailey and Gabby. "To answer your question, I don't know who will take care of the girls. I assumed their cousins in San Antonio would, but I've heard talk of other arrangements. One of my clients said the will named Nick legal guardian."

"You mean he's going to be Hailey and Gabby's new dad?"

My son's voice was so full of hope I hated to disappoint him, but how could an unmarried army officer take care of two little girls? Besides, from conversations with Ivana, I had the impression Nick wasn't interested in being a father. So, why had they given him custody?

I set down my coffee mug. "I don't think Nick is going to be the girls' new dad."

Travis's face fell before brightening with an idea. "Maybe they could live with us. I could share a room with you, and the girls could have my room."

I smiled at my son's generosity. He had such a kind spirit, just like his father and the rest of the Morgan clan. "I know you want to help Hailey and Gabby, but they can't move in with us."

"Why not?"

"They just can't, honey."

Concern marred his innocent eyes. "Will they have to go to an orphanage?"

"No, I'm sure their uncle will find other relatives to take them."

Travis's brow furrowed, and he tapped his spoon a little faster. "What would happen if you died? Where would I go?"

"Oh, sweetheart." I hated that the thought had crossed his mind. "You'd go live with one of your aunts.

Or your grandparents. But I'm not going to die. I promise."

His eyes narrowed. "Isn't that what Dad told you before he left last time?"

I shivered. "Your father had a very dangerous job as an infantry soldier. I cut hair for a living, and last time I checked, people don't die from carpal tunnel syndrome or sore feet."

My attempt to lighten the mood fell flat. Travis picked up the cat and ruffled its ears. "Hailey's mom didn't have a job, and she still died. People die even when they aren't doing anything dangerous."

How could I argue with logic like that? Life was dangerous, but it was my job to keep Travis safe. To create a bubble of protection around him and never allow anything to harm him. That's why I'd stayed on the island with my in-laws after Marcus died.

And that's why I would never leave the island, or fly, or do anything to jeopardize the sheltered life I'd built for my son and myself.

Chapter 3

Nick

I HADN'T INTENDED to run past Anna's house. I'd simply wanted to clear my head and take a break from my father and nieces. Seeing Anna standing on her back porch, albeit from a distance, was a welcome gift on this painful day.

How was I supposed to survive the loss of my brother and sister-in-law? Ethan and Ivana had been a source of strength and stability in my life. And except for my father, they'd been my only family.

To my bewilderment, the will had named me legal guardian for the girls. Why me, I had no idea. Then again, who else was there? Other than a cousin, Ivana didn't have any other family and Ethan only had me.

One of my army buddies had asked if I'd thought about keeping the girls myself. Of course, I had, but what did I know about being a father? I could make life and death decisions concerning my soldiers all day long, but taking care of two little girls? I didn't even know where to start.

No, Hailey and Gabby deserved a better home than I could provide. They deserved a father and a mother who didn't run off to war every few years. Somehow, I would find the perfect family to love and care for them.

Blood pounded against my skull as I raced up the porch steps of my brother's house. Today, I would lay Ethan and Ivana to rest. My soul ached, but I was determined to be strong. After all, nobody wanted to see a soldier cry.

Taking a deep breath, I pushed open the back door and found Gabby screaming alone in her playpen. I'd only been in Texas a few days, but already my ears rang from the baby's constant crying. Was there something wrong with her, or did she simply miss her parents?

Crossing the kitchen, I picked her up and awkwardly bounced her in my arms. "It's okay. Where's your grandpa? Did he feed you already?"

In response, the baby's cries grew stronger.

"Dad?" Cradling Gabby, I strode into the family room where my father stood in front of the large screen TV, holding a bottle of formula. His eyes were glued to the news coverage of Governor Williams and the first lady dancing at some fundraiser.

Anger snaked up my spine. Dealing with a screaming baby wasn't easy, but you'd think someone called *Grandpa* Jack would at least make an effort. "Dad, hand me the bottle."

Slowly, he turned around, his face grief-stricken. The skin under his eyes drooped, and his mouth trembled. He'd never been an overly involved or affectionate father, but at that moment, I realized how devastated he was by the loss of his eldest son and daughter-in-law.

Softening my tone, I asked again for the bottle, and he handed it to me. I offered it to Gabby and was grateful when she stopped crying long enough to guzzle it down. Last night, I'd accidentally screwed the lid on incorrectly, infuriating the child so much she'd slammed the bottle on the floor making a huge mess.

Now, she looked peaceful, staring up at me with curious eyes. To my surprise, she placed a chubby hand on my chin and grinned. I grinned back, feeling calmness spread through me. When Gabby wasn't screaming her head off, she was a real sweetheart.

On the TV, the governor's wife crinkled her mouth as if tasting something disgusting. My commanding officer had once chastised me for the same gesture, insisting it made me look nervous and weak. From that point forward, I'd tried to always look confident, even when I didn't know what I was doing.

My father turned off the TV and studied Gabby for a minute. I thought he might try to explain why he'd left her in the kitchen by herself. Maybe her screaming had gotten the best of him and he needed to take a break.

Instead, he tucked his sadness and all other emotion away by reverting to his usual mode of cold efficiency. "I have a conference call in five minutes that I need to take from my car, so I'll meet you at the funeral."

I shouldn't have been surprised it was business as usual for my father today. Jack was a workaholic whose quest for wealth and success never ended. While I had high ambitions of my own, at least I'd never been irresponsible enough to bring children into the mix.

My father straightened his tie. "I need you to talk some sense into Hailey. She's upstairs throwing a fit because I told her she can't wear jeans to the funeral. Have her wear the black dress Gina sent."

Gina was my father's latest fiancée—a cocktail waitress about the same age as me. Although I'd never met her, I assumed she was like the previous fiancées— gorgeous in looks, but empty on the inside and only interested in my father's money.

"Nick? Are you listening?" He shot me the *disapproving-Jack-Peterson* look he'd perfected over the years.

Gritting my teeth, I nodded. I'd seen enough death to know people processed grief differently, but my father's focus on work and appearances today made me sick to my stomach. Of course, at this point in my life, I should be used to my father disappointing me.

As Jack turned and walked out the door, Gabby removed the bottle from her mouth. "Bye, bye," she said, opening and closing her hand.

I shook my head in disgust. "Bye, bye, indeed."

She chuckled and shoved the bottle back in her mouth. I shifted her to my hip, ascended the staircase, and knocked on my oldest niece's bedroom door.

"What?" Hailey called, her voice angry and irritated.

"It's Uncle Nick. Can I come in?"

"I guess."

I pushed open the door and found her sitting on the floor, her back pressed against the bed. Her knees were pulled to her chest, and her face was buried in her arms. At her feet laid a pile of crumpled tissue.

"*Hailey*," I said, my heart crumbling. I crossed the room and sank to the floor beside her.

The baby offered her older sister the bottle, but Hailey shook her head. "No, Gabby. Don't."

I lifted Gabby and plopped her on the other side of me. Glancing cautiously at Hailey, I asked, "How are you doing, honey?"

"*Great, Uncle Nick,*" she said sarcastically, glaring at me. "Just great. Never better."

I blew out a slow breath. I understood her hostility. God had no right to take her parents from this world. As a child, I'd received a bag of candy in Sunday school class for memorizing a Bible verse from Psalms. *For the Lord loves the just and will not forsake his faithful ones.*

Then, why did He take Ethan and Ivana? They were the faithful ones, not me. No, I was the one who'd all but abandoned my faith. I seldom prayed, attended church, or read my Bible. I was a good person and still believed in the Almighty, but I couldn't understand why a loving God would destroy my brother's family like this.

Gabby used my leg to pull up to a standing position. Letting go, she wobbled on two unsteady legs and proudly clapped. I gave a weak smile and held out a protective hand to steady her before turning back to Hailey. "Grandpa said you want to wear jeans to the funeral?"

She looked up with puffy eyes. "I don't see what the big deal is. Does it really matter what I wear to my parents' funeral? This isn't a party, you know."

I glanced at the conservative, black dress hanging on the closet door. It didn't look that bad to me, but what did I know about the likes and dislikes of little girls?

"You don't like the dress Grandpa's fiancée picked out for you?"

Rage flashed in her eyes. "I *hate* that dress. Hate it!"

I exhaled slowly, trying to figure out how to respond. Ivana didn't allow Hailey to use the word hate, but maybe in this case it was okay.

"I'm not wearing it, Uncle Nick."

"No?"

"No." She balled her hands into fists so tight her knuckles turned white. "Why are you afraid of Grandpa? Dad was afraid of him. Mom was afraid of him. Even the pizza delivery man is afraid of him, but why are *you* afraid of him? You jump out of airplanes and went to Ranger school. You're friends with the president."

I felt ashamed by Hailey's confidence in me. Why was I still afraid of my father? Why could one critical glance take me back to that horrible summer day I struck out at the city-wide Little League championship game?

"You know, Hailey," I began, "the president and I aren't exactly friends. I met him when I graduated from West Point, but we don't hang out or anything. I've never been bowling at his house."

"*Whatever.*" She crossed her arms. "Just so you know, I'm not afraid of Grandpa. And I don't care what he says. I'm not wearing Gina's stupid dress to the stupid funeral."

Thrusting out her chin, she continued. "Didn't my parents put you in charge of me? Can't *you* decide what I'm supposed to wear?"

I could. In fact, until I relinquished custody to her new parents, I was responsible for her. I thought of my father marching out the door, using work as an excuse not to deal with today's heartrending challenges. And I thought of the faith Hailey had in me, and the faith I lacked in myself.

"Okay, Hailey Peterson," I said in my most authoritative voice. "I'm ordering you to wear jeans to the funeral."

Her eyes widened, and for the first time since my arrival, her mouth turned upwards with a hint of a smile. "Seriously?"

"Seriously." I lifted Gabby and bounced her on my knee. The baby giggled and kicked her legs in delight.

"What are you going to do about Grandpa?" Hailey tentatively asked. "He's not going to be happy if I don't wear the dress."

That's putting it mildly. "You let me worry about Grandpa, okay, kiddo?"

"Okay," she said, this time smiling for real.

Anna

I WORKED AT the salon all morning before collecting Travis from school and walking to the church, located just off the square on Church Street. The dark clouds from earlier had lifted, leaving behind sunshine and a bright blue sky that seemed almost sacrilegious for a funeral.

In the church parking lot, we ran into Nick standing next to Ivana's car, wearing his military uniform. My insides knotted. Even after all these years of living near a military post and having a father still on active duty, the uniform reminded me that my husband was gone. Cringing, I blocked out the last image I had of Marcus, waving from the bus that took him off to war.

"You look awesome!" Travis said, gazing up at Nick.

Nick shifted Gabby uncomfortably in his arms and gave a somber smile. "Thanks."

"My grandpa has a uniform like that," Travis continued, "but he has more medals."

"I imagine so. He's a sergeant major in DC, right?" Nick glanced at me for confirmation and I nodded.

"My dad was a soldier," Travis blurted out with little emotion. "He was killed when I was three."

My stomach dropped. Because Travis had very few memories of his father, Marcus's death was simply a matter of fact. Not the life-shattering event it'd been for me.

Nick's face tightened. "I'm sorry."

"And I'm sorry about Hailey's mom and dad," Travis said. "Mrs. Peterson taught me how to make sushi, and Mr. Peterson fixed my bike one time."

The lump in my throat turned to a boulder. Why had I thought it a good idea to come to the funeral? I'd wanted to support the Peterson family, but maybe I should just go home.

Travis tugged uncomfortably at the tie around his neck. "Is Hailey inside? Can I go see her?"

"She's in the sanctuary with her grandpa," Nick said.

Travis asked permission to join Hailey, then he ran off, leaving me alone with Nick and the baby. Nervous, I stepped forward and rubbed Gabby's back. "Hey, pretty girl."

The baby buried her face in Nick's shoulder, and he shifted clumsily so as not to drop her. I could tell that even though he didn't have a lot of experience with babies he was doing his best to care for Gabby.

I held out my arms. "Do you want to come to me, sweetheart?"

The baby giggled and snuggled deeper into her uncle's neck. Then, suddenly, she turned and lunged at me.

"Whoa," Nick said, holding on to her so she wouldn't fall. "Do you want Miss Anna to hold you?"

"Come here." I lifted Gabby into my arms and exchanged a smile with Nick. The simple gesture of taking a baby from a man stirred something inside me. I felt an unexpected yearning for something I couldn't name. Something I shouldn't want.

Pushing the desire away, I wrapped my arms around Gabby. On this sad day, I welcomed the reassurance a baby offered. Pulling her closer, I breathed in the sweet smell of baby shampoo, graham crackers, and something else.

Nick.

Some of Nick's spicy cologne had rubbed onto Gabby's sleeve, and the intoxicating scent made me lightheaded. A tingle of excitement swept through me, but I stopped the emotion before it could reach my heart. Despite the insane attraction I had to this soldier, he was not the man for me. He couldn't be.

"So, how's everyone doing?" I asked, focusing on the present.

Nick ran a hand through his short-cropped dark hair. "Other than the fact my father is going to have a conniption about Hailey wearing jeans to the funeral, we're doing okay."

I shrugged. "Hailey is a jeans and T-shirt girl. Something I can definitely understand."

Nick's gray-blue eyes quickly skimmed over my all-purpose black dress before returning to my face. "Honestly, I'm just glad she's here. She's spent the last few days lying on the couch watching *The Sound of Music* over and over and over. Last night, she insisted she wasn't coming to the funeral, so being here is a big accomplishment. At this point, I don't care what she wears."

"She didn't want to come today?"

"No." Nick sounded discouraged. Completely different from the confident man I'd met at the party a year ago.

I offered an encouraging smile. "What about you? How are you coping with everything? Ethan was your only brother, right?"

Agony encompassed his face, and I immediately regretted the question. What an insensitive thing to say. "I'm sorry—"

He shook his head. "It's okay. I'm doing as well as can be expected."

"If you need anything . . ."

"Sure. I appreciate that." He gestured toward the church. "I should go find my dad and Hailey."

"Of course. I'll carry Gabby inside for you."

"Thanks."

Chapter 4

*A*FTER THE FUNERAL, Travis and I joined the procession of cars headed to the gravesite. Rose Island was bike and pedestrian friendly, so I seldom drove. A wide bike path circled the entire island, conveniently passing in front of my house, taking me anywhere I needed to go.

Today, I'd driven my car because the cemetery was located on the other side of the island, near the army post. Tears stung my eyes as the motor patrol officers blocked traffic through town, allowing the mourners to travel together. Watching the other cars pull to the side of the road out of respect for the deceased released a flood of memories from the day we buried Marcus.

"Can I turn on the radio?" Travis asked, reaching for the controls.

I nodded, afraid my voice would break if I spoke. I'd been so numb during my husband's funeral I hardly remembered it. My parents and sisters had arranged everything, from the scripture readings to the songs.

I'd worn a long-sleeved, black dress but had no idea where it'd come from. One of Marcus's sisters must have bought it for me, or maybe my own mother had found it.

Regardless, the one thing that stood out from that horrible day was seeing all the cars pull to the side of the road as the procession accompanied the hearse to the cemetery. The considerate gesture moved me so deeply I'd never forgotten it.

"This song is awesome," Travis said, oblivious to my pain. He turned up the radio and sang along, pounding out a loud rhythm on the dashboard.

I smiled, grateful for his happiness. Without it, today would be unbearable.

At the cemetery, I parked the car but kept the motor running. Travis unbuckled his seatbelt and opened the passenger-side door while I remained seated.

"What's wrong?" he asked.

I stared at the above-ground tombstones, typical of many Gulf Coast cemeteries. Chairs and a canopy had been set up for the burial. Declining fall temperatures had turned the grass brown, but a white crepe myrtle bloomed as if holding out its arms and lifting its face in defiance of death.

Nick walked across the brittle grass holding Gabby, while Hailey clung to the hem of his uniform. His father followed several steps behind, keeping his eyes on the ground. I'd never seen Jack Peterson without his phone, and it was an odd sight. My heart ached for the entire family, but as much as I wanted to stay and show my support, I didn't know if I could make it through the burial. The funeral had been arduous, and I feared the beginning of a migraine.

"Mom?" Travis sat on the edge of the passenger seat, one hand on the opened door and one foot on the ground.

I rubbed at a rock hard knot on the back of my neck. "I'm not feeling well. Would you mind if we just went home?"

He pushed up his glasses and studied me carefully. "Is it because you're thinking about Dad?"

I nodded and held back the tears threatening to stream forth.

"I've been thinking about him a lot, too. Do I look like him? Aunt Jillian says I could be his twin, but Aunt Bianca disagrees. Aunt Vicki says I have his eyes, but I don't know. What do you think?"

I smiled sadly. Marcus had three older sisters, all of them with distinct personalities and opinions. Jillian was the oldest, followed by Bianca and then Vicki.

"If you compare your picture with your father's, it's difficult to see the resemblance. But your personalities are so much alike. I think that's what Aunt Jillian means when she says you could be his twin."

"Really?"

I nodded and brushed back his hair. "Your father had the same joyful optimism you have. He always saw the good in people, even when they disappointed him.

And like you, your father was a good friend. Not just to me, but to everyone he came in contact with."

Travis beamed as he closed the car door and put his seatbelt back on. "Okay, Mom. Let's go home."

I gave a sad smile in spite of my heavy heart. A knock at the driver's side window startled me, and I looked up to see Marcus's middle sister standing next to the car. Bianca owned The Last Tangle—the hair salon where I worked—and she'd been uncharacteristically reserved this morning. Her eyes were now red-rimmed, and her mascara smudged. She offered a weak smile as I rolled down the window.

"Are you coming?" she asked, motioning toward the canopy.

I glanced at Travis. As much as I wanted to go home and crawl into bed, now was the time to be strong and brave. Turning back to my sister-in-law, I nodded. "We're coming. Just give us a minute okay?"

"Sure."

I rolled up the window and watched her walk across the grass to embrace Vicki, the youngest Morgan sister. The two women were exact opposites. Vicki was petite and blond while Bianca was a larger woman with auburn hair.

"So we're staying?" Travis asked.

"I think we should, don't you?"

He nodded. "I want to stay for Hailey."

I turned off the engine and stepped out of the car.

Travis walked around to take my hand in a gesture that both comforted and surprised me. He hadn't held my hand in months, at least not in public, and the action deeply touched me.

"I love you," I said, squeezing his hand.

"Ditto," he replied, returning my squeeze.

Together, we moved forward and joined the mourners.

THAT NIGHT, MY mind raced with thoughts of the past. Sleep evaded me as I tossed and turned, unable to get comfortable. At some point, Travis crawled into my bed and proceeded to kick me every time I drifted off. No matter how far I scooted to the other side of the bed, his foot found me.

Eventually, I took my pillow downstairs to the couch in the living room. The cat, of course, thought that meant mealtime, so he meowed in protest until I fed him, even though it was only three in the morning.

When I finally fell asleep, I had wildly delicious dreams about kissing Nick on the back porch of the Petersons' house. As I threaded my arms around his neck, I noticed someone sitting on the railing watching us.

Marcus.

"Why are you doing this to me?" my late husband asked.

I jerked awake, gasping for breath as my heart raced. It didn't take a degree in psychology to dissect the meaning of *that* dream. I'd found true love with Marcus, and even though it'd been seven long years since his death, kissing another man, no matter how desirable, felt like an act of betrayal.

I managed to fall back into a fitful sleep for a few hours until the doorbell woke me in the morning. The cat walked over my chest as bright sunlight streamed through the curtains of the living room window. What time was it?

Travis thundered down the stairs and headed toward the front door. "Someone's here."

"Don't answer it," I insisted as the doorbell rang again.

Standing on tiptoes, he peered through the peephole. "It's Hailey!" Ignoring my warning, he opened the door wide for the entire world to see the morning version of his mother. Only, it wasn't just the whole world. Nick stood on the front porch, dressed in dark blue jeans and a charcoal cable-knit sweater that set off his eyes.

I folded my arms across my nightgown and tried not to panic. I could only imagine how frazzled I looked with no sleep, no makeup, and crazy lady hair. I asked Hailey if she was coming to school with us today, and she nodded.

"Come on in, sweetheart," I said, motioning with

my hand. "Just give me a minute to get dressed and we'll go."

Avoiding Nick's gaze, I dashed upstairs to my bedroom and threw on yoga pants and a sweatshirt. I pulled my hair into a messy ponytail and ignored the dreadful woman in the mirror. Why did I care if Nick saw me first thing in the morning? It wasn't like I was interested in him. It wasn't like I *liked* him.

Heading back to the living room, I stopped on the stairs and watched Nick in the entryway, looking at my family photographs hanging on the wall. Fully grown men seldom entered my home, so seeing his broad shoulders occupying so much space unnerved me. His height made the ceiling appear low, something I'd never noticed before.

My stomach tingled with a desire to walk up behind him, wrap my arms around his waist, and give him a big bear hug. I imagined the warmth of his sweater against my cheek and the strength of his hard muscles beneath my fingertips.

As he leaned toward my wedding photo, I held my breath. How many times had I removed that picture only to put it back up? I couldn't decide if it was better to be constantly reminded of Marcus, or better to forget.

I must've made a sound because Nick turned around and met my gaze. My stomach twisted at the intensity in his eyes.

"How old were you when you got married?" he

asked, pointing at my wedding photo. "You look so young."

I swallowed. "We were both nineteen."

"Nineteen." He shook his head and started to say something but stopped before giving a curt nod and changing the subject. "My father agreed to stay with Gabby this morning, and I have Ethan's bike." His voice faltered on his brother's name, but he pushed past it and offered to ride with the kids to school this morning.

Instead of a typical carpool, Ivana and I had taken turns riding bikes with the kids to school. It was a short ten-minute trip, and I enjoyed the exercise before work.

"I'll take them this morning," I said, grabbing my bicycle helmet from the hall closet. I called for Hailey and Travis, who were using the binoculars to watch a ship cross the bay. Hailey's eyes were still puffy, but they looked less red this morning than they had at the funeral.

Once outside, the kids raced down the creaky wooden steps to their bikes. Nick hung back on the porch as I closed and locked the front door. His silent presence gave me the ominous feeling he needed something. Slipping the key into the zipper pocket of my sweatshirt, I asked him if everything was okay.

He frowned. "I thought residents didn't lock their doors on Rose Island during the off-season."

"I'm probably the only one, but I don't like to take

chances."

He glanced over his shoulder at the kids, then back at me. "Can I ask you something?"

I braced myself for his question of why I'd ignored his e-mails and friend request on Facebook earlier this year, but instead, he asked something completely different. "Do you think it's okay Hailey goes to school today? She woke this morning on her own, dressed, and announced she was going. I told her she could stay home, but she doesn't want to. I haven't been around kids very much, so I just don't know if that's normal."

I released the breath I'd been holding and chastised myself for being so self-centered. Of course, Nick's question revolved around Hailey and not my immature response to his gesture of friendship. "If she wants to go to school, I'd let her. Maybe returning to her routine and seeing her friends will be helpful."

Nick's face relaxed. "That's what the grief counselor said, but I wanted your opinion. I know you're a good mom, Anna."

Warmth spread through me, and I smiled. "Travis means everything to me."

"I can tell." He scuffed his shoe across one of the wooden boards on the porch. "I have a meeting at ten with Ivana's cousin and his wife before they head back home to San Antonio."

"Doug and Caroline Kempner?"

He nodded and lowered his voice. "It's about them

taking the girls. Adopting them. Honestly, I still don't understand why the will named me as legal guardian instead of them."

"Ethan and Ivana never mentioned it to you?"

He shook his head. "No. Never."

Despite what I'd thought earlier about Nick's inability to raise the girls, seeing him care for them at the funeral yesterday had made me question my original assumption. "Maybe your brother and Ivana truly wanted you to raise their daughters."

A mixture of sorrow and panic flashed across his face. "No, I don't know anything about kids or being a parent. Plus, I have a three-year obligation to the army, and I'm supposed to deploy again next year. It wouldn't be fair for the girls to stay with me."

Frustration thickened his voice, making me feel guilty I'd implied raising the girls on his own would be easy. "I'm sorry. I know you just want what's best for them."

"I do," he said, looking relieved that I finally understood his dilemma. "So, do you think the girls would be okay with the Kempners? Besides my father and me, they're the only relatives."

I straightened my ponytail, not wanting to make things more difficult. The last thing Nick needed was a nosy neighbor telling him what to do. "I barely know Doug and Caroline. We met once at your brother and sister-in-law's housewarming party, and we said hello yesterday . . ."

"But you don't think I should leave the girls with them?"

My expression must've betrayed me because Nick said, "It's okay; tell me what you're thinking. I want to know your honest opinion. Is it because they home-school their children?"

"No, I think homeschooling is amazing. It's nothing I could do, but those Kempner boys are smart and polite." I checked on Travis and Hailey who'd ridden down the seashell driveway to the paved bike path and were now riding in figure eights. "I like Doug and Caroline a lot, but homeschooling and living with all those boys would be an adjustment for Hailey. Travis, on the other hand, could have his bags packed in five minutes."

Nick gave a sad smile. The Kempners had five boys under the age of eight. "Their very own basketball team!" Travis had enthusiastically observed. "And they don't even have to go to school. Can you believe that?"

I picked at a flake of paint on the railing. The house had been repainted just a few years ago but was already beginning to peel due to the harsh ocean environment.

"So, what are you going to do?" I asked.

He shook his head. "I don't know. But now that the funeral is over, I need to make a decision."

He looked defeated, and I scrambled to say something helpful. Before I could, Travis honked the rubber horn on his bike. "Come on, Mom. We're going to be late."

"On my way," I called.

I placed my helmet on my head and adjusted the chin strap. "Children adapt easily. Way better than adults. I'm sure both Hailey and Gabby will be fine with whatever you decide. The Kempners are great parents, and their boys seem happy."

Travis honked his horn again, and Nick shoved his hands into his pockets. "You'd better go. I'll see you later."

"See you later," I repeated, although I immediately regretted the words. I didn't need to see him later. I needed to avoid him, because whenever I saw Nick Peterson, I was consumed with a desire to throw my arms around him. I wanted to cling to him and help him through this difficult time. I wanted to take care of him and let him take care of me.

But as evidenced by our kiss on New Year's Eve and my desire to hug him this morning, throwing my arms around him would only lead to wanting more. And wanting more was not something I could afford when I had a child to raise and a heart to protect.

Turning away, I bounded down the stairs, determined to distance myself. When I reached ground level, however, Nick called my name.

"Yes?" I replied, turning around with an eagerness that was pathetic.

"Would you come with me to meet the Kempners? I'm . . ." He held out his hands in a surrendering motion. "I'm in way over my head and could really use your help."

One look at his pleading eyes had me saying yes. So much for resolving to maintain my distance. Fortunately, he'd be leaving soon, and I wouldn't have to fight my heart's foolish desires much longer.

Chapter 5

Nick

*L*ATER THAT MORNING, I met Anna and the Kempners at Casa Jose's, the festive Mexican food
restaurant on Harbor Street overlooking the bayside of
the island. Years ago, the building manufactured large
ships, but now it sold the best breakfast tacos in the state
of Texas.

Over the holidays last year, I'd eaten at Casa Jose's
with Ethan and Ivana several times. Being at the restaurant without them, especially given the reason for
today's meeting, proved more difficult than I'd anticipated. In fact, everything about being on the island
without my brother and his wife proved more difficult. I
kept imagining that instead of dying, they'd gone on a
cruise and had convinced me to babysit the girls for a
few days.

Inside the restaurant, I placed Gabby in a high chair
and handed her a graham cracker before sliding into the
booth next to Anna. Doug and Caroline Kempner sat

across from us with two-year-old twins who epitomized the phrase *active toddlers.* The boys clambered over their parents, played with the sugar packets, and hid underneath the table.

The Kempners' three older boys, ages eight, six, and four, occupied a separate booth where they'd constructed an interesting structure made entirely from salt and pepper shakers. "It's the Great Pyramid of Giza," the oldest one said.

Anna grinned. "Impressive!"

Despite my misgivings about the girls living with the Kempners, I could tell Doug and Caroline were good parents who loved their children. Like Anna, they were patient and treated their children with a respect I often saw missing in other parents.

The adults made small talk until our food arrived. Just as I took the first bite of my omelet, Gabby lifted her sticky hands in the air and screamed, begging to be rescued from the confines of the high chair right now. The twins imitated her by screaming and lifting their own hands before bursting into bouts of laughter. As if insulted, Gabby screamed even louder.

I dug through the enormous diaper bag until I found the baby wipes. Then, as patiently as possible, I set to work on the intricate process of cleaning my niece's chubby fingers. Of course, Gabby didn't want her hands cleaned, so she arched her back and shrieked.

I couldn't help but laugh at the incredibly loud and

obnoxious sound such a little thing could produce. "If you hold still, this will only take a minute. Honestly, how can one tiny baby be so controlling?"

Doug chuckled. "It's a special talent they're born with."

When Gabby was finally clean, I pulled her out of the high chair, sat her on my lap, and patted her shoulder. "Now, that wasn't so bad, was it?"

She giggled and touched my face as if her tantrum had been all for show. I glanced at Anna and saw she was smiling at us. I smiled back, hoping she didn't regret coming with me this morning.

Doug gestured toward Gabby. "She's quite a handful, isn't she?"

"She's precious," Caroline said, her eyes suddenly moist. She sniffed as if trying to hold back tears, and the twins engaged in a round of dramatic sniffing and giggling.

Doug placed a loving arm across his wife's shoulders. "It's going to be okay, honey."

I had no idea what was going on, but I had a feeling they wouldn't be adopting Hailey and Gabby.

"Caroline adores the girls," Doug began. "We both do, and we're devastated by the loss of Ethan and Ivana. We want to help, but—"

"I'm pregnant," Caroline said, forcing a smile. "With triplets."

If I was a character from one of the cartoons Ethan

and I used to watch on Saturday mornings, my jaw would've hit the table. Instead, I simply stared, speechless.

Anna spoke, voicing my thoughts exactly. "Wow. That's unbelievable."

Caroline nodded. "We're thrilled, of course. And shocked. You may know that our three oldest sons were adopted. The twins were a surprise, but this pregnancy—"

"We're overwhelmed," Doug said. "Thrilled, but completely overwhelmed. I just found out I'm being laid off, and Caroline's Etsy store doesn't bring in a lot of money. Plus, she was on bed rest with the twins, and we worry about that happening with this pregnancy."

"We want the girls," Caroline said, blinking. "We'll make room for them, love them, and raise them as our own, but perhaps another family—"

"I understand," I said. Gabby grew fussy in my arms, and I found her beloved binky, making her happy for a brief moment. But then she arched her back, let out a wail, and spat the pacifier out of her mouth. It flew across the table and landed in Doug's coffee cup, causing coffee to splash onto his shirt.

"It's fine," Doug said, laughing as he attempted to clean up the mess with a syrupy napkin.

I apologized, but Caroline waved a dismissive hand. "Don't worry about it, Nick. We're used to it. It's part of being a parent."

As if to prove her point, there was a sudden blood-curdling scream from the other booth. The youngest of the three older boys turned to reveal blood gushing from his nose. "He hit me!" he shouted, pointing at his brother.

The middle boy, looking extremely guilty, said, "No, I didn't."

"Yes, you did," the oldest one said.

"But I didn't mean to. My hand just slipped."

Chaos ensued, and Gabby emitted another high-pitched shriek as though traumatized by the sight of blood.

"I'm so sorry," Caroline told Anna and me as she held a napkin to her son's nose and escorted him to the bathroom.

The waitress brought the check, and Doug reached for his wallet, but I handed over enough cash to cover the entire bill plus a generous tip. When Doug protested, I shook my head. "You can get it next time."

Standing, I flung the diaper bag over my shoulder, a gesture that ironically reminded me of grabbing my rifle before heading out on maneuvers. Gabby's cries grew louder, so I tried placating her by bouncing her up and down, but that only seemed to fuel her temper.

"It was an accident, Dad," the middle kid insisted.

Doug grabbed his wife's purse and hoisted the twins into his arms. "We'll talk about this in the car, son. Let's go."

As we headed out to the parking lot, I could feel the disapproving glances from the other customers. Outside, Anna gave me a bemused smile and held out her hands for Gabby. "Can I try?"

Willingly, I handed over the baby, relieved to have her in the arms of an expert instead of my inept ones. Doug corralled his children into the minivan, and shortly after, Caroline and the bleeder exited the restaurant.

"I'm so sorry," Caroline said, placing a hand on my arm. "I want you to know things aren't always this crazy. Well, maybe they are. But we'd love to have the girls, and we can make room for them. Plus, I have faith that Doug will find another job."

"I'm sure he will." I glanced at the minivan where one of the twins was digging through Caroline's purse, examining each item with fascination before tossing it into the front seat.

"Your girlfriend seems really sweet," Caroline said, either not noticing what was going on with her purse, or not caring.

I turned my attention to Anna who'd successfully managed to calm Gabby. "She's sweet, but she's not my girlfriend."

"No? Well, she's wonderful."

I nodded as Gabby laid her head on Anna's shoulder and closed her eyes.

Caroline gave me a hug good-bye before joining her

family. The toddler handed his mother the empty purse, and Caroline scooped up all the items as if not the least bit annoyed. Doug started the engine, and everyone waved and hollered good-bye as they drove out of the parking lot.

Anna walked over to me and spoke in a hushed whisper so as not to wake the baby. "I think I'd have a nervous breakdown if I was pregnant with triplets and had five other boys."

I smiled. "No kidding. Never again will I complain about Gabby's crying or Hailey's insistence that I cut her sandwich in triangles instead of squares."

"You cut her sandwich in squares?" Anna asked, pretending to be outraged. "What were you thinking?"

"I have no idea." Anna and I grinned at each other, then I said, "I know you need to get to work, but thanks for coming with me this morning. I hope you weren't too bored."

She laughed at my joke, and Gabby jerked but didn't wake. "Do you want me to put her in the car seat for you?" she asked, rubbing the baby's back.

I nodded and opened the back door. Anna expertly buckled up Gabby before placing a blanket over her legs.

"Can I give you a ride to work?" I asked, wanting to spend more time with her.

She motioned toward her bike, leaning against the restaurant. "Thanks but I have my own transportation."

I shoved a hand through my hair. "Maybe you could show me how to use the baby carrier on Ethan's bike. I think Gabby might enjoy that, and I'd be able to help take the kids to school."

A strange expression crossed her face. "Sure, anytime."

Anna

AS I RODE away from Nick, I tried not to picture him strolling around the island on a bicycle with the adorable Gabby waving from the bike seat behind him. Could anything tug at my heartstrings more than this strong man and precious baby?

Chastising myself for being weak and so easily lured by romantic notions, I cycled up to Main Street. The heavenly scent of freshly baked bread from Vicki's Bakery greeted me, and colorful pansies spilled over terracotta planters in front of every shop. Bianca had been responsible for the flower initiative, and this year, the winter flowers were spectacular.

I passed the bakery and continued next door to The Last Tangle where I found my sister-in-law checking the large appointment book that sat on the front counter separating the waiting room from the hairstylists.

Bianca, dressed in an expensive silk blouse and a Hermes scarf, greeted me with a smile. Although she was talented enough to make more money working in

KRISTIN NOEL FISCHER

an upscale salon in Houston or on a movie set, Bianca loved living on the island and owning her own business. The salon had room for two more stylists, but currently, we were the only two who worked there.

"How'd the meeting go?" she asked, brushing back a strand of auburn hair. At thirty-six, she was a stunning, full-figured woman. She'd never been married but had been briefly engaged to her college sweetheart who'd broken her heart when he chose to marry someone else.

I hung my bag on the hook next to my station. "The Kempners are pregnant with triplets."

Bianca's eyes bulged. "Wow."

"That's what I said."

"Their little boys are so cute," Bianca said. "But triplets! They'll have eight boys under the age of nine."

I nodded. "Hailey would probably be a real blessing to Caroline."

"More like cheap labor," Bianca said sarcastically. "So, what's Nick going to do? Did you ask him about keeping the girls himself?"

I sighed. "He says he can't because of his job, but he's so good with them. Patient, kind, loving. Plus, Ethan and Ivana must've had some confidence in him to name him as the girls' legal guardian."

Bianca narrowed her eyes and studied me carefully. "Oh, wow."

"What?" I looked down, thinking I must have coffee or something on my shirt. "I don't see anything."

"You like him," she stated.

A warm tingly feeling danced through my body. "Who? Nick? No, I don't." Grinning, I walked to the front of the salon and opened the blinds. I flipped over the "We're Open" sign and waited for my racing pulse to slow.

"Are you saying you don't like him?" Bianca asked in her typical middle child, provoking way.

"I'm saying he's nice and good-looking, but we're just friends."

"You kissed him."

My lips and cheeks tingled at the memory. "That was almost a year ago, and it didn't mean anything."

"Of course it meant something. You're not exactly the kind of girl who goes around offering meaningless kisses to handsome men. By the way, you're blushing. A sure sign that you're enamored with Nick Peterson."

I refrained from touching my face and forced a casual laugh. "Enamored? That's a very big word to use this early in the morning."

Humming a popular love song to herself, Bianca ran a finger down the names in the appointment book. "It's okay, you know."

"What's okay?"

"Being enamored with Nick. Feeling something for him. Even falling in love with him is okay."

My breath stalled. "I'm not falling in love with him or even enamored. I'm just trying to help him sort out things with the girls. He's leaving next week, and I feel sorry for the whole family, don't you?"

Bianca's face crumpled. "Oh, honey, I do. My heart breaks for those little girls, Nick, and even grumpy Grandpa Jack. The whole thing hits too close to home, reminding me of losing Marcus."

"I know," I agreed.

Chapter 6

*F*OR THE REST of the week, I focused on work and taking care of Travis. Around two in the afternoon on Friday, Nick entered the salon, holding Gabby and the Vera Bradley diaper bag.

My throat went dry at the sight of him. Why did he have such a profound effect on me? All week long, I'd been successful at keeping my distance—waving from the safety of my bike and exchanging quick text messages regarding taking the kids to school. Sure, I'd helped him figure out Gabby's bike seat, but I hadn't lingered.

Now that he was in the salon, avoiding him would be impossible.

Bianca clapped her hands and strode across the floor to greet him. "Look at you, all domesticated." She gave him a big hug like they were best friends. She'd met him briefly at the New Year's Eve party last year and again at the funeral. But that was Bianca. Despite being overweight, she had the confidence of a Sports Illustrated swimsuit model.

"How are you?" Nick asked, slightly taken aback.

"I'm fine. Now hand over that baby, so we can paint

her little bitty toenails."

Nick caught my eye as he passed the baby to Bianca. Fearing I might blush, I avoided looking at him and focused on my sister-in-law. "You can't paint a baby's toenails."

Bianca frowned. "Why not?"

"Because she still puts her fingers and toes in her mouth, right, Nick?"

He shook his head and grinned. "Oh, no. Don't you dare drag me into this. I know better than to get in the middle of an argument between two women."

Both Bianca and I laughed. "This isn't an argument," I insisted. "Just common sense."

Bianca carried Gabby over to her station. "What about a bow? Will the *Nail Polish Police* allow me to put a bow in the baby's hair?"

I rolled my eyes. "I'm sorry to ruin your fun, but I have a problem allowing a baby to ingest a potentially harmful substance."

"You have a problem with anything potentially harmful," she shot back.

I placed a hand over my heart with mock indignation. "Ouch."

Shaking her head, Bianca turned her attention to Nick. "Did you know Anna used to be an award-winning helicopter pilot?"

Nick raised his brow. "Seriously?"

"I won employee of the month," I said, refuting my

sister-in-law's exaggeration. "It wasn't a big deal, and it was a long time ago. Now, I'm a successful hairdresser who's adamantly opposed to putting nail polish on babies."

Nick carefully studied me. "Do you still fly?"

"No," I said.

"Why not?"

I picked up a broom and began sweeping around my station even though it was already clean. "It's a long story, but basically, I wanted to try something different."

He said nothing as he continued staring at me. Tightening my grip on the broom, I spoke with a forced lightness. "Are you here for a haircut today, Nick?"

He touched his hair self-consciously. "No. I wanted to ask you about Monday. I'm going to Houston for Gabby's wall-baby appointment, and—"

"A *what* appointment?" Bianca interrupted, her voice clearly amused.

"A wall-baby appointment?" he repeated, slightly uncertain now. "At least that's what the pediatrician's office told me over the phone."

Bianca threw her head back and roared with laughter, the sound shaking the salon. Tears spilled down her cheeks.

"What's so funny?" Nick asked, confused.

I smiled. "I think you mean *well*-baby appointment. Babies get them every few months to make sure they're *well.*"

He readjusted the diaper bag, looking embarrassed. "I guess that makes sense." One corner of his mouth tugged upward in that quirky smile I found downright adorable.

Bianca kept laughing. "What'd you think? They put the baby on the wall to see if she stuck?"

"I didn't know what to think. This baby thing is completely foreign to me. Besides, the pediatrician's office called during one of Gabby's screaming episodes, and it's impossible to hear or think straight when she's freaking out like that."

"Wall-baby appointment," Bianca repeated, laughing again as she reached into a drawer and found several hair bows.

"Anyway . . ." Nick turned back to me. "Gabby's appointment is up in Houston, and since there's no school on Monday, I'm going to take Hailey with me. She's been talking about visiting the pet store."

"Bubba's Pets," I said. "Travis loves that place."

"Yes, that's why I stopped by the salon. I was hoping you'd let Travis come with us."

Panic fired in my brain, and I let out a deep breath. "I don't know. It's kind of far away, and last time, they had this venomous snake named Cuddles. Not for sale, just on display . . ."

Nick looked offended and confused. "Could he come with us if I promise not to let him touch the venomous snake? It'd be good for Hailey to have a friend along. She's having a hard time. Her teachers say she's doing fine in school, but when she comes home, she sinks into a horrible depression. I thought Travis could lift her spirits."

I nodded, wanting to say yes for Hailey's sake but nervous about letting Travis leave the island without me. Rose Island offered a safe and idyllic life not found elsewhere. What if Travis wandered off and became lost? What if Nick had a car accident? What if someone tried to harm them?

Nick must've sensed my fear because he took a step back and raised his hands. "Sorry, I didn't mean to push. I'm just trying to help Hailey, but the bottom line is I can't fix the fact she lost her parents. I can't force her to be happy."

Guilt washed over me. The rational part of me knew I was being ridiculous. Hadn't I told Travis that Hailey needed a friend like him?

Plus, with Travis gone for the day, I could pick up a few more appointments and make a little extra money for Christmas. My parents were coming for the holiday, and I wanted to take some time off in December.

"Ta-da!" Bianca disrupted the tension by swirling the chair around, causing Gabby to giggle. The baby reached a tentative hand to her head and touched the bows.

"Doesn't she look beautiful?" Bianca asked.

Both Nick and I nodded.

Bianca lifted the baby into her arms and addressed Nick. "Now, we're going to show off Gabby's new hairstyle at the bank while you stay here and convince Anna you're not going to kidnap her son."

"I'm not worried about that," I insisted.

"No, but I'm sure that crazy mind of yours has come up with all sorts of worst-case scenarios. Talk to the man about Monday or give him a haircut. Either way, Gabby and I will be back."

With a wink, she headed out the door. Nick glanced nervously around the salon, taking in everything but me. His eyes landed on the wooden sign hanging above the sinks on the back wall.

"The higher the hair, the closer to heaven." Grinning, he ran a hand over his head. "I was thinking about getting my hair cut, but maybe I shouldn't go any shorter."

I returned his smile. "It does seem a little long for the military. Are you leading a rebellion or something?"

His expression faltered. "I was waiting in the barber shop on post when my father called about Ethan and Ivana."

I winced. "I'm sorry."

"It's fine."

"I'd be happy to cut your hair," I offered.

He surprised me by agreeing and taking a seat at my station.

Smiling apologetically, I held up two bibs. "Our men's selection is rather slim today. You have your choice between pink polka dots and daisies."

"How about I hold onto my man card and forgo a gown?"

"Okay." I stood behind the chair and locked eyes with him in the mirror before running a hand through his dark hair. Usually, there was nothing sensual about touching a man's hair, but this felt different. Special. Almost intimate.

Suddenly, I was struck by an insane longing to lean over and kiss the back of his neck. Run my hands over his shoulders and down his arms. Thankfully, I came to my senses before doing anything reckless.

"Okay, let's start with a shampoo," I said, gesturing for him to follow me.

He gave me a blank stare. "Why? You don't need to do that."

Returning to him, I tugged at a tuft of hair. "Let me guess. The baby ate carrots for breakfast? Maybe strained green beans for lunch?"

He brought his hand to his head, and I guided it to the spot matted down, compliments of Gabby. "Well, that's attractive," he said, sarcastically.

We shared a laugh, and together, we walked back to the sinks. Sitting in the first chair, he leaned back and closed his eyes.

I tried to maintain a professional demeanor as I

dampened his hair, but once again, my attraction to him overwhelmed me. I hadn't been seriously interested in anybody since Marcus. Although I'd gone out on several dates and had even kissed a few men good-night, nothing compared to the explosion of emotion I felt toward Nick.

I lathered his hair with shampoo, the rich scent of sandalwood filling the air. He kept his eyes closed, giving me the opportunity to really look at him without fear of being discovered. No wonder I continued to think about kissing him.

He was magnificent. Broad shoulders, solid biceps, flat stomach, long muscular legs. Nick was nothing if not solid and dependable, both in body and personality.

After New Year's Eve, I'd run a background check on him, and it hadn't even turned up a speeding ticket. It was ridiculous not to trust him with Travis. So, why was I afraid? Just general anxiety issues, or something more?

A large drop of water splashed onto the ragged scar at his temple. He opened his eyes and stared up at me as if reading my thoughts. For a moment, neither one of us moved, then, placing a fingertip over the rough skin, I brushed aside the water.

"How did you get that scar?" I asked.

He let out a slow breath. "When Ethan and I were kids, we shattered a glass table in the living room. This is where a piece got stuck, and Ethan pulled it out with a pair of tweezers."

"Your dad let him do that?"

He shook his head. "Our father wasn't there, and we never told him. We weren't supposed to be wrestling in the house, so we cleaned up the mess and never said anything."

I frowned. "Didn't Jack notice the missing table or the gaping hole in your head?"

Nick gave a derisive grunt. "No. He was working on an important business deal, so as long as we stayed out of his way, he tended not to notice us."

"That must've really hurt."

He shrugged. "It wasn't too bad."

I rinsed his hair, then dried it with a towel. I imagined the shard of glass in his head, and his father not noticing hurt more than Nick cared to admit, but I didn't ask him about it.

"What scares me the most about taking care of the girls," he began without preamble, "is the fact that Ethan and I didn't have a lot of supervision growing up. Our mother left when we were little, and our dad worked all the time. Ethan wanted a different life for his kids."

Clients often revealed personal information while I washed or cut their hair, but I was surprised to hear Nick speak so candidly about his childhood. Like a lot of military guys, he kept a tight rein on his emotions.

"Your brother was extremely involved with both his

daughters," I said. "Even though he worked hard, his family was most important."

"I know." Nick sounded frustrated, and he scooted to the edge of the chair as though preparing to stand. He took the wet towel off his head and tossed it in the hamper. "So tell me, how am I supposed to find someone to replace him? For that matter, how am I supposed to find someone to replace Ivana? In some ways, she was like a mother to me—sending me care packages when I was away, insisting I took the time to visit, and embracing me as a member of their family."

"You'll figure it out." Wanting to encourage him, I rested my hand on his shoulder and gave it a reassuring squeeze.

Something between us shifted as he covered my hand with his. I sucked in a quick breath when he laced our fingers together and came to his feet. Still holding my hand, he stood just inches away and stared at me with his beautiful, beautiful, beautiful eyes.

A flutter of anticipation shot through me. I told myself to step back. Don't let this happen.

But when he placed his free hand at my waist, I held perfectly still. There was a moment of hesitation. A moment when I could've distanced myself, but I didn't want to. Didn't want anything more than to feel his lips on mine.

With a gentle tug, he brought me closer and lowered his mouth to mine. His touch consumed me, and I threaded my arms around him, wanting more. Briefly, I lost myself in the comfort and desire of his kiss.

And then, warning bells clanged in my head so loud my entire body stiffened. Once again, I pushed him away.

"Anna," he said, immediately releasing me.

"It wasn't your fault. I can't . . ." I pressed a hand to my hammering heart and took a deep breath.

A million different thoughts charged through my mind. "It's not that I don't like you or don't find myself attracted to you, but you're leaving in a few days."

"I'm staying until after Christmas," he said, as if that made any difference at all.

I shook my head. "Okay, but you're a soldier, and I can't ever be involved with another soldier. I was a military wife for nearly four years. I've served my time. I've seen the stress my mother has endured with my father, and I don't want to ever do that again."

"I know," he said, looking away.

"I shouldn't have kissed you last New Year's Eve, and I shouldn't have kissed you now."

"It's okay."

I opened my mouth to speak, but he stopped me. "Anna, it's fine. Don't worry about it, okay? I'll go."

He excused himself with a quick nod and strode across the salon. Everything inside me screamed for him to stay. I wanted him to turn around and fill the emptiness that had become my constant companion—not

KRISTIN NOEL FISCHER

since I'd lost Marcus—but since Nick had taken my hand to jump into the air at the stroke of midnight.

I knew I could stop him by calling his name. Instead, I remained silent, letting him go.

And letting a piece of my heart go with him.

Chapter 7

*O*N MONDAY MORNING, my son went to Houston with Nick, Hailey, and Gabby. Before they left, I gave Travis strict instructions to stay with Nick and to keep away from the snake at Bubba's pet store.

All morning, I tried to focus on my work, but my mind continued drifting to Nick. I was like a kid in middle school, obsessed with something that wasn't good for me.

"What exactly happened while you were washing Nick's hair?" Bianca asked as we cleaned our stations between clients.

She'd asked the question earlier, but I'd avoided it by luring her into a conversation about an old episode of *Downton Abbey*. This time, I tried distracting her with questions about reordering shampoo.

She pinned me with her gaze. "I know you don't want to talk about it, but I'm not going to let you off so easily."

To my relief, the salon door opened, and my oldest sister-in-law, Jillian, entered. Jillian worked as a nurse in elder care. She was a divorcée with two teenage boys, and she had the most beautiful, thick, long honey-brown hair.

As Jillian followed me back to the sinks to have her hair washed, Bianca trailed behind, excited to relay the news that Travis had gone to Houston with Nick and the girls today.

"Am I missing something?" Jillian asked, taking a seat. "I have a feeling I should be outraged."

Bianca leaned against the counter. "Well, Anna doesn't know Nick very well, so I'm surprised she let a *stranger* take her son off the island. Last time I wanted to take Travis to the Rose Museum, she practically made me take a driving test."

"No, I didn't." I turned on the faucet and held my hand underneath the water to test its temperature. "Anyway, Nick isn't a stranger. He's my next door neighbor. I figured if the United States government can trust him with equipment worth millions of dollars, maybe I should, too."

Bianca scoffed and addressed her older sister. "All I know is, when he stopped by the other day, I took the baby to run errands while Anna cut his hair. I wasn't gone more than five minutes when he came rushing into the bank, insisting he had to leave. His hair was wet, and I noticed a dab of lipstick on his bottom lip."

"That's not true." I protested. *Was it?*

Bianca tapped her own bottom lip. "Right here. It was a coral color, kind of like . . . hey, it was kind of like the color you're wearing, Anna."

My cheeks reddened, but I lathered Jillian's hair and tried to ignore Bianca's accusations. "Give it a rest. Please?"

"*Oh, my . . .*" Bianca said.

Jillian brushed water off her forehead. "What?"

"It's worse than I thought." Bianca's tone was dramatic. "She *really* likes him."

I turned off the water and wrapped a towel around Jillian's head. "Nick and I are friends. That's all."

Bianca winked at Jillian. "And that's why she kissed him again. Right here in the salon. Probably here at the sinks, in that very same chair you're sitting in, Jillian."

I tried to hold back my smile, but it refused to stay hidden. "I honestly don't remember."

"You did!" Bianca clapped her hands. "That's wonderful and deliciously unprofessional at the same time. Give us the details."

Shaking my head, I walked Jillian back to my station as Bianca skipped alongside, begging for information.

"Don't you have something more important to do than meddle in my personal life?" I asked.

She shook her head. "No, not really."

Jillian sank into the salon chair, her expression somber and lacking the excitement of Bianca's. "Nick is the soldier you kissed last New Year's Eve, right? He's Ethan Peterson's brother."

"That's right," Bianca said. "Of course, you didn't

get to meet him because you went with *Bryan* to his parents' house in Dallas instead of spending New Year's with your family. And you missed the funeral because you were picking up *Bryan* from the airport."

Jillian rolled her eyes. Bianca wasn't one to hold back her opinion, and she often expressed disdain for Jillian's new boyfriend, secretly calling him Boring Bryan.

The front door opened, and Bianca's next client, the Morgan family's favorite veterinarian, Dr. Lindsay, entered the salon. "How are y'all doing?" she asked in her usual cheerful manner.

"Wonderful," Bianca answered. "We're discussing Anna's new love interest. That gorgeous Nick Peterson."

Dr. Lindsay tucked a strand of strawberry blonde hair behind her ear and smiled at me. "You have a new boyfriend?"

"No, I don't."

Bianca waved a dismissive hand. "Don't listen to her. Come on back, and I'll tell you all about it while I wash your hair."

I shook my head, refusing to engage in the usual salon gossip and banter, especially since it involved me. Turning back to Jillian, I combed out my sister-in-law's hair.

"I can't stop thinking about the Peterson girls," Jillian said. "And then I think about Travis growing up without knowing his father . . . it just seems so unfair."

I rested a hand on her shoulder. "It's a shame that Travis hardly knew Marcus, but he knows you and your boys. He knows Vicki and Bianca and your parents. Every day, he experiences his father's goodness reflected in your family."

She wiped her eyes. "Have you been in therapy or something, Anna? You sound so well adjusted."

I laughed. "Therapy, yes. Well-adjusted? I don't know about that. I'm just trying to—"

"Move on?" she offered.

I bristled. *Moving on* sounded too much like forgetting, and I didn't want to forget about Marcus. "I'm trying to be grateful for what I have and not dwell on what's missing."

She nodded. "That's a good policy. I'm trying to focus on the positive in my life as well. I think there's something valid to the whole gratitude movement."

"I agree."

Over the next several minutes, I lost myself in the rhythm of my work . . . dividing Jillian's hair into sections, grasping a strand between my fingers, and cutting it at an angle to give her the soft look that best framed her face. A country station played in the background and various artists sang about love, God, America, and old pickup trucks.

When I finished Jillian's haircut, she asked if the Kempners were planning on adopting Hailey and Gabby.

"I'm not sure." I described the chaotic meeting with Caroline and Doug's family. "Nick doesn't think he can provide the girls a stable home, but I don't know what he's going to do."

Jillian glanced over her shoulder at Bianca and lowered her voice. "Is she right in saying that something is going on between you and Nick?"

I couldn't help but smile as I slid smoothing gel over Jillian's hair. "Nothing's going on. I kissed him again, but nothing can come of it. He's here only temporarily. Once he figures out the girls' situation, he's leaving."

"So you don't see yourself getting involved with him?"

"No. He's army. You know what that's like."

"Yes, I do." Jillian's tone was bitter. It was no secret she blamed the military for her divorce.

Her ex-husband, Keith Foster, had been the company commander when Marcus was killed. I'd never held Keith responsible for Marcus's death, but Keith hadn't been able to overcome the loss. Marcus's death dramatically changed him, leaving him angry and prone to alcohol abuse.

"You know," Jillian began with a false cheerfulness, "Bryan has a golfing friend. A dentist named Mitch Norman. He's recently divorced, handsome, and very sweet. And he just bought a house on the island because he's planning on staying. I think you'd really like him. How about I set something up for the four of us?"

Bianca glared from across the salon and mouthed the words, "Don't do it."

"I think you met Mitch at church a few Sundays ago," Jillian continued. "He's that good-looking guy with the straight white teeth?"

"Oh, sure. I remember him." I'd spoken to Mitch briefly, and while he was pleasant, I hadn't felt any spark between the two of us.

"Well, what do you think?" Jillian asked. "Are you interested?"

I thought about it for a minute. Maybe going on a date with Mitch would take my mind off Nick. "Sure. Why not?"

"Okay, I'll see what I can do."

Later, after Jillian and Dr. Lindsay left, Bianca shot me a disapproving glare. "Are you seriously going to let my sister fix you up with one of Bryan's golfing friends? *Boring Bryan*? Mr. Excitement himself?"

"Bryan's not so bad."

"Well, he's no Nick Peterson," she insisted.

No kidding, I thought.

AFTER LUNCH, NICK called to explain they'd had car trouble and were stuck just north of the island waiting for parts. Tense, I hung up the phone and explained the situation to Bianca who didn't see any need for alarm. "I don't know why you're worried. They'll be home soon."

"I know." Of course I agreed it wasn't healthy to worry, but that was the problem. I couldn't seem to stop unfounded fears from taking over my thoughts.

Bianca made a disapproving clucking sound. "I can only imagine what's going through that irrational mind of yours. Why don't you stop biting your lip and throw in a load of laundry."

"Yes, boss." I scooped the towels out of the hamper and took them to the washing machine. Would I ever be able to conquer my anxiety issues? Would I ever be able to trust God's promise that all things worked together for good for those who loved Him? And what about flying? Would I ever find the courage to get back in the helicopter?

The rest of the afternoon passed quickly as I was fully booked and had little time to think, let alone worry. Around five, I talked to Nick over the phone. He said the mechanic was installing the broken part, and they'd be home shortly. I tried to feel relieved, but I desperately wanted to jump in the car and pick up Travis myself.

"Why don't I bring Chinese takeout to your house so you don't have to wait alone," Bianca suggested, wiping down the counter.

"You don't have to do that. I know they're fine. I just need to work through my anxiety."

"Are you still taking the medicine the doctor gave you?"

I shrugged. "Not really. I don't like how it makes me feel flat and unmotivated."

"Well, flat and unmotivated might not be such a bad thing because you're about to chew off your lip, and it's freaking me out."

I pressed my lips together and reminded myself to breathe. "I'll be fine."

"Will you? I'm afraid if I leave you alone to wait, and it takes longer than expected, I might read about your breakdown in the *Island Sun* tomorrow morning."

"Very funny." I pressed my palms together and shifted my weight to stand in tree pose, one of the few yoga positions I regularly practiced. "I've gotten better, haven't I?"

"You have. But let me bring you dinner tonight. Besides, I need a change of scenery."

Bianca lived in a studio apartment above the salon. Many of the shops on Main Street boasted upstairs living quarters, including Vicki's Bakery. Both sisters loved the convenience and excitement of being downtown, but the arrangement could occasionally become stifling.

"If I'd be doing you a favor by allowing you to bring me Chinese food, then how can I refuse? Should we invite Vicki?"

Bianca shook her head. "She has a date. Besides, it's difficult to indulge in Huan's greasy egg rolls when Ms. Skinny Minnie is around."

I laughed. "True."

We closed the salon and I rode my bike home, grateful for Bianca's friendship. From the beginning, I'd liked all of the Morgan sisters, although I was closest to Bianca. Not just because of our work situation, but because she made me laugh and helped me put life's problems into perspective. We also shared a love of reading, greasy Chinese food, and romantic comedies.

At home, I made myself a cup of hot tea and ran upstairs for a quick bath. Slipping beneath the suds, I drank my tea and tried to relax. What I needed was something to distract me from constantly worrying about Travis. Nick's face immediately popped into my mind, but I pushed it away, determined not to entertain that impossible idea.

What if I went back to school? Lately, I'd been toying with the idea of taking a few classes at the local community college. Because I'd dropped out of college after my first semester, I'd always regretted not finishing my degree. At the time, I didn't see the point of staying in school when my ultimate goal was to get my pilot's license. Plus, Marcus and I had broken up, and I didn't want to continue attending the same college, running into him, and pretending everything was fine.

Against my parents' advice, I'd paid for a commercial pilot's training program with the money I'd inherited from my grandparents. By the time Marcus came home for the summer, I'd obtained my Certified

Flight Instructor's credentials and had begun earning money while logging the hours needed to be competitive in the job market.

Marcus and I had resumed our relationship that summer, and I'd wound up pregnant. Although I hadn't planned on getting married and having a baby at nineteen, I'd truly loved Marcus, and we'd made the best of a less than ideal situation. He'd enlisted in the army while I divided my time between flying and taking care of Travis. Life wasn't always easy, but for four years, we were happy.

Then he died, and I gave up flying. While everyone assumed I'd stopped out of fear of an accident that would leave Travis orphaned, I sometimes wondered if I was motivated by guilt. Guilt that I was still alive, able to live my dream, while Marcus was gone.

Bianca had encouraged me to go to cosmetology school, and although I enjoyed working at the salon, it wasn't my dream job. For starters, I didn't make very much money. Not that I needed a lot, especially given that I paid very little to live at the beach cottage. But there were things I wanted to provide for Travis that I couldn't because of my limited income, and I feared those needs would only increase as he grew older.

Was it too late to go back to school and change professions? And what about Travis? Did he really need me to be so busy with both work and school?

All these thoughts bounced around my head as I

soaked in the tub, failing to relax. But the thought that played most on my mind—the thought that refused to leave me alone—was Nick.

I WAS STILL soaking in the bathtub when the front door opened followed by urgent and joyful shouts from Travis. "Mom! Mom! Where are you?"

"In my bathroom," I hollered back, relieved he was home. I drained the water and climbed out of the tub. As I was drying off, there was a scuffling sound outside the bathroom door. "Travis? Are you okay?"

"Yes," he replied, impatiently. "When are you going to be out? I want to show you something."

The scuffling sound increased. "What's going on out there?"

"Nick bought me an early Christmas present. Come see it."

I hung up my towel and reached for my bathrobe. "It's not a snake, is it?"

"*Yes, Mom,*" he said, exasperated. "That's exactly what it is. I brought home Cuddles."

As I pulled on my bathrobe, something barked. Surely, Nick hadn't bought my son a dog, had he? Flinging open the door, I was shocked to see a black and brown puppy scoot under the bed.

"Travis Marcus Morgan!"

Travis positioned himself between me and the bed.

"Mom, I know what you said about getting a dog, but Nick bought him for me. He's a gift, and you can't just refuse a gift. You don't want me being rude, do you?"

"Rude?" I was outraged. "It's a puppy, Travis. A living, breathing puppy. I already told you I didn't want a dog. That's why I bought you the cat."

He thrust his hands together and begged. "Please, Mom. I promise to take care of him. I'll do everything. You won't even know Yoda's here."

"That's what you said about Felix, and do you know who feeds and changes the litter box every day? Me!"

"But this is a *dog*." His voice was full of sacred awe at the word dog. "Grandpa Walter is always saying a boy needs a dog, and Yoda is the best."

"Grandpa Walter wanted to give you a purebred yellow lab, not a mangy street dog."

At that moment, the mangy, street dog in question peeked out from under the bed. His large brown eyes met mine, taking away some of my outrage. Like all puppies, he was adorable. One of his fangs was longer than the other, giving him a lopsided expression that bordered on silliness.

I couldn't deny his cuteness, but I hardened my heart, because like I'd told my father-in-law, dogs were messy, smelly, and lots of work, not to mention expensive. Even a *free dog* needed visits to the vet, shots, and dog food.

Travis turned toward the bed, knelt, and patted his

leg. "Come here, Yoda. Here, boy." The dog's pointed ears twitched, and he slowly crept toward Travis who showered him with hugs and praise. "Good boy, Yoda. That's a good boy."

Pleased with himself, the dog wiggled away and pounced on the designer handbag Bianca had given me for my birthday last year. Although the purse outweighed the puppy by several pounds, he shook it hard, causing all the contents to fly out. Makeup, receipts, a hairbrush, and several cough drops skittered across the wood floor.

"Stop!" I shouted.

Instantly, Yoda obeyed and dropped the purse. He fell to the floor and rolled onto his back in a submissive pose, staring up at me with big, innocent puppy eyes that held the power to melt away my anger. Although I wasn't a dog person, I'd always thought Labrador retrievers were cute, and I guessed this dog was part Lab, part German Shepherd, part mutt, and one-hundred percent trouble.

"Ah," Travis said, rubbing Yoda's belly. "He's sorry, and he won't do that again. Will you, boy?" Yoda jumped up and licked Travis's glasses. Travis fell to the floor, laughing and rolling around with the puppy.

I picked up my damaged purse. Bianca had paid a fortune for the handbag, and now it was ruined. This had been the exact reason why I'd refused to get a puppy in the first place. Keeping him would only mean more destruction.

What in the world had Nick been thinking, buying my son a dog?

The doorbell rang, and I marched down the stairs, expecting to find an apologetic Nick. Instead, Bianca stood on the porch holding two large bags of Chinese food. "Who's ready for dinner?"

Chapter 8

Nick

AFTER THE LONG day, I was exhausted. I bathed Gabby, gave her a bottle, and rocked her to sleep. In the nursery, above the dresser hung an ornate mirror engraved with the words, "I am a child of God." Something about that statement chipped off a piece of my heart. *What about me? Was I a child of God?*

The question troubled me as I wanted to believe in a benevolent creator who cared about me, but in the darkness, I wasn't so sure.

Standing, I laid Gabby in the crib and gently patted her back. "Sleep tight, sweet pea."

Downstairs, I found Hailey, curled up in the laundry room with her three new puppies, all of them sound asleep. Smiling, I snapped a picture with my phone. Maybe buying an entire litter of puppies was overkill, but the happiness on Hailey's face during the ride home had made it all worthwhile.

Bending over, I scooped up my niece and carried her

upstairs to tuck her into bed. I pulled the covers over her shoulders and gently kissed her forehead. "Sweet dreams, honey."

Hailey turned over in her sleep. "Love you, Uncle Nick."

My chest tightened. I hadn't grown up saying *I love you*, but Ethan and Ivana had used the phrase liberally.

"I love you, too," I repeated, feeling vulnerable and exposed. Love had never served me well. I must've loved my mother as a baby, but I had no idea if she'd returned my love. I loved my father, of course, and I assumed Jack loved me in his own indifferent way, but that love had never made me feel safe.

Love had consequences. Love hurt and could leave you weak and injured.

And love, after all, was the reason I couldn't leave the girls with Doug and Caroline Kempner. Instinctively, I believed their frenzied family wouldn't be a good fit for Hailey and Gabby.

My father thought I was acting ridiculous, wasting so much leave time, but I refused to be bullied, even by him.

Recently, one of my friends from college had adopted two little boys. He'd used an agency in Houston and had given me the name and number. After meeting with the Kempners, I'd called and spoken with a lawyer named Lucy Jenkins. Lucy had been very sympathetic and encouraged me to make an appointment. Today,

I'd driven past the address to check it out.

From the outside, the business looked legitimate and professional. But could I really leave Hailey and Gabby with strangers who weren't even related to them? And if I did, would I later regret it? Would my father care that his only grandchildren wouldn't be raised by relatives? And how would that affect my relationship with the girls?

I wanted to do the right thing for my nieces, but what did that mean?

Back downstairs, I took the puppies outside to use the bathroom, changed their newspaper in the laundry room, started the washing machine, and loaded the dishwasher. Just as I finished cleaning the kitchen, the doorbell rang.

To my surprise, I found Anna standing on the front porch, glaring at me. "Your shirt is sopping wet."

Confused as to why she was so upset about my shirt, I looked down and shrugged. "I guess it got soaked when I was bathing the baby."

Her face filled with panic. "You didn't leave Gabby in the bathtub by herself, did you?"

"Give me some credit," I said, slightly offended. "I may not know what kind of cereal to buy, or how to braid Hailey's hair, but I'd never leave a baby unattended in the bathtub."

"Well, where is she?"

I studied Anna carefully. Why was she so mad?

"Gabby's sound asleep in her crib."

Anna's entire body relaxed, and she placed a hand over her heart. "Sorry. I have an awful fear of babies and drowning."

I nodded. "Yeah, me, too. That's why I would never leave her alone."

Awkward silence followed, and then I asked Anna inside. She started to turn down my invitation, but sounds of the puppies barking from the laundry room interrupted her. The scowl on her face deepened. "You bought Hailey a puppy, too?"

Her contempt was obvious, and being the genius I was, I concluded she was mad about Travis's puppy. "I take it you disapprove of Yoda?"

She squared her shoulders. "You bought my son a *dog* without my permission." She said the word *dog* like one would say the word sewer or politician.

"Travis insisted you'd be okay with it," I said, only half joking.

"He's ten. Of course he said I'd be okay with it. What ten-year-old boy would ever refuse a puppy?"

Stepping back, I opened the door wider. "Come inside, Anna. I want to show you something."

She planted herself firmly in place and folded her arms across her chest. "No, I can't stay. I only came to express my frustration about the dog. You can't give my son a dog, or anything else, without my permission. Do you understand?"

"Yeah, I understand, and I'm sorry. But please, come inside."

Anna

RELUCTANTLY, I STEPPED over the threshold and followed Nick through the living room to the kitchen. The Blue Crab shared a similar floor plan, but the Petersons' house was much larger and more recently built. High quality windows enhanced the spectacular view of the ocean, and a large wooden deck wrapped around the entire first floor.

In the kitchen, pots and pans dried on the counter while the dishwasher hummed quietly. A pile of laundry, neatly folded and stacked, sat on the table. I found the tidy scene comforting. Nick was somewhat of a neat freak; something I admired in a man.

He led me into the laundry room where three puppies similar to Yoda scrambled to the baby gate, vying for attention. "How many puppies did you buy?" I asked.

"All of them."

"All of them? Are you serious?" The man was insane.

Removing his phone from his back pocket, he scrolled through his photos. "I thought you should know we didn't buy the dogs from the pet store."

"No?" His comment confused me because what did that have to do with anything?

"There was an elderly woman in the town where the car broke down." He handed me his phone, and I stared at a picture of an extremely thin and wrinkled woman, sitting on the ground next to a shabby trailer. Four puppies surrounded her, including one I recognized as Yoda.

"I know they're just mutts," Nick said, leaning against the doorframe, "but I felt sorry for them. This woman had no money, and she was trying to earn a living by selling the puppies. I paid a fortune for them, but I couldn't say no. And I'm pretty sure someone as sweet as you, Anna Morgan, would've done the same thing."

I gave back his phone and stared down at the puppies. "I understand taking pity on her and the dogs, but if you wanted to help, why didn't you just *give* her money? Why did you insist on buying the dogs?"

He shook his head. "Nobody wants to be a charity case."

I understood that sentiment. Bianca had helped pay for beauty school, but I had returned the money as soon as I could. And each month, I gave my in-laws a check for rent, even though they'd offered the beach cottage free of charge.

I studied Nick carefully. "I appreciate what you're saying, but more responsibility is the last thing either one of us needs right now. Don't you have enough going on in your life without adding all these puppies to the mix?"

He gave me a sly smile. "That's why I was hoping you'd take another one."

"What?"

His grin spread across his face, and I knew he was joking. I smiled back at him and shook my head. "I'll keep Yoda, but I'm not taking another dog, so don't get any ideas."

He nodded. "Look, if you don't want Yoda, I'll take him back. What's one more puppy when you already have three?"

I sighed. "No, I told Travis he could keep him, especially since he insisted that means I'm no longer obligated to give him anything for Christmas, his birthday, or any other holiday for the rest of his life. And he promised to feed and take care of Yoda without my nagging."

"It sounds like a good deal."

I gave a grunt of disbelief. "We'll see. But do you have any idea the amount of work a puppy requires, let alone *three* of them?"

My question caused Nick's face to fall, making me regret offending him. But seriously, what kind of person bought three puppies when they were in the middle of a crisis?

"My father used that excuse whenever Ethan and I asked for a dog," he said. "And the thing is I have no idea how much work a dog requires because I've never had one before. I'm sorry I gave Travis a dog without asking you, but I don't regret buying them, so please don't lecture me."

"You're right," I conceded, remorseful. "I'm sorry."

He looked at me with those penetrating eyes. "We had a rough weekend, and I wanted to make Hailey and Gabby happy. You should've heard them giggling on the way home. Hailey hasn't giggled since the accident. And tonight, she fell asleep without me having to lie on the ground beside her bed."

I pictured Nick keeping guard as Hailey slept. I could've used someone like that after Marcus died.

Even though buying four mutts was overkill, how could I fault him for trying to make his nieces happy? I smiled up at him. "Are you sure you're in the military? You're kind of a softie."

He laughed, the sound rumbling in his chest and making my knees weak. "I'm not a softie. I've been called all sorts of insulting names, but when it comes to Hailey and Gabby, I can't say no. There isn't anything I wouldn't do for those girls."

"I understand."

We turned our attention back to the puppies and watched them play for a little bit. Then he asked if Travis had told me about Gabby's ear infection.

"No," I said.

"That's why she's been crying so much. I feel horrible I didn't take her to the doctor sooner, but I thought she was crying because of her parents. I've never taken care of a baby before, and I didn't know."

"It's all right," I said. "She can't tell you her ear hurts. Lots of parents would've missed that. Is she on antibiotics now?"

"Yes." He exhaled and gave a hopeless look. "Taking care of the girls is overwhelming."

"I'll help you," I offered before I could stop myself.

"You will?"

"Of course. That's what neighbors do. They help out each other."

He took my hand and gently squeezed it.

I looked down at our entwined hands, remembering this was exactly how our last kiss began. Why, why, why did I have to be so attracted to this man? "I better get back to Travis." Reluctantly, I slid my hand from his and walked toward the front door.

I'd made my point, and now it was time to go home before I did something foolish. When Marcus died, I'd been so devastated that getting out of bed was difficult. With each day, my strength and courage increased, and I learned to live without him.

Now, here was Nick, threatening the independence I'd worked so hard to achieve. I couldn't let him break down my walls and take me back to that place of vulnerability.

Nick followed me through the living room to the front door. "So, do you have any words of wisdom about what I should do regarding the girls?"

I turned to face him, diverting my eyes from the large family portrait of Ethan, Ivana, Hailey, and Gabby hanging above the fireplace. "Just follow your heart. As clichéd as that sounds, it's the only thing that really matters."

He exhaled deeply. "My heart says not to leave the girls with the Kempners, so that means finding someone else to take care of them."

I nodded. "Do you have any ideas?"

"I do."

The air between us filled with a tense silence I didn't understand. Nick was holding something back. He rubbed his knuckles across his chest before speaking. "I've been in contact with an adoption agency in Houston."

An *adoption agency*? That sounded so cold and sterile. Was Nick thinking about leaving the girls with strangers? Would they have to go through the foster care system?

"I know it sounds horrible." He shifted his weight from one foot to the other. "But what other choice do I have? The lawyer I spoke to at the agency is confident she can find the perfect family for the girls. We'd arrange an open adoption, so I'd still be a part of their lives. They'd still know me as their Uncle Nick, and my father and I could visit anytime we wanted.

"You said you'd help me," he continued. "Will you

help me with this? I have an appointment tomorrow morning back in Houston. Will you come with me? Be my second set of eyes and ears and watch that I don't make a mistake?"

"What about your dad?" I asked, thinking this should be a family decision.

"My father's in Japan on business for the month."

"Japan? Isn't he going to help you with the girls?"

"No." A pained expression filled his face. "My father has never been in the running for grandfather of the year. Or father of the year for that matter. He thinks I'm making a big deal out of nothing."

I was appalled by Jack Peterson's apathy and knew I couldn't refuse Nick's request for help. "I'll have to reschedule my appointments, but yes. I'll go with you."

"Thanks." His entire body relaxed, and he opened his arms for a hug. I walked into his embrace as if it were the most natural thing in the world. He pulled me close and rested his chin on top of my head.

With my arms around him, it would be so easy for this innocent hug to turn into more than a comforting gesture between friends. But friends were all we could be. We needed each other's support right now. Anything more would only make things difficult when he left.

"See you tomorrow," he said, letting me go.

"Okay. See you tomorrow."

Chapter 9

*I*N THE MORNING, I straightened my hair and pulled on a baby blue sweater dress with black tights and boots. At Nick's request, I hadn't told Travis I was leaving the island today, and I felt guilty about that. On the other hand, I certainly understood why Nick didn't want Hailey to know about the adoption agency.

Hailey believed she and Gabby would eventually move in with their cousins. Although she wasn't pleased with the idea of living in a house full of boys, at least she was familiar with the Kempners. Finding out Nick was looking for another family might upset her.

When Nick pulled into the driveway, I placed the puppy in the kitchen behind the enclosure I'd bought at the pet store with Bianca last night. Yoda whined, but I gave him a chew toy, promising that Bianca would stop by later to feed him.

Felix sauntered into the kitchen, his tail raised in annoyance at all the commotion. The cat didn't seem too impressed by our new addition to the family. Yoda, on the other hand, was obsessed with Felix, and he barked repeatedly until the cat curled up in the kitchen sink out of sight.

"It's okay, boy," I said, rubbing the puppy's head. "Felix will play with you later."

With the pets taken care of, I hopped into Ivana's Tahoe. Would I ever come to think of it as Nick's Tahoe? Probably not since he wasn't planning on staying and would soon be selling the vehicle.

From the back seat, Gabby squealed. I turned around and tickled her sock-covered feet. "How are you doing this morning, Fancy Face?"

"I'm doing just fine," Nick answered, not missing a beat. "What about you?"

I smiled. "I can't complain. Any problems dropping off Hailey and Travis?"

"No flat tires or bike wrecks if that's what you mean."

"Ha, ha."

He winked. "Everything went fine. I think Gabby really enjoys the morning bike ride, and she's finally used to wearing the helmet."

"That's good. How's her ear infection?"

"Better. The doctor said it might take a while for the antibiotic to kick in, but she slept all night and woke up happy."

"What about the puppies? How'd they do?"

He groaned. "Please don't say 'I told you so,' but the puppies were *way* worse than the baby."

I laughed. "You must've given us the good one, because Yoda did better than I expected. Travis slept on the kitchen floor with him, and I didn't hear them until this morning."

"Lucky you."

We exchanged a smile and continued down the road in companionable silence for a few minutes. I looked out the window at the ocean gently lapping against the sandy shore. I loved living at the beach. Loved the community, my church, and everything about Rose Island. While many residents developed *island fever*, I never felt a need to leave.

"So," Nick said, tapping his fingers on the steering wheel. "You told me your father was stationed here at Fort Xavier when you were a kid?"

I nodded. "Twice, actually. Once when I was in the sixth grade and then again my senior year. After Marcus and I married, I stayed on the island working while he went through basic training. I joined him at Fort Benning where we had Travis, but our last tour was back here."

"And you worked as a helicopter pilot out of the Rose Island airport?"

"That's right. I was a flight instructor and also worked for a company giving sightseeing flights to tourists." Suddenly, I was filled with the uncomfortable sense of dread that accompanied any mention of my previous career. Why had I been so forthright with my answer to Nick's question? I should've given a simple "yes," instead of revealing my life story.

Nick briefly took his eyes off the road to study me. "You haven't been able to fly since your husband died?"

I shook my head. Everyone, including my parents and in-laws, had thought it foolish for me to quit flying after spending so much time and money on flight school. And the thing is, I agreed with them.

What disappointed me the most was the fact I'd given up on my dream. I tried telling myself raising Travis in a safe environment was my dream, but sometimes I wanted more.

"So, did Bianca and her sisters grow up here?" Nick asked.

"They did. Luella, my mother-in-law, vacationed here as a child. When she and Walter married, they came down for their honeymoon and ended up staying."

Nick grimaced.

"What's wrong?"

"Luella was the name of my father's fifth wife," he explained.

"Fifth wife? How many times has he been married?"

"Six. He's engaged again and swears Gina is *the one.*"

I tried to suppress my judgment. "Has he ever found *the one* before?"

"Nope. But there's a first time for everything, right?"

Before I could follow up, Nick asked where my in-laws lived on the island. I explained they owned a small hobby ranch on the mountain. The mountain was actually a large hill in the center of the island, home to many organic farms, free-range ranches, and a few farm-to-table restaurants.

While several species of wild roses thrived on the mountain, the island had actually been named for the Rose family who fled Mexico during the rebellion against Spain in the early 1800s. On the mountain's highest peak, Franco Rose had built a mansion for his large family that currently housed the island's historical museum in addition to operating as a quaint bed-and-breakfast.

"And you rent The Blue Crab from your in-laws?" Nick asked.

I nodded. "Luella and Walter lived there until their family grew, and they decided to buy a small farm. They used the beach cottage to generate rental income, but when Marcus died, they bribed me with it."

"Nice bribe."

I smiled, self-conscious that maybe I was talking too much. Usually, my dates droned on about their own accomplishments and past relationships. Not that I considered this outing to be a date. Regardless, I found being with Nick refreshing. He seemed genuinely interested in what I had to say.

As we drove over the causeway that connected the island to the mainland, I breathed easily. Usually, crossing the bridge bothered me, but today, Nick's presence calmed me.

"So, why the bribe?" he asked.

I smoothed back my hair. "Part of it was their desire to have a solid relationship with Travis, and part of it was Luella's guilt. I was a little nervous at first, but the arrangement has worked out nicely. I can't imagine living anywhere else."

"I can understand that. The island is beautiful, and you seem happy."

"I am."

A beat of silence fell, then Nick asked about Marcus's mom. "You said your mother-in-law felt guilty? Why is that?"

Through the sideview mirror, I watched the island disappear. Although my problems with Luella were in the past, and I'd completely forgiven her, I felt compelled to answer Nick's question. "Marcus and I weren't married when I conceived Travis. Against his parents' wishes, he proposed, dropped out of college, and joined the army. At the time, I thought the military was a good idea and my parents supported it.

"Jillian's ex-husband was in the army. Actually, he still is. He tried to talk Marcus into finishing college in order to enter as an officer, but Marcus wanted to take immediate responsibility for me and the baby."

"That's understandable," Nick said. "And honorable."

"Yes, but you know what happened. He was killed

in Iraq—"

"Wait a minute." Nick's eyes widened. "Sergeant Morgan? That was your husband? I didn't realize . . . he was the soldier who saved Governor Williams and the reporter Lyla Gray. She wrote a book about the sacrifices of several soldiers and included a chapter on your husband, right?"

My chest contracted. "Yes."

"I'm so sorry. I had no idea. I know you'd rather have him alive, but he was an amazing soldier. I read the book a few years ago, and I remember the part about him."

Hot tears stung my eyes, but I blinked them away, determined not to cry. "I am very proud of him. He was a good man."

Nick reached over and squeezed my hand. "Hey. I'm sorry, that was a stupid thing to say. I didn't mean to be insensitive."

I squeezed back. "It's okay. I know what you meant; it's just hard. Not something I've ever been able to get used to."

Letting go of his hand, I pulled a tissue from my purse. Nick said nothing as I dabbed at my eyes and tried to compose myself. "I was angry and depressed for a long time. It's still hard, and I know I'm often afraid for irrational reasons, but I've grown a lot."

He gave a silent nod, and I continued talking. "After Marcus died, I lived with Bianca until Jillian helped smooth things over with her mother. Then I moved back to the ranch until they offered me the beach house."

"What do you mean, *smoothed things over*?"

I chastised myself for saying so much, but I had to finish the story. "Well, at first, Luella blamed me for Marcus's death. Not directly, but he never would've joined the military had I not gotten pregnant."

Nick tightened his grip on the steering wheel. "You never would've gotten pregnant had he not impregnated you."

"True, but Luella lost her son, and . . . well, we all kind of went crazy for awhile. Later, she apologized, insisting she had no right to blame me. But it doesn't matter anymore. We're very close, and I've forgiven her."

Nick stared straight ahead. "It was unfair she held you even the least bit responsible for her son's death. Every soldier accepts risk when he or she joins the army. Especially when they deploy."

"You're right." Nick's adamant insistence of my innocence both surprised and touched me. I hated seeing him upset by something that'd occurred years ago and was no longer important. At the same time, his loyalty moved me. Nick was the kind of guy who protected his friends.

"I'm glad you worked things out," he said. "I don't know if I would've been as forgiving."

"Life is all about forgiveness. People make mistakes, and if you let resentment dominate your thoughts, you'll be disappointed. Besides, I can't sit in church every Sunday and not believe in forgiveness."

He frowned. "Do you go to church every Sunday?"

"I try. Do you?"

His face tensed. "I used to love going, but other than the funeral, I haven't been in a long time."

I made a mental note to add *doesn't go to church* to the list of reasons why I shouldn't get involved with Nick.

"How long has Jillian been divorced?" he asked, changing the subject.

I gave him an odd look. "You like to ask a lot of questions, don't you?"

"I'm just trying to get to know you better, Anna," he said with a bashful grin.

My stomach jolted. What was that supposed to mean? Tamping down on my anxiety, I turned the tables and asked a question of my own. "What about you? Have you ever been married or divorced?"

He laughed and shook his head. "No, I've always wanted a career in the military."

"And that means you can't get married?" I teased. "Is there a new vow of celibacy I'm not aware of?"

He laughed again, the rich, deep sound filling the car. "No, I just think with all the continuous deployments it wouldn't be fair to a spouse. I think marriage is hard enough without that added pressure, don't you?"

"Of course, but . . . you *never* intend to marry?"

"My father's had six wives. I didn't exactly grow up with the best view of marriage. If I ever marry, my wife would have to understand the sacrifices military spouses endure. And she'd have to be willing to put up with those sacrifices. I think a woman like that would be hard to find."

I gave an involuntary shudder because I completely agreed with him. Throughout the years, I'd watched my parents struggle with the deployments, politics, and sacrifices of army life; and I'd made those sacrifices myself while married to Marcus.

Moreover, I'd seen Jillian's marriage crumble under the pressure. So, while I deeply admired military families, army life wasn't anything I wanted to experience again.

Our conversation drifted to more neutral topics, including the latest product from Apple and a recent movie we both wanted to see. Nick talked about Ranger school and the first time he jumped out of an airplane. I told him about Fin's Steakhouse, my favorite restaurant on the River Walk in San Antonio.

When we pulled into the parking lot of the adoption agency, disappointment washed over me. We'd had such a nice drive, I'd temporarily put the reason for the trip out of my mind. Now that we'd arrived, I wanted to turn around and go back home.

Nick parked the car next to a hawthorn tree, and as soon as he turned off the engine, Gabby began to cry. She settled down when he leaned into the back seat and unbuckled her.

"Did you have a nice nap, cupcake?" he asked, lifting her into his arms.

She gave a sleepy smile and pointed at me as if surprised I was still there. Leaning forward, I started to kiss her chubby fingers, but before I could, Nick spun her out of my reach.

She chuckled and so did I. Nick grinned at the both of us, and everything inside me melted.

A thick raindrop hit the windshield, causing Gabby to jump. The baby laughed as the rain increased, and I smiled at Nick.

It would not be difficult to fall in love with this man who so easily blended strength with tenderness. Hardening my heart, I looked out the window at the sign for the adoption agency and reminded myself I was here to help Nick. Not to complicate matters.

Chapter 10

INSIDE THE ADOPTION agency, I entertained Gabby while Nick completed several forms. A young and pregnant girl no older than sixteen sat across from us, playing on her phone. She had well-manicured nails and expensive shoes. Was she here to give up her unborn baby? Maybe she'd changed her mind and had come to cancel her arrangement.

I glanced at Nick, his head bent over the clipboard. Would the agency really be able to find a loving family for the girls?

Nick returned the completed forms to the receptionist and took a seat next to Gabby and me. He unzipped the diaper bag and fixed a bottle as the baby squirmed in anticipation.

"I think she's hungry," I said.

"I think you're right." He handed Gabby the bottle, and she thrust it into her mouth with a grunt of pleasure. Her wide blue eyes darted between Nick and me as if trying to make sense of it all.

"My little piglet," he said, smiling as he rubbed a large hand over the baby's head.

Gabby pushed the bottle out of her mouth and let out a belch. Nick placed a hand over his heart. "Such a talented child," he teased.

Both Gabby and I giggled.

After a while, the receptionist led us down a carpeted hallway where a tall, thin woman with curly brown hair greeted us. "I'm Lucy Jenson. It's nice to finally meet you in person, Mr. Peterson. This must be Gabby. What a cutie-pie."

The baby buried her face in my neck and giggled. Nick leaned over and took her from me, leaving me feeling empty.

We entered Lucy's cheerful office, which was lit by the sun streaming through large windows. Several purple African violets lined the windowsill. Nick and I sat next to each other on a comfy couch while Lucy took the straight-back wooden chair beside us.

With incredible calmness, Nick spoke about his desire for an open adoption, so he could maintain a relationship with his nieces. "Giving them up is a difficult decision, but keeping them isn't something I can do right now."

"I completely understand," Lucy said. "We have a number of families that would meet your criteria and are open to adopting a sibling pair, especially given the girls' circumstances. Why don't I take you into our conference room where you can use our computers to get started? Afterwards, we can talk about what appealed to you, and I can get a better sense of what to look for."

I had a strange feeling of déjà vu. Recently, I'd helped Jillian look for a new house. At the real-estate office, the realtor—whom Jillian was now dating, the one Bianca called Boring Bryan—had said almost the same thing regarding prospective homes. How much more important was this decision than finding a dream house?

Lucy showed us the conference room and issued instructions on how to use the *Family Find Program*. "I'll come back and check on you in about half an hour, but if you need anything, don't hesitate to ask."

"Thank you." Nick set Gabby on the floor with a chunky board book, which she promptly stuck in her mouth.

Sitting at separate computers, we scrolled through the list of prospective families. Each profile showed a happy couple, boasting various hobbies, favorite children's books, and holiday traditions. Many of the couples had posted pictures showing them baking, swimming, and playing at the park with their nieces and nephews.

I never imagined there'd be so many couples looking to adopt a baby. I didn't know whether I felt sadder for the couples without kids, or those with just one who wanted another child. I'd grown up as an only child, and it'd been lonely. My mother had desperately wanted another baby, but it'd never happened. Had my parents ever considered adoption?

Sometimes I felt sorry Travis was an only child. I consoled myself with the fact that at least he had his cousins, Matt and Drew. When Travis was younger, he often talked about his imaginary brother, but it'd been a long time since he'd mentioned Ole Meatball Tutu. While I had no idea how he'd come up with that crazy name, it made me laugh every time he said it.

As I sifted through the list of families, I could see Hailey and Gabby living with several of them. Maybe adoption was Nick's best option.

But just like searching for a house, until you met the families face-to-face, how would you know? And even then, it took a while to make a final decision. If Nick was supposed to leave after Christmas, he didn't have much time. Thanksgiving was next week and Christmas would soon follow.

I clicked on the next page and froze. "I know this couple. It's the Woodalls. She was Travis's kindergarten teacher, and he's a principal at the middle school. They've been trying to have a baby for years. They'd be perfect parents for Hailey and Gabby. Nick, take a look."

Turning my computer screen toward him, I glanced up to gauge his reaction. He gave a cursory glance at the screen, then looked down at Gabby who sat on the floor, pulling out the baby wipes one by one.

"Nick?"

His Adam's apple bobbed up and down. Without a word, he leaned over, clasped my hands, and closed his eyes. My heart cracked wide open as he took several ragged breaths.

"I can't do this," he whispered.

Gabby crawled across the floor and pulled herself up, using Nick's leg for balance. He bent down and scooped her into his arms. "Hey, sweetheart."

I started to ask what he'd meant by not being able to do this, but Lucy entered the room. "How are we doing in here?"

Nick came to his feet and shifted Gabby in his arms. "We need to head back home, but I'll call you tomorrow."

Lucy studied him closely. "I know this is an emotional decision for you, Mr. Peterson. Is there anything I can do to help? Anything you need me to clarify or want to discuss?"

"Not now, but I'll be in touch."

I put the baby wipes back in the container and repacked the diaper bag. Then Nick and I walked outside. The rain had stopped, and bright sunshine warmed the earth. The grass and trees were green and alive, reminding me of spring instead of late fall.

"Are you okay?" I asked Nick once we reached the car.

He gave a sad smile. "Yes, but I'm hungry. What about you?"

"Starving."

"And what about you?" he asked Gabby, tickling her tummy. "Are you starving?" She giggled and he kissed her fat little cheek.

Smiling down at me, he said, "I know this fabulous hamburger place. I'm sure it can't compare to Fin's Steakhouse on the River Walk, but I'd love to buy you lunch."

"I'd like that."

As I climbed into the car, I wondered how many people at the restaurant would assume we were a happy, little family.

I also wondered how wrong it was for part of me to wish it were true.

Chapter 11

*I*N BETWEEN CLIENTS at work the next day, I iced my back. Unlike Bianca, who could work for hours without complaint, I often suffered from aches and pains associated with standing on my feet all day, washing, cutting, and coloring hair.

I loved being a hairstylist and making people feel beautiful, but it didn't compare to flying. No job compared to flying. Completing the Flight Instructor's training had been one of the hardest things I'd ever done. Afterward, my confidence had exploded, making me believe I could accomplish anything.

And now? Now, I was a mess of nerves and anxiety. As Oprah would say, I wasn't living my *Best Life*.

Rocking side to side in the salon chair, I thought about Nick's difficult decision regarding the girls. On the drive home, I'd tried talking to him about a few of the prospective families, but he'd quickly changed the subject.

"Don't look now," Bianca called, wiping down the front window. "But Mr. Sweet and Spicy is coming this way."

"Nick?" I asked, my heart involuntarily leaping out of my chest.

"No, not Nick," she hissed sarcastically. "Some other six-foot, dreamy-eyed, gorgeous hunk of a man who happens to be into you."

I rolled my eyes. "He's not *into* me."

"*Please.*"

"Well, it doesn't matter. It's not like he's going to stay. Eventually, he'll go back to the army, and you know how I feel about that."

Bianca batted the air with disgust. "Until then, would it be so wrong to enjoy a little romance with the man?"

"Romance?"

"Yes. Dinner, dancing, a little handholding. Maybe a little walk on the beach or a little kissing under the harsh fluorescent lighting of the salon. Nothing permanent or too serious, but an enjoyable short-term diversion."

Her teasing transported me back to being a teenager, and I buried my face in my hands and shook my head. "Can we *please* talk about something else? He's here for Hailey's appointment." Standing, I tossed the ice pack into the sink.

Bianca opened the door, and Travis and Hailey stepped inside, followed by Nick, who wore jeans and a black T-shirt. He carried Gabby in a baby backpack, and her sweet face peaked over his shoulder, taking in everything.

My emotions exploded at the tender sight. Heat rose to my face, but I dismissed it by focusing on Travis. "How was school today? Everything go okay with your math test?"

"It was fine," he answered.

Upon spotting Bianca, Gabby let out a squeal of delight and tried to climb out of the backpack. Fortunately, she was well secured and didn't get far.

"Sorry, baby," Bianca said, gathering her purse. "I know you want me to put more bows in your hair and take you to the bank, but I can't stay. I need to run errands before my next client."

I smiled at Hailey. "Are you ready for your haircut?"

"Yes, Miss Anna." Hailey kept her head down as she took a seat in the salon chair. A horrible sadness clung to her, and while I knew a new hairstyle couldn't erase her pain, I hoped I could at least make her feel better.

"Want to play a video game?" Travis asked Nick. "It's in the kid room."

Nick looked at me for permission.

"Go ahead. We'll be okay without you. Travis, find the bucket of baby toys for Gabby, okay?"

"Right-O, Mommy-O," he merrily answered, leading the way.

Nick glanced at Hailey before following Travis through the salon. From my station, I could see into the kid room, which contained a couch, TV, table, and several buckets of toys.

Travis had outgrown most of the toys, but whenever he came to work with me on a Saturday, he'd pull out the blocks and Lincoln Logs to build an enormous city. There was something innocent and sweet about toys that didn't need charging or syncing.

Nick put Gabby on the floor with the laundry basket of brightly colored baby toys, then he took a seat on the couch and listened as Travis explained the game in minute detail. It was amazing how much my son could remember when it came to video games. If only he could be that passionate about his schoolwork.

Turning my attention to Hailey, I fingered the child's tangled hair. Ivana never would have allowed her daughter to look like this. Nick cared about his nieces, but he probably didn't realize he needed to remind Hailey to wash and brush her hair every day.

I smiled at Hailey's reflection in the mirror. "What are you looking for today? A trim like last time, or would you like something different?"

Hailey avoided my gaze in the mirror. "Will you give me a bob, so it's shorter in the back and comes to about here?" She placed her hands just below her chin.

I swallowed. "Like your mom wore it?"

She looked at me, her eyes hesitant. "Yes."

Patting her shoulder, I nodded. "We can definitely do that."

We headed back to the sinks, and as I shampooed

Hailey's hair, I listened to Nick and Travis laughing about blowing up some building. I'd never understood the attraction to video games, and I had no idea why Travis and Jillian's boys found so much joy in destroying things.

Even before Marcus died, I'd been opposed to anything that glorified violence, including video games and toy guns. My father had taught me how to shoot, and I often went with Marcus to the rifle range, so I wasn't opposed to guns. I just didn't believe they should be used as toys.

Then I'd had Travis, a boy through and through, who could turn a paper plate or church hymnal into a gun. I'd struggled with his attraction to weapons but Marcus had finally won me over.

"It's instinct," he'd insisted. "You have to let the boy be a boy. Just because he enjoys destroying things doesn't mean he's a psychopath."

Judging by how Nick and Travis were shooting it up in the game room, it was obvious Nick felt the same way. Travis must've made an impressive move because Nick gave him a high five and said, "Way to go, buddy!"

My pulse thudded. What would it be like to have a man in my life? A man like Nick? A man who could be not just a husband to me, but a good father to Travis? And what would I be willing to sacrifice in order to have that?

I'd loved Marcus so much, but I'd been young, naïve, and fearless. Could I ever love another man with the reckless abandon of youth?

Nick's kindness and confidence spoke to my heart. Last night, I'd dreamt about him again and had awoken eager to see him. Maybe I should follow Bianca's advice and open my heart to a little romance. I wouldn't mind a candlelit dinner or a walk on the beach at sunset with Nick.

In the end, however, the result would be another broken heart. And this time, I feared I might never recover.

"Miss Anna?" Hailey asked. "Are you all right?"

I turned off the water. "Sure, sweetheart. I'm fine. I was just lost in my own thoughts."

"Oh." She lifted her head so I could wrap a towel around her wet hair. "For a moment, you looked really sad."

I gave her shoulder a motherly pat, and we walked back to the station in silence. I spent a long time painstakingly combing out her hair, careful not to pull on the tangles. "I'll send home some conditioner with you. If you use it after you shampoo your hair, it will be easier to brush."

"Okay," she said.

I separated her hair into layers and began cutting it. "I think it's going to look so pretty."

She stared at the floor. "I hope so."

Nick

WHEN THE BABY grew fussy, I excused myself from the video game. I made a bottle and carried Gabby through the salon to check on Hailey.

"You can have a seat here," Anna said, motioning to the empty chair beside her.

I sat and stared down at Gabby as she drank the bottle. I loved how her eyes closed and her body grew heavy as she drifted off to sleep. Often, she rewarded me with a sleepy smile, which I found encouraging. Maybe I was doing okay when it came to caring for her.

In contrast, Hailey never smiled in her sleep. I knew that because I always checked on her before going to bed. Last night, I'd found all three puppies snuggled under the covers with her. Even then, her hands were balled into fists and her brow was deeply furrowed.

Should I be doing more to help her cope with the death of her parents? I'd mistakenly told my father Hailey was seeing a grief counselor. Jack had disapproved, insisting most quacks were quacks themselves. I didn't dare admit I'd not only seen a shrink last year, but I'd found the session worthwhile.

Admitting you needed help wasn't a sign of weakness. At least, that's what I'd told my men after we'd lost one of our own to suicide.

The first time I'd seen the psychologist, I'd felt foolish talking about my personal problems.

Yes, I obviously had issues with commitment stemming from being abandoned by my mother and ignored by my father. Yes, losing buddies in battle continued to haunt me. Yes, I felt personally responsible for the suicide in my unit even though the soldier had been under medical care.

Regardless of how difficult I'd found the session, however, I'd left with some coping skills and had been motivated to return. Lately, I'd been thinking about making an appointment for myself on Rose Island. I thought it might be helpful to talk to someone about losing my brother.

Living in Ethan and Ivana's home, surrounded by all their personal belongings, wasn't easy. Part of me wanted to box up everything and forget they'd ever existed. Yet, how could I do that when Hailey seemed comforted by her parents' things? Whenever she was feeling particularly sad, I'd often find her curled up in her mother's bathrobe or wearing one of her father's baseball caps.

Yesterday's trip to the adoption agency had been tough. Reading about all the couples who desperately wanted a child of their own had disturbed me, making me question my decision to put the girls up for adoption. Was it wrong for me to think about keeping them myself?

Last night, Hailey made dinner for us. She'd set the table with Ivana's fine china and a vase containing wilted flowers from the funeral. As we enjoyed our meal of cereal, carrot sticks, and chocolate chip cookies, we'd talked about how best to train the puppies and what we should name them. I thought since Travis had Yoda, our puppies should have *Star Wars* names as well, but Hailey insisted on Liesl, Friedrich, and Louisa. Names from the *Sound of Music,* a movie I'd secretly come to love almost as much as *Star Wars*.

How was I supposed to turn my back on all this? How was I supposed to sign the papers giving custody to someone else?

Yet, how could I assume responsibility when I didn't have the skills required to be a parent?

I'd often wondered if my mother had been mentally ill. How else had she been able to so easily abandon her children?

And my father? Since the funeral, Jack had called only once, and that was because *Gina* wanted me to bring the girls to Dallas for Thanksgiving. What kind of normal grandfather ignored his granddaughters after their world had been turned upside down?

Then again, maybe I was the one with the mental illness. Maybe I was too soft and needed to accept the fact the girls were better off living with someone else. Besides, even if I wanted to keep them, I couldn't abdicate my military obligation.

To drive that point home, my commanding officer had called this morning, asking if I had any interest in being an aide to General Sanchez. Any interest? Of course! I'd met Sanchez during Officer Basic Course when the superior officer, then Colonel Sanchez, had taken an interest in me. We'd run into each other again at graduation and several other times over the years. If I could serve as the general's aide, that would put me in a prime position for further advancement.

And that's what I needed to focus on. Any thoughts of domestic bliss needed to be forgotten because the girls required more than I could give right now. They *deserved* more than I could give. Tonight, I'd force myself to look through the list of possible families and find a home for Hailey and Gabby.

The sound of Anna turning off the blow dryer broke my musings. She spun the chair around and gave Hailey a handheld mirror to see the back of her hair.

"Well, what do you think?" Anna asked, obviously pleased with the results.

Hailey's lip began to tremble, a sure sign she was about to cry. Just as I predicted, her hand shot to her face, and she burst into tears.

Anna turned ashen. "Oh, Hailey. I'm sorry. I can change it. Tell me what you want, and I'll change it."

I stood, careful not to wake Gabby. "It's okay," I told Anna, squeezing her arm. Then I squatted so I was eye level with my niece. "Don't cry, honey. Anna said she'd change it for you. Tell her what you want, okay?"

Hailey shook her head and wiped her eyes. She lifted the mirror and turned her head from side to side. Her previously tangled blond hair was now cut in a way that looked healthier. Anna had applied some sort of gel to make it smooth and shiny.

"I like it," Hailey said, giving a brave smile. "It's just—"

The bell above the door jingled as Bianca entered the salon. "Oh my goodness," she squealed, catching sight of Hailey's new hairstyle. "Don't you look just like your mother. That bob is fabulous on you. Fabulous!"

I worried Bianca's observation would set off a round of fresh tears, but Hailey smiled, swooshing her head from side to side. "I asked Anna to cut it like my mom's."

"Well, she did an amazing job," Bianca said. "You look just like your beautiful mother."

I lifted Gabby to my shoulder and patted her back. "You really do look pretty, Hailey."

Hailey beamed with pride. She looked at me, hesitating just a moment before flinging herself at me. Wrapping her arms around me tightly, she said, "Thanks, Uncle Nick. Thanks for bringing me to get my hair cut."

My heart swelled so big, I thought it might burst. And that's when I realized I'd do pretty much anything for this little girl's happiness.

ON TUESDAY EVENING, I could barely keep my eyes

open. Gabby hadn't slept well the night before, and she'd missed her afternoon nap. When she finally went down before dinner, I allowed myself a quick siesta on the couch.

"I'll make us something to eat in about half an hour," I called to Hailey who was working on her homework in the office.

"Can I play on your computer when I finish my math assignment?"

"Sure," I said, grateful Anna had showed me how the parental controls worked on my laptop. "Just wake me up in thirty minutes, okay?"

I collapsed on the couch only intending to sleep a few minutes. When I awoke, however, it was dark outside, and the house was silent. I called Hailey's name, but she didn't answer.

Upstairs, I searched the bedrooms, slightly concerned I couldn't find her. In the past, she'd always responded right away, but maybe she was in Gabby's room. Quietly, I pushed open the door to the nursery.

When I didn't see Hailey, a sickening feeling took hold of me. My heart began to beat faster, and as my eyes adjusted to the dark room, fear shot through me. Not only was Hailey not there, but I couldn't see Gabby.

I headed toward the crib, my worry escalating with each step. When I saw the empty crib, I couldn't breathe.

"Gabby! Hailey!" I spun around the room, scanning every possible hiding place. Had Hailey taken Gabby outside to look at the stars? Urging myself to remain calm, I rushed through the house to the porch, but they weren't there.

Panicked, I returned inside, racing down the hallway, frantically searching each room, turning on lights, and calling their names.

Had they been kidnapped? News of Ethan and Ivana's deaths had covered the front pages of several local newspapers. The home address had been listed along with the ages of the girls. Maybe someone viewing Hailey and Gabby as easy targets had taken them.

My stomach roiled. I tried to call on my military training, but I wasn't prepared for this. I didn't know what to do.

Lord, don't let anything happen to them. Please. Protect them and help me find them. Tell me what to do. Show me where they are. Guide me!

Hands trembling, I dialed 911 and was connected to the sheriff dispatch. As calmly as possible, I explained the situation.

"Are there any signs of disturbance?" the woman on the other end of the line evenly asked.

"Any signs of disturbance!" I felt out of control. "Yes, my nieces are missing!"

"A car is on its way, Mr. Peterson. Try to remain calm."

Chapter 12

Anna

*S*OMETIMES I WORRIED my son was destined to become the next featured hoarder on one of those reality shows. Like his paternal grandmother, Luella, Travis was a collector. Empty cereal boxes, unusual rocks, bottle caps, string, and an assortment of other items littered his bedroom.

Tonight, I'd forced him to part with two large garbage sacks of junk. Before he could regret tossing out some random trinket, I put on my coat and hauled the garbage down to the dumpster.

Gutting Travis's room was never fun, but with my parents coming for Christmas next month, I needed to begin tackling the enormous chore. I could hardly wait to see my mom and dad. As much as I loved my in-laws, nothing compared to the comfort of being with my own parents.

A bitter cold wind whipped past me as I tossed the trash into the dumpster. Shivering, I pulled my jacket a little tighter. Since last week, the temperature had dropped. Tonight, clouds in the dark sky blocked out all moonlight, making the night feel eerie.

I glanced up at my house, happy to see the light in my cozy kitchen. When I went back inside, I'd make a cup of hot tea and crawl into bed early so I could have plenty of time to read the latest Grace Greene book. I loved this author's ability to describe the beach so beautifully; and her stories stayed with me for a long time.

A sound underneath the porch steps startled me. At first, I thought a family of raccoons had taken residence. When I looked closer, I realized there was a child with several puppies. "Hailey? What are you doing out here? It's freezing."

She responded in a shaky voice. "I don't care about freezing, Miss Anna."

"Oh, sweetheart. What is it?" I squatted and petted the puppies as they jumped up and down with their greetings. Like Yoda, they were full of energy and growing bigger every day.

Something in Hailey's lap began to cry, and that's when I realized Gabby was there as well. My chest clenched with fear that something terrible had happened. Taking the baby, I held her close, wanting to keep her warm.

I looked at the Petersons' house and noted every single light was ablaze. Where in the world was Nick, and why were the girls outside alone? "Sweetheart, I think we better call your uncle. I'm sure he's worried about you and Gabby."

"Nick doesn't care about us," she said, trembling.

"That's not true. Nick loves you."

She shook her head. "I saw on the computer. He's sending me off to *strangers*!" A loud sob racked her body, and she buried her face in her arms. "He doesn't want me. He's going to put me up for adoption!"

My heart lurched. "Oh, Hailey, Nick just wants what's best for you."

"No, he doesn't. He wants to get rid of me. I don't know what he's going to do with Gabby. Probably sell her to the highest bidder on eBay. Babies bring in a lot more money than older kids like me. But I won't let him separate us. I won't. Gabby and I *have* to stay together. And the puppies, too."

"Come on, let's go inside and talk about this." I stood with the baby, but Hailey made no effort to move.

"No, thank you, Miss Anna. I'm just going to stay out here and freeze to death."

I bit my bottom lip, trying to figure out how best to handle the situation. I needed to call Nick, but I'd left my cell phone in the house.

"Hailey," I began, holding out one of Gabby's chubby hands, "your little sister is cold. Her fingers feel like ice cubes. Let's take her inside so she doesn't get sick, then if you want to come back outside, you can."

Hailey stared at me suspiciously. "I'm only coming if Liesl, Friedrich, and Louisa can come, too."

"Of course," I agreed. "As long as they stay in the kitchen with Yoda. But let's get your sister inside."

With that settled, we climbed the steps to the house. Travis met us at the door, excited to see everyone. He helped settle the puppies in the kitchen as Yoda barked and ran around in circles, thrilled to be reunited with his siblings. Felix jumped on the kitchen table and looked down at the reunion with disgust. The cat had learned to handle one puppy, but three more were out of the question.

Before I could call Nick, my phone rang. "Hailey and Gabby are missing!" he shouted. "And so are the puppies. I fell asleep on the couch after putting Gabby to bed, and when I woke, they were gone."

"They're at my house," I said.

"I just called 911!"

"Well, call them back because the girls are here in my kitchen."

"Are you sure?"

"Positive."

"Okay, I'll be right there."

I could only imagine the state of sheer panic Nick had experienced as he called 911 to report the girls missing. I also imagined relief would only come once he arrived and saw for himself that they were safe.

Moments later, there was a pounding at the front

door immediately followed by Nick rushing into the house. "Hailey! Gabby!"

He took the baby from me and pressed her to his chest. Then he sank to the floor next to Hailey, hugging her with his free hand. "Honey, promise me you'll never leave the house again without telling me first. I had no idea where you were."

Goosebumps prickled my arms. Nick loved these girls so much.

"I've never been more scared in my life," he said. "I don't know what I'd do if anything happened to you or your sister."

Hailey stiffened and shoved him away. "Then why do you want to get rid of us?"

"What? I don't," he insisted.

"Yes, you do. I saw on the computer. You're going to give us up for adoption."

Nick's face fell. "Oh, Hailey, I didn't want you to find out like that. I wanted to tell you myself."

"Then it's true." She glared at him with all the anger, fear, and resentment a little girl could possess. "You do want to get rid of us."

"No. I . . ." His shoulders slumped, and he adjusted Gabby on his lap. "I understand now why you're upset, but let me explain, okay?"

She shrugged. "Whatever, Uncle Nick."

He flinched at her harsh reaction, then composed himself and spoke with control. "I don't want to get rid of you, but I do want you to be happy. I want to find a family with a mom and a dad who will love both you and Gabby. I know how you feel about living with your cousins, so I've been trying to find someone different. I didn't tell you because I didn't want you to worry until I figured out everything."

Hailey picked up one of the puppies—Louisa, I think—and tried to smooth down its ear, but it popped right back up again. "Why can't we just stay with you?"

Nick thrust a hand through his hair. "I wish you could, but my job is with the army. They paid for my recent training, and I made a promise to serve for the next few years. I can't break that commitment."

Hailey's brow furrowed into tight lines as Nick continued. "My job involves going wherever the army sends me, and sometimes I'm gone for a long time. You and your sister need a mom and a dad who can take you to school, help you with your homework, and tuck you in at night. And I'm sorry, Hailey, but I can't do that. Not because I don't want to, but because of my job. That's why I've been trying to find you a family, not because I want to get rid of you."

"So, if you weren't in the army, you'd keep us?"

I expected Nick to hesitate, but his response was instant. "Yes. I'd keep you if I could. You and Gabby are the only connection I have to my brother, and I miss him so much. I love you girls, and I wish I could keep you—"

"But you can't," she finished, sounding more resolved than angry. Exchanging the puppy in her lap for another one, she nodded. "I get it."

I suspected she was simply putting on a brave front. Deep down, she had to be devastated to learn Nick was considering placing Gabby and her with a different family.

"What about my mom?" Travis asked, joining Nick and Hailey on the floor. "Couldn't you marry my mom so we could be one big happy family? I need a dad, too, you know."

My breath hitched at the suggestion. Nick's eyes sought mine, and my world held still.

Could I marry Nick for the sake of the kids? The idea was absurd, but throughout history, people had married for less noble reasons. Library shelves were filled with romantic tales of marriages of convenience. Was it insane for me to entertain such a crazy idea? Standing in my warm kitchen, staring down at Nick and the kids, I could almost imagine making it work.

Something shimmered in Nick's eyes. Was he thinking the same thing? For a brief moment, I wondered if my life was about to change.

Then Nick looked away and shook his head. "Anna and I are friends. We're not getting married."

"Why not?" both Travis and Hailey asked.

Nick avoided my gaze. "Because that's not how marriage works."

"Oh," Hailey said, disappointed.

I forced a smile. "That's right. Nick and I are just friends, but I've been helping him look at families, and I know we'll find the perfect home for you and Gabby."

"You're going to help him find me a new mom and dad?" Hailey asked.

I nodded. "Yes."

She jutted out her chin. "They have to want the puppies, too."

Nick laughed and gave Hailey a quick hug. "We'll find someone who's always wanted two little girls and three puppies, okay?"

Not quite convinced, she asked, "What about Six Flags? Are you still taking me to Six Flags on Saturday during Thanksgiving break like you promised?"

Nick chuckled. "Of course. I would never break a promise to you."

"Can Travis and Miss Anna come?"

"Yes," Travis said, his voice completely serious. "We'll definitely come."

Nick raised an eyebrow at me. "What do you say? Would you and Travis like to come with us? I have complimentary tickets."

I shook my head. "I don't think so."

"*Mom*," Travis said. "Why not?"

The question flustered me, and I scrambled for an excuse. I wasn't a fan of amusement parks. Roller coasters and crowds scared me. Plus, Six Flags was way off the island. "Oh, I'd hate to leave Yoda for so long. And it's Thanksgiving weekend. We're supposed to spend time with your grandparents and cousins."

"Thanksgiving is Thursday," Travis pointed out. "Church and Sunday brunch are on Sunday. Six Flags is on Saturday, and we're not doing anything on Saturday."

Hailey stood and edged closer to me. "Will you please come, Miss Anna? That way, you can help Uncle Nick with Gabby so he can go on the rides with us."

I started to offer another excuse, but Hailey stopped me. "How are you going to help Nick find us a family if you don't spend time with Gabby and me?"

I smiled, knowing I was defeated. Hailey had given me the perfect reason to come, and there was no getting out of it.

TRAVIS AND I spent Thanksgiving Day at Luella and Walter's house with the rest of the Morgan family. Bianca and Vicki were there, along with Jillian, Matt, Drew, and Jillian's boyfriend, Bryan.

As usual, Luella had decorated the house with all the Thanksgiving decorations her kids and grandchildren had ever created. Pilgrims made out of construction paper, handprints turned into turkeys, and papier-mâché cornucopias covered every available wall and surface.

On the refrigerator hung the pilgrim Marcus had decorated with macaroni noodles when he was in the third grade. I ran a finger over the pilgrim's hat and imagined my husband as a little boy, his face scrunched in concentration, glue smeared on his hands.

During dinner, Travis dominated the conversation with talk about Nick. In endless detail, he described all of his medals, muscles, and amazing video game skills. "Did you know Nick might become an aide to General Sanchez?"

I frowned. I hadn't heard that. My father had worked with the general several years ago and deeply respected the man. Becoming Sanchez's assistant would greatly advance Nick's career.

Vicki, who seldom ate carbs despite owning the bakery, buttered another one of her mother's delicious homemade buttermilk rolls. "Nick brought Gabby into the bakery the other day. I took a break and had a cup of coffee with him."

"Oh? What'd you talk about?" I tried to keep the unexpected twinge of jealousy out of my voice. Vicki was hands down the cutest Morgan sister with her petite figure, short blond hair, and naturally red lips. Men found her adorable, but her unrealistic high standards kept her from finding Mr. Right.

"Nick said you and Travis are going to Six Flags with him on Saturday," Vicki said.

Travis pumped his fist in the air. "It's going to be

awesome. Nick has special military tickets, so we get in free and can eat all the hot dogs we want."

"Sounds like fun," Bianca said.

Travis continued talking about *The Great Nick Peterson.* Walter seemed intrigued, but Luella appeared uncomfortable with the conversation, so I attempted to change directions by asking about the Dallas Cowboys. I didn't know much about football, but as I'd anticipated, Matt and Drew took over the conversation, discussing the quarterback's latest injury.

Travis, however, wouldn't be distracted. He launched into a detailed story about all the stray dogs in Afghanistan and how that influenced Nick to buy the entire litter of puppies.

Luella cleared her throat. "And he gave you one without your mother's permission? That seems very irresponsible."

Travis threw his head back and laughed. "Mom was angry at first, but she loves Yoda now. Don't you, Mom?"

"He's growing on me," I conceded. "But if I had my choice—"

A thick tension filled the room. Luella never enjoyed hearing about my dates, but Nick in particular seemed to really bother her. Perhaps it was the military connection or the fact that Travis was so infatuated with him. Whatever the reason, I desperately wanted to distract Travis and restore peace to the holiday.

Luella rapped her fingernails on the tablecloth. "Anna, I can't believe you *let* that man buy your son a dog without your permission."

I was trying to be sensitive to my mother-in-law's pain, but I couldn't ignore the unfair condemnation in her voice. "Even though I never would've bought the dog myself, I'm happy Travis has him. He's always wanted a dog, and it's pretty cute seeing Yoda and Felix sleeping together."

"Speaking of cute . . ." Bianca began.

I glared at my sister-in-law. I didn't need Bianca joining Travis in singing Nick's praises. Especially not in front of Luella. Pushing away from the table, I stood. "Who wants more pecan pie? Vicki? Walter?"

Vicki placed a hand on her non-existent belly. "I've eaten way too much already. I'm going to have to spend the next week doing a juice fast and double workouts to take off all this extra weight."

"You aren't allowed to talk about weight during a holiday meal," Bianca spat. "Especially before it's over. That's a major violation of Miss Manners."

I agreed. "For your punishment, I'm going to bring you a huge piece of pie with whipped cream and make you eat the whole thing."

"No," Vicki insisted, horrified.

We all laughed, but out of the blue, Jillian's youngest son Drew brought the conversation back to Nick by asking if he was my boyfriend.

"No," I said firmly. I stole a quick glance at my mother-in-law's stricken face. "I'm going to make some more coffee. Can I bring you another cup, Mom?"

Luella looked down at her empty mug. "No, thank you. I think I'll step outside for a breath of fresh air."

"Are you okay, honey?" Walter asked, placing a concerned hand on his wife's shoulder.

She gave a weak smile. "Yes, darling. I'm fine. I just have a little headache."

"My mom gets headaches," Travis said knowingly. "Nick says the best thing to prevent a headache is exercise. He runs three to five miles every day, and last year, he did an Ironman. That's a 2.4-mile swim, a 112-mile bike ride, and then a whole marathon."

"*Travis*," I called sharply.

"What?"

"Come help me in the kitchen." I gave my best do-as-I-say look, and miraculously, it worked because he joined me without arguing. As we entered the kitchen, his little hand slid into my elbow. "Mom, do you think I could run an Ironman one day?"

I closed my eyes and wondered how in the world I was going to stop this obsession with Nick. And not just for Travis, but for myself as well.

Why did the man have to sweep in and take over our life? Perhaps if I'd never kissed him, I wouldn't be so preoccupied with him.

"Mom?" Travis's voice brought me back to reality.

"What?"

He pushed up his glasses and squinted at me. "Are you okay? Your face is all red and sweaty, and you have the crazy look in your eyes."

"I'm fine," I said, embarrassed.

"Good, 'cause I want to tell you about the Thanksgiving Nick spent in Qatar."

Chapter 13

*A*FTER THE DISHES were washed and everyone had settled in to nap or watch the football game, I made two cups of tea and went searching for my mother-in-law. I found her sitting in the office looking through an old photo album. "I brought you a cup of tea, Mom."

"Oh, you didn't have to do that," Luella said.

"I know, but I wanted to." I handed her the mug and sat beside her on the couch. "I'm sorry Travis upset you by talking about Nick."

She took a sip of tea and placed it on the sofa table. "You have a new man in your life, and while I know it's only natural, I am surprised. You haven't been interested in anyone since . . ." Her voice faltered as she had difficulty speaking her son's name.

I gently touched her arm. "I'm not interested in Nick as anything more than friendship. Travis has a little hero worship thing going on, but Nick and I are just friends. I've been helping him with his nieces. That's all."

Sadness washed over Luella. "Those poor girls. To lose both their mother and father at the same time. How are they managing?"

"I think they're doing okay, considering the circum-stances."

She nodded. "Children are resilient like that."

"I know," I agreed, remembering I'd said the same thing to Nick regarding his concerns about Hailey and Gabby living with the Kempners.

Luella returned her attention to the photo album on her lap and pointed to a wedding picture of Marcus and me standing on the church steps. "You two were so young."

I gave a sad smile. Marcus had worn a simple black suit, and I'd borrowed a dress that successfully hid my pregnancy.

It had rained during the ceremony, and thunder had shaken the church as we said our vows. I could've interpreted the storm as an omen, given what happened to Marcus, but I never regretted marrying him. I'd loved him completely and only wished we'd had more time together.

Running a finger over the wedding photo, I sighed. "He was sure good-looking, wasn't he?"

Tears sprang to her eyes. "He was beautiful, and I think about him every day."

"So do I," I admitted.

That seemed to make her happy, but I wondered what would happen if there ever came a time when I didn't constantly think about Marcus.

And more than that, what would happen if I managed to push my husband far enough aside that I created room for someone else?

SATURDAY MORNING, I tried on several different outfits for the trip to Six Flags. I wasn't trying to impress anyone. I just wanted to be comfortable. At least, that's what I kept telling myself as the pile of discarded clothes in the corner of my closet grew. Finally, I settled on a pair of jeans and a long-sleeved T-shirt.

At seven forty-five, Nick pulled into the driveway. "Thanks for inviting us," I said, feeling nervous as Travis and I climbed into the Tahoe.

Nick flashed a confident grin. "We're glad you could come."

The baby gurgled from her car seat, and I turned around to say hello. "Did you go see Gina and your grandpa up in Dallas? Did they feed you Thanksgiving turkey and pumpkin pie?"

Gabby laughed and kicked her legs, but Nick gave a derisive grunt.

"Thanksgiving was awful," Hailey explained from the back seat.

"Really? What happened?"

"Nothing unusual," Nick said with great sarcasm. "Just your typical, dysfunctional Peterson holiday."

I turned to study him. He wore sunglasses, a baseball cap, T-shirt, jeans, and worn leather loafers. I hadn't seen him in several days, but he was even more handsome than I remembered.

From the back seat, Hailey enthusiastically elaborated on the disastrous holiday. "Grandpa's fiancée got the stomach flu, so we didn't get to meet her. Then the puppies ate Grandpa's couch! There was so much stuffing on the living room floor, it looked like snow."

I stifled a laugh. "You're kidding? You didn't take all three puppies up to Dallas, did you? I thought you were going to board them."

"No, I brought them with us," Nick said, adjusting his sunglasses. "And that was mistake number one."

"What was mistake number two?"

He shook his head. "I'll spare you the details, but the girls and I ended up spending the night at Motel 6 and eating dinner out of the vending machine."

"We had cheese crackers for our main course and candy bars for dessert." Hailey spoke as though the experience hadn't been unpleasant at all, but rather a great adventure. In fact, for the first time since the accident, she seemed genuinely happy.

"What about the food at your dad's house?" I asked.

Nick shook his head. "We had reservations for the steakhouse, but my father took a business call from Europe, so we never made it to the restaurant. We tried to reschedule, but they were completely booked. Then the couch incident happened, and everything went downhill from there."

I frowned. "Your family doesn't cook for Thanksgiving?"

"No." Nick gave a sardonic laugh. "My father has never cooked anything more elaborate than cereal. I'm just mastering the art of grilled cheese myself. It wasn't until college that I learned most people don't eat cereal for breakfast *and* dinner."

"Seriously? Is that what you ate growing up?"

He shrugged. "Sometimes we ordered takeout. One of our nannies cooked, but she quit after a few months."

I had so many wonderful memories of cooking with both my parents and my in-laws, I couldn't imagine eating Thanksgiving dinner at a restaurant. Travis was only ten, but already he could fix a handful of decent meals. Maybe I should offer to teach Nick how to cook. I imagined him wearing an apron around his narrow waist, and his strong forearms flexing as he chopped an onion.

"How was your Thanksgiving?" Nick asked, interrupting my fantasy.

"It was nice." I thought about the laughs I'd shared with Marcus's sisters while we peeled sweet potatoes and drank glasses of Chardonnay before dinner. After the game, we'd gone for a long walk, then played a few hands of Hearts.

"You went to your in-laws' ranch?" he asked.

"We did."

"And you know what, Nick?" Travis shouted from the back seat. "Grandpa thinks you must be half crazy for buying me a puppy without asking my mom's permission."

Nick chuckled. "I'm glad he thinks I'm only *half* crazy."

"Yeah," Travis said. "It's my Aunt Jillian's boyfriend, Bryan, you have to be worried about. He thinks you're *certifiable*. Whatever that means."

Nick burst out laughing, the intoxicating sound rumbling through the car, filling the hollow of my bones. As though reading my thoughts, he smiled at me. "Well, I'm glad the man has such a high opinion of me."

"I don't know, Nick," Travis said. "I think certifiable is a bad thing."

Nick and I both laughed.

The rest of the trip was uneventful. The kids played car bingo while Nick and I chatted easily about everything from the best Mexican food restaurants to the worst TV shows.

Signs for Six Flags came into view, and both Hailey and Travis shouted joyfully. Gabby joined in the excitement, clapping her hands and blowing bubbles.

Nick parked the car, and we made our way toward the entrance. For late November, the weather was unseasonably warm, so lots of families had turned out to enjoy the beautiful fall day.

"We're hitting the Texas Giant first," Nick declared, after we passed through ticketing and security.

The children voiced their approval and set off across the park. Nick led the way, pushing Gabby in the stroller and maneuvering through the crowd at breakneck speed. I had to run in order to keep up with everyone.

At the ride, I placed my hands on the baby stroller. "I'll wait here with Gabby while you go with Travis and Hailey."

Nick eyed me suspiciously. "Okay, but I'll be back, and it will be your turn."

"We'll see." Statistically, I knew roller coasters were relatively safe, but I had no intention of getting on that deathtrap. Although Nick gave me an odd look as if sensing my apprehension, he said nothing as Hailey and Travis dragged him toward the ride.

"It's just you and me," I told Gabby, lifting her out of the stroller. Sitting on the bench, we enjoyed the sunshine and engaged in one of my all-time favorite activities—people watching.

A heavily tattooed and pierced couple in their early twenties strolled past, arm in arm. At that age, I truly believed Marcus and I would be together forever.

How wrong I'd been. Yet, my inexperience had allowed me to love Marcus without limits. Without fear or judgment. Maybe it was only possible to truly love another person when you were young and unafraid. I'd always believed I'd never love another man like I'd loved my husband, but Nick stirred something in me. Desire, obviously. But it was more than that. A need to let him into my life. To take a chance. To be brave.

Gabby giggled and pointed at Nick who jogged toward us. Sunlight hit his hair and the smile on his face made me tingle.

"All right," he said, taking a seat on the bench beside me. "Your turn. I'll watch Gabby so you can ride with the kids."

I held on to the baby for protection and shook my head. "Thank you, but I'll pass."

Nick studied me carefully. "You're not afraid, are you?"

"Yes," I admitted. "You figured it out. Roller coasters scare me. Can you believe it?"

He rubbed a hand over his firm bicep. "What are you afraid of, Anna?"

"Dying, throwing up, flying off the track, waking up in a coma—"

He frowned. "I don't think you can *wake up* in a coma."

"Ha, ha." I tapped him playfully on the arm. "You know what I mean. Amusement rides just aren't my thing."

He looked up at the roller coaster zooming by. "I don't get it. You used to fly helicopters for a living, and now you don't even ride roller coasters?"

"No."

He pressed his lips together as if forming his words carefully. "There are a lot of things you're afraid of, aren't there?"

"Maybe, but why do you care?"

"Because I do."

A powerful beat of silence followed, and my throat went dry. Nick had answered my flirty and flippant question with a seriousness I didn't know how to interpret. His gaze locked on mine, and I thought about kissing him again. When had I become so *boy-crazy*? So *Nick-crazy*?

An older lady stopped in front of us and placed a hand on Gabby's back. "You have a beautiful baby. She looks just like you, Mom."

Gabby giggled and snuggled closer. "Thank you," I said, choosing not to correct the assumption. Part of me knew the explanation would only make matters awkward, and another part of me—the part deep down—wished it were true.

After the lady left, Nick shook his head. "She doesn't look anything like you."

I shrugged. "People see what they want to see."

He studied me carefully, and I held still as his eyes grazed over my face and down to Gabby. "She looks good on you. Do you ever think about having more children?"

I hesitated. "Sure, but it would have to be with the

right guy. Someone who was just as good with Travis as he was with me. Someone who—"

"Wasn't a soldier?" he suggested, his voice flat and devoid of any humor.

I nodded. "That would be part of my expectations, but he'd also need to have a good job and want to stay on the island. My in-laws have been through a lot, and I don't want to take Travis away from them or his cousins."

Nick removed his baseball cap and ran a hand through his hair. "I understand. Rose Island is your safe haven. Bianca, Vicki, and Jillian are your best friends, and you get along with Walter and Luella. Leaving them would be difficult."

A gloomy mood settled between us. I hadn't meant to offend him. I'd only wanted to be honest and protect both of us from getting hurt. I might dream about Nick and think about him all the time, but the truth was, just as much as he wasn't the man for me, I wasn't the woman for him. He wanted a military career, and in order to be successful, he couldn't have a resentful wife.

Changing the subject, I asked about his progress regarding the list of prospective families for the girls. He sighed and placed a finger in Gabby's hand. The baby lowered her mouth and began gnawing.

"It's not a French fry," he said, removing his finger from her mouth. He scooped her up, and she laughed, lunging for his hand again. "Silly girl."

I smiled and gave Nick a moment to digest my question. Finally, he said, "Ever since Hailey ran away and asked me why I couldn't keep her, I haven't been able to look at that list. Lucy Jensen from the adoption agency keeps calling, but I don't want to talk to her."

"Have you thought any more about keeping the girls yourself?"

He sighed. "I want to do the right thing. I thought that meant adoption, but I've since read that giving up a child means waiving all legal rights. Even if we arrange an open adoption, the new parents could ultimately decide they don't want me in the girls' lives. I could challenge that decision in court, but I wouldn't want to put the girls through an ugly legal battle."

I refrained from clasping his hand and telling him everything was going to be okay. "Aren't there single parents in the military?"

"There are," he conceded. "But they have a lot of help from extended family. At the very least, someone needs to be appointed to your Family Care Plan in order to take care of the kids during deployment. My father won't do that, and I don't have any other relatives."

"Have you talked to your dad about it?"

"No."

I crossed my legs and swung my foot. "What about hiring someone? Like a nanny?"

"I thought of that, but what would happen if she quit? I couldn't exactly find someone new from the battlefield."

"True." At that moment, I wanted to volunteer to take care of the girls while he was gone. The words were right on the edge of my lips, then rationality kicked in. I couldn't take on the responsibility of two more children. I had a hard enough time working and raising Travis on my own. How could I possibly support myself and Travis with two additional children—one of them a baby?

Guilt pressed down on me, but I remained silent. "I'm sorry, Nick."

He gave a curious smile. "Why are you sorry? It's not your fault."

But it was. By refusing to take the girls, I left him with few options. "I'm sorry you have to go through this."

"I couldn't even be doing this part without your help. So, thank you." Reaching out, he took my hand. "And now, Anna Morgan, I'm going to do something to help you."

"Me?"

He grinned. "Yep. I'm going to convince you to ride the Texas Giant."

Chapter 14

Nick

*A*FTER A WONDERFUL day at Six Flags, followed by pizza at the Pelican Pub, I found myself humming as Hailey helped me get Gabby ready for bed. Over the past few weeks, the three of us had fallen into an easy nighttime routine consisting of baths, pajamas, reading, and prayer.

At first, Hailey had done all the praying, but lately, I'd begun adding a few sentences of my own. Tonight, I thanked God for the lovely day and the blessing of funnel cake.

Although my father had taken Ethan and me to church when we were kids, and I still considered myself a Christian, I'd fallen out of the habit of praying or spending much time on my spiritual life. Seeing Anna live out her faith so naturally made me want a closer relationship with God.

I wasn't quite sure how to make that happen, but I'd started reading the children's Bible to Gabby and Hailey each night. Some of the stories seemed a little farfetched, but I loved reading about the miracles of Christ. What would it be like to walk on water? To have your sight restored after years of living in the darkness? To have Jesus remove a demon from you?

"And please help Uncle Nick find a new mom and dad for me, Gabby, and the puppies," Hailey said, concluding the prayer with a somber *Amen!*

"Amen!" Gabby repeated, clapping her hands.

I felt a pang of guilt that my niece had to worry about such an unsettling topic. The sooner I resolved this issue, the better. I tucked Gabby into her crib, gently covering her with her favorite pink blanket. "Sleep tight, pumpkin."

"I love you," Hailey told her little sister.

"Wuv you," Gabby said.

"I love you, too," I said easily. Telling the girls I loved them was becoming less awkward. I supposed the words could easily become rote, but I appreciated having a phrase that expressed how I felt. I loved Gabby and Hailey so much it scared me. With each day, I grew closer to them, making the idea of leaving more difficult.

Downstairs, I took the dogs outside to use the bathroom, then I tucked them into bed with Hailey. Despite being mutts, the puppies had quickly grasped the idea of house training, and they now slept in Hailey's room every night.

After wishing her sweet dreams, I stepped onto the back porch and gazed up at the stars. When my cell phone rang, I dug it out of my back pocket to discover my father was calling. I hadn't spoken to him since the fiasco on Thanksgiving, and I was tempted to ignore the call. At the last minute, I answered with a brisk hello.

"How are you, son?" Jack asked, his voice somber.

"I'm fine, sir. You?"

He hesitated. Something he never did. Was something wrong or had he hung up on me? "Dad?"

"Yeah, I'm here. It's just that . . . I want to apologize for Thanksgiving."

"Excuse me?" I was certain I'd misunderstood. As far as I knew, my father never apologized for anything. Ever.

"I know, son. It's a long story, but Gina felt it was unfair of me to put business first on Thanksgiving. I'd like to apologize for that. And for overreacting with the dogs. As Gina pointed out, it was only a couch. An ugly one at that."

I didn't know what to say. Since my father's fiancée had been sick over Thanksgiving, I'd still never met her, but I was beginning to like her. Or at least beginning to grow less suspicious of her.

"I hope you'll forgive me," Jack said, sounding nothing like himself. "I'd like another chance."

I almost asked if this was some kind of crank call. Then I thought about what Anna had said regarding forgiveness. *Life is all about forgiveness. People make mistakes, and if you let resentment dominate your thoughts, you'll be disappointed in life.*

"I forgive you, Dad."

"Oh, really?"

"Yeah," I said, thinking it felt good to voice those words.

"Well, that's great," he stammered, as if forgiveness was the last thing he'd expected.

A moment of awkward silence ensued, then Jack said, "So, how about that Cowboys game? Can you believe that catch?"

I smiled to myself. "It was pretty incredible."

Anna

IN ALL MY life, I had never met anyone as ambitious, successful, and organized as PTA president Kate Tate. On Monday morning, Kate entered the salon for her appointment at precisely 11:00.

Kate was a curvaceous woman with perfectly round, lifted breasts, compliments of her ex-husband's surgical skills. She also had perfectly colored and styled caramel brown hair that hung just below her shoulders, compliments of me.

Every time she came into the salon, I struggled with feelings of inadequacy as she talked about all she did for the school. She'd earned Rose Island's prestigious

Volunteer of the Year award three years in a row.

"I saw you're working the face painting booth again this year," Kate said, referring to the upcoming school carnival.

"I wouldn't miss it for the world."

She gave a curt nod. "And how was your date with Nick on Saturday?"

Goodness. Was there no limit to Kate's knowledge? Apparently not.

Vicki, who was having her roots colored by Bianca, asked a question of her own. "You were pretty quiet at brunch yesterday, but now that it's just us girls, tell us, did Nick kiss you good-night again?"

"Again?" Kate raised a perfectly arched brow. "So the two of you are definitely dating?"

"No," I insisted, laughing it off. "Nick and I are just friends."

"Keep repeating that, and maybe you'll convince yourself it's true," Bianca said.

Kate pursed her lips. "Spending the entire day with a man definitely sounds like a date to me. And if you kissed him—"

"We took three kids to Six Flags," I explained. "It wasn't a date. And no, he didn't kiss me good-night. Nick and I are strictly platonic." *Except for two kisses, a few hugs, and some innocent hand-holding*, but I wasn't about to divulge that information to this hungry pool of sharks.

"Afterwards, you stopped at the Pelican Pub for pizza and video games," Vicki added. "And that definitely counts as a date."

I stared openmouthed at my sister-in-law. "How in the world did you know about that?"

She jingled her phone in the air. "Hailey posted it last night."

"Great," I said, sarcastically. "So now I'm being stalked and judged based on a pre-teen's social media status?"

Kate twisted one of her diamond stud earrings. "We're certainly not stalking or judging you. Simply commenting on the facts."

"Hey, if you won't tell us what's going on in your love life, we have to find out somehow," Bianca said.

Kate nodded. "They do have a point."

I smiled. Taking the kids to Six Flags yesterday had been one of the best days of my life.

In fact, every day with Nick was wonderful. Being with him just felt right. I hadn't realized how lonely I'd been until I met him. Sure, I had a full life with friends, family, church, and my job, but spending time with Nick filled me like nothing else.

The hardest part was the guilt. I kept telling myself that Marcus would want me to be happy, but I continued struggling to believe it.

THAT NIGHT, MATT and Drew slept over at my house while Jillian worked an overnight shift. Usually, our parents watched the boys when Jillian worked, but tonight, they were teaching a class on baptism at the church.

I adored my nephews. When they were little, I frequently watched them, but as they'd grown and had become more involved in school and sports, I seldom saw them outside of church and Sunday brunch.

Sitting at the kitchen table, I said a blessing over the food. As soon as the boys joined me in saying "Amen," my phone rang.

"Your boyfriend is calling," Drew said in a singsong voice as he gestured to Nick's name on my caller ID.

"He's not my boyfriend." I silenced the phone, sending the call straight to voice mail. Travis and I had adopted Luella and Walter's strict rule of no phone calls during dinner. If Nick left a voice mail, I would return his call after we ate.

If he didn't . . . well, I'd probably obsess over why he'd called without leaving a message, but that was beside the point.

Travis snuck Yoda a piece of pepperoni. "You know, Mom, it'd be okay if Nick was your boyfriend. I really like him."

"No kidding," Matt said. "That's *all* you ever talk about. *Nick this and Nick that.*"

Travis shrugged and took a bite of pizza. Matt and

Drew were both older and often teased Travis, as boys tended to do. I tried not to interfere, but I hated seeing my son so harshly criticized.

"I like Nick, too," Drew said, sticking up for Travis.

Matt groaned. "You don't even know him."

"Maybe not, but he seems cool."

"He is," Travis said. "He's amazing."

My phone rang again with another call from Nick, and Travis squeezed my arm tight. "Mom, you should answer that because it might be an emergency. Hailey might've run away again."

I heard the worry in Travis's voice, something that had been absent lately. Even so, I didn't want to fall into a bad habit of picking up the phone during dinner. Nor dropping everything for Nick.

"I'll call him when we're finished," I said, proud for being such a strong, independent woman. "He can always text if it's an emergency."

The boys looked skeptical but returned to their pizza. Two seconds later, Nick texted, "Need help. Please call ASAP."

Worried, I called him back immediately. He answered on the first ring. "Hailey is freaking out, and I can't get her to calm down. She's locked herself in the bathroom and won't talk to me."

I pushed away from the table. "We'll be right there."

Chapter 15

*L*EAVING YODA AND Felix in the kitchen, Travis, Matt, Drew, and I raced over to the Petersons' house. Nick met us at the front door with Gabby in his arms, followed by all three puppies, who tried to scoot outside but were blocked by Travis.

The boys each picked up a puppy and filed into the living room to watch the game. Nick motioned for me to come upstairs with him.

"She's locked herself in the bathroom and won't stop crying or tell me what's wrong," he explained. "When I picked her up from tennis lessons this evening, she was quiet, but she didn't seem upset. Next thing I knew, she was screaming in the bathroom, refusing to tell me what happened."

"I'll talk to her." I stepped forward and knocked on the bathroom door. "Hailey? It's Anna. Can I come in?"

Nick leaned past me and pounded on the bathroom door. "Open up, Hailey."

I feared he might break down the door if Hailey didn't answer right away, so I pleaded with her to let me in. After what seemed like ages, but was probably only a few seconds, she finally unlocked the door, cracking it open just a bit. "Only Miss Anna," she whispered, her voice wobbly and eyes puffy from crying.

"What is it?" Nick demanded. "Did someone hurt you?"

"I just want to talk to Miss Anna right now."

Nick stepped back as though physically wounded. "Okay, but I'll be right here with Gabby if you need me."

I slipped into the bathroom. When I saw Hailey wasn't in danger, I gave Nick a reassuring smile. "Why don't you wait downstairs with Travis and his cousins? I'll call if we need help."

I could tell from the expression on his face that waiting downstairs was the last thing he wanted to do. Reluctantly, he nodded and I closed the bathroom door. I walked across the tile and sat on the edge of the tub next to Hailey who pressed a bloody washcloth to her shin.

"I'm so stupid," she cried, removing the washcloth to reveal a deep gouge. "I just wanted to shave my legs so the kids would stop calling me *gorilla legs*, but now I've made it worse."

I placed an arm around the little girl's shoulders. "You're not stupid, honey. You just need someone to teach you how to shave without cutting yourself. Will you let me help you?"

She nodded.

Using the washcloth, I blotted the cut. I'd been older than Hailey the first time I'd shaved, but I remembered being embarrassed by the dark hair growing on my legs. "Girls can be so mean, can't they?"

"Just to me," she said.

"I know it can seem like that, but I bet the other girls feel picked on as well."

"I doubt that."

I turned on the bath water and rinsed out the razor. "One time when I was a little older than you, my friends and I were doing this thing where we held each other's hands and spun around. It was a lot of fun, but then one of the girls slipped out of my grip and fell on the rough asphalt. She cried and all the other girls blamed me! They said I did it on purpose."

"Did you?"

"No, of course not. But they wouldn't stop asking why I pushed Tyra and why I was so mean. Even though I told them it was an accident, they wouldn't believe me. Every time they passed me in the hall, they called me Pusher. When I sat down to eat lunch at our table, they moved to another one."

Hailey looked up with a horrified expression. "You had to eat by yourself?"

"I did." I shuddered at the memory, surprised an event from so long ago could still hurt. It'd been almost twenty years, but I remembered every shameful detail. "It felt like everybody hated me, and I didn't have any friends."

"I know what you mean," she said.

I lathered her legs with soap and gently guided the razor over her skin. "Now you try."

She took the razor and followed my instructions. "Like this?"

"Exactly."

"So, what finally happened with those girls?"

I gave a sad smile. "I wish I could tell you everything was better the next day, but they held a grudge for a long time. I actually stopped eating my lunch in the cafeteria and hid out in the library by myself."

Hailey winced. "At least I only get harassed at tennis lessons or when I wear shorts."

"That's good. For me, hiding in the library turned out for the best because I became friends with a very nice boy who offered me the most delicious, homemade chocolate chip cookies."

Hailey rinsed out the razor. "Was it my Uncle Nick? Was he the boy with the cookies?"

I smiled. "No, it wasn't your uncle. I didn't know him when I was younger, but I could see him doing something like that."

"Oh," she said, disappointed. "Well, was the boy cute?"

"He was very cute." Unexpected tears pooled in my eyes as I pictured Marcus standing in the library with his mother's cookies. Sixth grade had been the first time we'd met, when he'd befriended me after the mean girls' incident. My family had moved away a year later, but when we returned to Rose Island my senior year of high school, Marcus and I had easily resumed our friendship.

That fall, he'd asked me to homecoming. I wore a green dress because it was his favorite color, and from that moment forward, we were inseparable. I'd never wanted anyone else. He'd been my first. My only. And even after all this time, there were days when the pain of losing him hurt so much.

Wiping my eyes, I offered a weak smile. "I'm sorry. That boy in the library became my husband. Travis's dad. It's really difficult when someone you love dies. But you already know that."

Hailey nodded. "I hate it when people say 'Time heals all.' It makes me want to punch them in the face."

I smiled at the heartfelt statement. "I know what you mean."

"So, it never gets better? I'm always going to miss my mom and dad?"

I chose my words carefully. "I'll tell you the truth. Missing them never goes away, but it becomes bearable. You learn to accept things have changed, and eventually, you find happiness again. But you'll never forget them. And that's why there's always a little sadness when you remember they're gone."

Hailey scrunched up her face, taking it all in. "Travis's dad died in the war, right?"

"That's right."

"Uncle Nick showed me the book he's in. I never knew Travis's dad was a war hero. He saved both the governor and that reporter's life."

The lump in my throat expanded, making it difficult to breathe or swallow or think. I blinked back tears. "I'm very proud of Travis's dad and what he did—"

Hailey placed a hand on my leg. "But you wish he hadn't died?"

I nodded. "I'd give anything to bring him back."

She looked down at the cut on her shin, which had finally stopped bleeding. She rinsed the razor and made a smooth pass over her leg, carefully avoiding the gouge. "Nick is going to the war, you know. Once he finds me and Gabby a family, he's leaving. He's probably going to die, so we'll never see him again."

"Oh, honey." My soul twisted. "You don't know that. And even if he does deploy, lots of soldiers come home safely. My dad has been in the army for years, and he's never been hurt. Never been shot, or broken an ankle, or anything."

She shook her head. "I'm not going to be so lucky. God doesn't like me anymore. When Nick goes to war, he's going to die. Just like my parents."

My breath caught. Placing a hand on her back, I offered a silent prayer. *Give me wisdom to comfort this child, Lord. Help me say the right thing and speak your truth.*

"Hailey, sometimes life is tough. People we care about get hurt, but even then, God loves you. He's always there for you, especially when you don't think so."

I could tell she wasn't convinced, so I tried to find another way to make my point. "You love your little sister, right?"

"Yeah."

"Even though you love her and would never wish her harm, sometimes she falls and gets hurt, right?"

"Yes, but . . ." She gave a disapproving groan. "I know what you're trying to say, Miss Anna. I just don't think God really feels that way about me."

I nodded, remembering I'd felt abandoned after Marcus died. It'd taken me a long time to feel God's love again and accept the fact that sometimes bad things happened to good people. It didn't mean He didn't care about me. Just that He had a different plan for my life than I'd envisioned.

"Don't let fear stop you from loving Nick," I said. "He's your father's brother, and there's so much he can teach you about your dad and about being a Peterson. Don't shut him out, Hailey. He needs you as much as you need him."

"You think Uncle Nick needs me?"

I pulled her close for a side hug. "I know he does, sweetheart."

She finished shaving her legs and rinsed them off

with running water. As I stood to find a bottle of lotion, she called my name. "Miss Anna?"

"Yes?"

Taking a deep breath, she wet her lips. "I think Nick needs you, too. We all do."

I'd been afraid of that. But even more, I'd been afraid of how much I'd started to need Nick and the girls.

Not knowing what to say or how to respond, I returned to Hailey and gave her a hug. "You're a very special girl."

She smiled and hugged me back. "Thanks, Miss Anna. I think you're special, too."

Nick

SITTING ON THE couch, I tried to watch TV with Travis and the other boys, but my mind continued drifting to Hailey and Anna upstairs. If only I knew what was wrong, then I might stand a chance of fixing it.

Overall, I was a capable guy. I'd played football at West Point, was Airborne, and had survived Ranger school. I'd successfully trained dozens of soldiers, led combat missions, and had received countless military awards.

When it came to Hailey and Gabby, however, I was getting a beating. Obviously, these little girls needed someone more qualified than me. Yet, every time I tried to look through the list of prospective families, I couldn't do it. And every time Lucy from the adoption agency called, I sent her straight to voice mail.

When things were going well—when the baby was happy and I understood Hailey's homework—I loved taking care of the girls. I could even imagine creating a life with them.

But when stuff like this happened, I felt so far out of my expertise, I knew I wasn't capable of replacing their parents.

Every night, Hailey and I prayed that God would bring us the perfect family. I wanted to believe our prayers would be answered, but so far, God had remained silent.

The sound of Anna descending the stairs brought me to my feet. I scooped up Gabby and strode across the room. "Is Hailey okay?"

Anna smiled. "She's fine. It was just girl stuff, but she's fine."

Uncertainty took hold of me. "What kind of girl stuff?"

She spoke in a hushed tone so Travis and his cousins couldn't hear. "The other girls have been making rude comments about her hairy legs. I taught her how to shave, so it was an easy fix. She's much better now."

My stomach churned. While I was relieved it hadn't been as serious as I'd feared, I chastised myself for not paying more attention. "I didn't know girls her age shaved."

"Some do. I think if it makes her feel better about herself, then it's okay."

I exhaled and placed the *hairy legs issue* in the category of *I-won't-worry-about-this-today.* "Let's go outside, okay?"

"Sure."

On the back porch, we sat on Adirondack chairs overlooking the ocean. Anna held Gabby who snuggled in tight as a gust of wind swept through. With a muffled giggle, the baby reached out a hand and tried to capture the breeze. Every time she did something cute like that, I found myself becoming more attached to her.

"She's adorable," Anna said, kissing Gabby's cheek.

"She is," I replied, smiling at both of them. "I can't believe I used to be afraid of babies. It's strange because in some ways, taking care of her is easier than dealing with the unpredictability of Hailey."

"Little kids, little problems. Big kids, big problems," Anna said. "At least that's what Jillian tells me. She's had a lot of issues with her oldest son, Matt, this year."

I looked inside at the teenage boy who seemed fine to me. Turning back to Anna, I exhaled slowly. "When Hailey opened the bathroom door, and I saw blood on the washcloth, I was worried she'd tried to hurt herself."

Anna's face crumpled. "Oh, Nick. It wasn't anything like that. She's doing really well considering everything that's happened to her. Girls her age can be ruthless. Hailey simply wanted them to stop teasing her, so she tried to take care of it herself."

"I wish she would've told me."

Anna patted Gabby's chubby leg. "She was probably embarrassed. I'm very close to my father, but growing up, I never talked to him about shaving or problems at school."

I knew Anna was trying to make me feel better, but her words only shed more light on my inadequacies to parent the girls. I placed my ankle on top of my knee and rapidly shook my foot. "Last spring, one of the guys in my unit committed suicide."

"Oh, Nick. That's horrible."

"Yeah. I knew he was depressed, but I had no idea how serious it was. I should've been more proactive. I made sure he saw a doctor, but I should've done more for him. I don't want to mess up with Hailey like that."

"You won't. You care about her, and you're with her all the time. You take her to the counselor and provide a safe environment for her to talk about her feelings. Honestly, Nick, she's doing fine."

I stared out at the ocean, wanting to believe Anna. A person living at the beach could easily become immune to the peaceful movement of the waves, but I concentrated on the sound, wanting to distract myself and avoid burdening Anna with any more of the details.

"It wasn't your fault, you know," she said, somehow saying exactly what I needed to hear. "Most depressed people don't hurt themselves. You couldn't have possibly known what he was going to do."

I allowed myself to look at Anna and take in her beauty. She was absolutely gorgeous. Both on the inside and outside. She had an incredible ability to believe in others and encourage them to become their best self. She did that with Travis, the girls, her sisters-in-law, and she did it with me. Too bad she couldn't seem to do it with herself.

Anna kissed the top of Gabby's head. "Hailey told me you showed her the book with the chapter about Marcus."

I nodded. "She asked me how he died. Ethan had the book in his study, and I've been reading it again, so I let her read about Marcus. I hope that's okay."

"Of course, but she's afraid you'll go back to the Army and won't make it home."

I tapped my foot. "I didn't know she was worried about that."

Another cool breeze whipped across the porch, and Anna shivered. "It's getting cold. Maybe we should go inside."

"Hold on. I'll be right back." I wanted to keep talking to Anna, so I went into the house and returned moments later with a thick fleece blanket. Leaning down, I placed it over her and Gabby, tucking in the sides to keep them warm.

She surprised me by resting her hand on my shoulder. "Thank you, Nick."

I nodded, afraid speaking would reveal the over-whelming emotion rushing through me. *Why was I allowing myself to fall in love with this place? With my nieces? With Anna? Why had she touched me like that? She understood I couldn't stay, didn't she? Understood I was going back to the army?*

Pulling her hand away, she leaned back in the chair. "Is it stressful to know Hailey's concerned about you?"

I sat in the other chair. "It's a little stressful, but I'm glad you told me. I'll be sure to mention it to her counselor."

I gazed up at the stars, silently naming the constellations I'd learned throughout the years. One of the army chaplains had insisted the complexity of the universe proved the existence of a God who not only deliberately designed the world, but continued to sustain it today.

At the time, I'd taken great comfort in that statement. Of course the universe hadn't just randomly popped into existence one day. And of course the Creator responsible for this amazing world still cared about His creation.

Right now, however, my life seemed so complicated. Did God really care about my little problems when there were more important things to worry about?

I brought my gaze back to Anna's blue eyes. "I've wanted to be a soldier my whole life. I'm good at my job, and I can't imagine doing anything else for a living.

But Hailey and Gabby have challenged me beyond anything I could've ever imagined."

"Kids have a tendency to do that."

I blew out a slow breath. "Sometimes, I can see myself taking care of them permanently. But tonight, I feel so inadequate that I can't understand why making a decision and moving forward is so difficult."

Anna peered at me over the top of Gabby's head. "Perhaps you're having a hard time making a decision because it's the most important decision you've ever had to make."

I nodded and looked down at my hands as if they held the answers to all my problems. Maybe I should resign my commission and find a civilian job. But then what? How would I pay my bills? Although Ethan and Ivana had left enough life insurance to cover the girls' living expenses, there wouldn't be enough for things like college and weddings. Plus, I wouldn't feel right relying on that money for my own expenses.

Perhaps I could ask my father about taking care of the girls during my deployment. I could hire a full-time nanny, give my dad power of attorney, and resume full custody when I returned.

But was taking care of the girls something Jack could actually handle? And what about me? Could I learn how to be the parent Hailey and Gabby needed?

"Did you look at the family I told you about?" Anna asked. "The Woodalls?"

"Not yet," I said, feeling discouraged.

"I think they'd be good parents. And they live on the island, so Hailey and Gabby wouldn't have to leave."

"Okay, I'll look into it." I couldn't talk about this anymore, so I changed the subject. "Do I need to buy some special kind of razor for Hailey? I've seen those pink ones in the store."

Anna gave me a questioning look, obviously recognizing I was avoiding the issue of adoption. She didn't call me on it, however. Instead, she nodded and said, "A pink razor would be nice, then Hailey wouldn't have to use your manly man ones."

"Great. I'll put pink razors on my shopping list." I felt a momentary reprieve from the difficulties of my life. After all, while the girls continued to overwhelm me, I was becoming quite proficient when it came to grocery shopping.

Chapter 16

Anna

$\mathcal{E}$VERY YEAR IN December, the elementary school hosted a holiday carnival with games, entertainment, and delicious home-baked goods. I finished my shift at the face-painting booth, then purchased several raffle tickets for the silent auction.

Taking my time, I walked up and down the hallway, carefully studying the baskets and deciding how to spend my tickets. In the end, I divided my chances between the scrapbooking basket and one entitled, *Organize Your Life*.

"Put a ticket in the jar for the Jet Ski," Travis urged, pointing at the shiny red vehicle donated by Island Water Sports.

I thrust a hand to my hip. "No way! Do you know how dangerous those things are? Honestly, they're like motorcycles on water."

PTA president Kate Tate, who'd obviously over-heard the conversation, scowled. "Here's an idea, Anna.

If you don't want to win the Jet Ski, don't enter. But don't ruin the prize for the rest of us. As a member of the PTA, and a concerned parent, you should be happy for the donation."

I blinked. Kate's words stung, especially given the fact they were true. "I'm sorry, Kate. You're right. For my penance, I'm going to allow Travis to put my last ticket in the Jet Ski jar."

Kate rolled her eyes. "Let's not get radical."

Travis grabbed the ticket and shoved it into the jar before I could change my mind. "Done! Now I just need to keep my fingers crossed until we win."

"Oh, dear." Kate rapidly tapped a pen against her clipboard. "We'd rather the winner be someone who is excited and not opposed to the Jet Ski."

I shook my head. "Don't worry. Statistically, winning would be impossible."

A deep voice from behind spoke with mock sincerity. "Anna Morgan, I never pictured you as one for adventure on the high seas."

Anticipation shot up my spine as I spun around to see Nick grinning down at me. Gabby slept in the baby backpack, her thumb shoved deep into her mouth and her head resting on Nick's shoulder.

Putting a stranglehold on my emotions, I straightened. "I think we both know my name and high adventure don't belong in the same sentence, but I'm all about the cause."

He leaned so close I caught the faint scent of laundry detergent on his T-shirt. In a challenging voice, he asked, "What are you going to do if you win?"

"*When* we win," Travis said, breaking the moment, "we'll show our appreciation by using the Jet Ski every day. Maybe even twice a day."

"Heaven help us," Kate said, walking away.

"Will you keep it if you win?" Nick asked.

I shook my head. "No, if we win, which isn't going to happen, we'll sell it and use the money for braces or some other sensible purchase."

"*Mom,*" Travis said, horrified. "You can't be serious."

Nick shifted the straps on the backpack, causing Gabby to pop open one eye before falling back asleep. "Don't you think if you win, it means you're supposed to have more excitement in your life?"

"Yes," Travis agreed. "That's exactly what it means."

I lifted my chin, refusing to be railroaded. "I happen to have a lot of excitement in my life."

"I'm sure you do," Nick teased, winking at Travis. Both of them laughed, then Travis ran off to join his friends.

Nick smiled at me. "I'm sorry I made fun of you. Can I buy you a chicken burrito to apologize?"

"Oh, you don't have to do that," I stammered, suddenly feeling foolish.

A slow grin crept up his face as if amused by my refusal. "It's a burrito, Anna, not steak and lobster."

Heat scorched my face. Why was I being so difficult, resisting his simple offer of friendship? I agreed to the burrito, and we joined the line where Nick asked if I was worried about winning the Jet Ski.

"No. Definitely not," I insisted.

"Then let's make a deal. If you win—"

"I'm not going to win."

"Well, if you do, you have to promise you'll let me take you out on the water and show you how much fun it is before you sell it."

I eyed him warily. "I'm not going to win."

"Then it shouldn't be difficult to make a simple promise."

Heaving a great sigh, I relented. "Okay, I promise."

"Pinky-swear?"

"What?"

He shrugged. "It's something I learned at Ranger school."

"Really?"

"No," he said, laughing. "I'd get beat up for something like that. It's a Hailey thing."

I looked down at his hand and wrapped my little finger around his. There was a softening in my chest that both thrilled and scared me. "Okay, it's a deal," I said.

Nick paid for our food, and we found a table at the back of the crowded cafeteria. I spotted a small boy about four holding Carrie Woodall's hand. The child seemed a little young to be the kindergarten teacher's student. Maybe he was her nephew?

I greeted Carrie with an embrace. We talked about Travis for a moment, then I introduced Nick, and Carrie introduced the little boy. "This is Colton. He's been living with us for awhile, and we just found out we're going to be able to adopt both him and his baby sister."

A cry of joy broke from my lips. "Oh, Carrie! That's wonderful. I'm so happy for you."

Colton clasped Carrie's hand and beamed up at me. "She's going to be my real mom."

I squatted and looked directly into the little boy's eyes. "You're going to have one of the best mommies in the world."

"I know," he said, grinning. "And guess what?"

"What?"

"I'm getting a daddy, too!" He covered his mouth with both hands and gave a little squeal of joy.

I embraced Carrie again, thrilled at the good news. It was only as she and Colton walked away I realized the Woodalls probably wouldn't be interested in adopting Hailey and Gabby now that they had Colton and his sister. I experienced a minor sense of loss, but overall, I was happy for them.

On stage, Kate spoke into the microphone. "Testing, one, two, three. Testing, one, two, three." She gave a thumbs up to the sound director, then began frantically buzzing around, issuing orders to everyone.

Nick nodded toward Kate. "She's very efficient, isn't she?"

"That's the understatement of the year."

He took a bite of his burrito and washed it down with a sip of soda. "My father said she'd make the perfect military wife."

"She would," I agreed, my heart suddenly aching. It was ridiculous to be envious of Kate, especially given my determination to keep my distance from Nick. But I was incredibly jealous.

Nick opened a package of salsa and squirted it on his burrito. "After the funeral, Kate brought me two weeks' worth of neatly labeled homemade frozen meals. They were delicious, especially her artichoke frittata with Cotija cheese."

Selfish and immature thoughts raced through my mind. Artichoke frittata with Cotija cheese? How in the world did you make that?

"Kate is very talented," I offered, resisting the temptation to say something unkind. I didn't want to be petty, but did Nick know who was responsible for Kate's beautiful hair? Did he know that without me, Kate would be completely gray?

"She reminds me of my father's third wife," Nick said. "All business. Very serious about life and how to reheat artichoke frittata. It's as if she believes our national security depends on preheating the oven properly. A little too high maintenance for me."

Relief flooded me. Nick wasn't romantically interested in Kate, unless comparing her to one of his many stepmothers was a positive thing.

"What about me?" I asked in a snarky voice. "Which one of your father's wives do I remind you of?"

I expected him to laugh. Instead, the moment grew serious as his eyes swept across my face and down to my lips. "Actually, Anna, you don't remind me of anyone but yourself."

My heart hammered. "Is that a good thing?"

"Yeah. It's a really good thing." His gaze stayed on my lips, and I wondered if he was going to kiss me again. Embarrassed by the idea, I looked away, warning myself not to go down that path.

Nick must've shared my sentiment because he shifted the conversation back to his father. "Ever since Thanksgiving, phone conversations with him have been strange."

"Strange?"

"He actually apologized for Thanksgiving, saying he should've had the meal catered so we could've stayed home with the girls. And now, he wants to bring Gina to the island for Christmas."

"You don't sound happy about that."

"I don't trust him. Apologizing and making plans for Christmas isn't like him."

"Maybe he's trying to change," I suggested.

He gave a look of disbelief. "I doubt that."

"What? You don't think people can change?"

"Not really. At least, not my father."

I paused. "You attended Sunday school growing up, right?"

"Yeah."

"Well, have you ever heard of the Apostle Paul from the New Testament? He went around persecuting Christians until God transformed him into one of the greatest men in the Bible."

Nick laughed. "Yes, of course I've heard of Paul who was once called Saul."

"Well? Don't you think if God could change Paul's heart, he could soften your father's?"

Nick stared down at his hands, something I noticed he did whenever deep in thought. "I wish my faith in God and humanity was as strong as yours."

I refrained from reaching out and clasping Nick's hand. "Have you asked God to give you the gift of faith?"

"Not in so many words."

"You should try it sometime. He wants to connect with you. All you have to do is ask."

Nick gave a sad smile, and I hoped I hadn't overstepped or offended him with my talk of God and forgiveness. My faith was important to me, but it wasn't something I wanted to shove down anyone's throat.

And yet, Nick seemed to be searching for answers only the Lord could provide. How could I not share my faith with him?

Kate's confident voice snapped across the cafeteria. "Ladies and gentlemen. Thank you so much for coming to the carnival and showing your support for Rose Island Elementary School. This year, we have some very exciting prizes, including a Jet Ski donated by Island Water Sports."

The room erupted with loud applause and whistles of approval. Gabby opened her eyes for a brief moment before closing them and falling back asleep on Nick's shoulder. I motioned to the baby. "I can't believe she's sleeping through all this noise."

"She loves the backpack, and as long as she's there, she can sleep through anything." He patted her little hand. "And I admit, it's really nice having her here. Plus, the backpack has a pouch for her diapers and bottles, so I don't have to carry around that enormous, girly diaper bag."

I smiled, feeling the tenderness of the moment spread through me. On stage, one of the students withdrew a ticket from the first basket. Kate announced the winner, and I clapped politely.

When they reached the *Organize Your Life* basket, I crossed my fingers, but ironically, Kate's name was called. The already competent woman giggled endlessly as she took her prize.

Nick leaned toward me and whispered, "Maybe now she'll finally get her life together."

A shiver rushed through me as Nick's breath brushed against my ear. Laughing it off, I gently shoulder-bumped him, taking care not to wake Gabby. "No kidding."

The names of more raffle winners were announced, including mine for the scrapbooking basket.

"What are you going to do with all this stuff?" Nick asked after I returned from the stage with my prize. He picked up a package of stickers, examining it as if it were from a foreign country.

I cocked my head to the side, uncertain if he was joking or serious. "Well, Bianca, Vicki, Jillian, and I get together every few months to scrapbook. I'm way behind, but maybe this basket will motivate me."

"Scrapbook?" he asked, confused.

I nodded. "We arrange photos and other memorabilia into books for our families. Have you never heard of scrapbooking?"

"I don't think so."

I studied him carefully. "Are you teasing me?"

"No. Is it like a photo album or something?"

"Kind of, but it's much more elaborate than just a photo album. Next time you come to my house, I'll show you my books. Travis's life has been very well documented."

He nodded but continued to look clueless. Maybe

nobody had ever compiled an album for him or Ethan. I was about to ask when loud applause echoed through the cafeteria in response for the final raffle item.

"Here we go." Nick crossed his fingers and grinned. "Are you ready to walk back to the stage when they call your name?"

I smiled. "I don't think so."

"Drum roll, please," Kate said.

The students banged their hands on the tables and floor as Kate withdrew a name from the jar. "And the winner is . . ." She glared at the paper and frowned.

"Who is it?" the principal asked, joining Kate on stage.

Kate shook her head and handed the winner's name to Mrs. Abbott. The principal squinted at the paper and whispered something to Kate who nodded. Grabbing hold of the microphone, Mrs. Abbott said, "On behalf of Rose Island Elementary School, I'm pleased to announce the winner of the Jet Ski is . . . Anna Morgan."

Chapter 17

I FROZE, CONVINCED winning the Jet Ski was a joke. I'd never known Kate or the principal to have a sense of humor, but there was a first time for everything. The audience clapped and stared right at me.

"This can't be real," I told Nick.

He burst into laughter. "You won! I can't believe it, but you actually won."

"No." I shook my head. "They're just teasing me."

The audience continued applauding as the principal jingled the keys and spoke into the microphone. "Anna Morgan, please come to the stage immediately to claim your prize. It's yours whether you want it or not."

I shook my head with disbelief as Nick laughed so hard, tears rolled down his face. Travis bounded toward me, trembling with excitement. "We won, Mom! We won! Can you believe it? We only put in one ticket and we won."

"I think it's a mistake," I said. "In fact, I'm sure of it."

My statement caused Nick to laugh even harder. Gabby opened her eyes and began crying. Nick reached behind his back and pulled the baby into his arms. "It's okay, sweetheart," he said between bouts of laughter. "Sorry to interrupt your nap, but we're in the midst of a Christmas Carnival miracle."

I stood on shaky legs to claim my prize. At that moment, I didn't know which I was more afraid of: winning the Jet Ski, or the terrifying sense of warmth and affection spreading through me as I watched Nick laugh.

Nick

"WHEN ARE WE going to take your new toy for a spin?" I asked, walking home with Anna, Travis, Hailey, and Gabby after the carnival ended. I'd laughed so hard when Anna won the Jet Ski that my stomach ached as though I'd done a thousand sit-ups.

"How about tomorrow?" Travis suggested.

Anna shook her head. "Tomorrow, we're going to church with Grandma and Grandpa and then to their house for Sunday brunch like always."

"Can't we go out in the afternoon?" Travis asked.

I tousled the boy's hair. "Don't worry, buddy. I'm not going to let your mom weasel her way out of this. She's going on that Jet Ski even if I have to toss her over my shoulder and haul her down to the water kicking and screaming."

Both Hailey and Travis laughed, but Anna didn't

seem amused by my threat. Instead, she withdrew and remained quiet the rest of the way home. When I asked if she was okay, she gave a nonchalant shrug. "Just tired."

I saw Anna and Travis safely to their cottage before taking the girls home. Once Gabby was down for the night, I tucked Hailey and the puppies into bed.

"Uncle Nick?" Hailey called as I turned off her light. "Do you think we could go to church tomorrow?"

I'd been contemplating that same idea all the way home. "I'd like that."

"Can we sit with the Morgans in the front row?"

I wanted to sit with Anna, but I wasn't sure her in-laws would approve. I'd met Luella at the bakery the other day, and for being such an outgoing person, she didn't seem pleased to meet me.

"We better sit in the back in case Gabby gets fussy and I have to take her out," I said.

Hailey fluffed up her pillow. "Actually, the cry room is near the altar, so we should sit up front."

Agreeing with her logic, I left her room and took my iPad onto the balcony. Moonlight danced on the water and lit up the beach. Glancing at The Blue Crab, I wondered if Anna would be pleased to see me at church tomorrow. I thought of her sweet face and smiled.

Every time we were together, I wanted to pull her into my arms. I'd been attracted to other women before, but this was different. Something about Anna made me question what I wanted out of life. She made me want to be a better man and do whatever possible to make her happy.

Placing a hand on my stomach, I pushed on the muscles that were sore from laughing so hard at the carnival. I did sit-ups on a regular basis, but tonight, I'd used muscles I didn't normally exercise. The irony of that fact didn't escape me.

For as long as I lived, I would never forget the look on Anna's face when she won the Jet Ski. Of all people to win the grand prize!

Smiling at the memory of her shocked and beautiful face, I turned my attention to my iPad and logged onto my e-mail. Lucy from the adoption agency had written again, including a link that would supposedly lead to the perfect family for Gabby and Hailey. I stared at the iPad, wanting to click on the link but unable to do so.

Was it wrong to raise Hailey and Gabby by myself? Was doing so unfair to them?

As a child, I'd attended Boy Scouts with a neighbor boy. I'd loved camping, fishing, rock-climbing, and experiencing many other activities with the troop, but having a workaholic father had been tough. I'd been constantly jealous of the other boys and their involved fathers, and I swore I'd never raise a child without two parents who could share the responsibility.

And yet, Travis seemed to be thriving with only Anna. Maybe a kid's well-being depended on the parent.

After all, George Lucas, the creator of *Star Wars*, had raised three children on his own while building a multi-million-dollar empire.

I allowed myself to visualize what it would be like to keep the girls. I saw myself picking them up from daycare after work and eating dinner together. I imagined taking them to the park and the zoo on the weekends. Attending their school functions and helping with homework.

And then I pictured saying good-bye when I deployed. I saw their little lives disrupted by having me gone for months at a time. I imagined myself being distracted with worry and causing an injury at work because of my inability to focus.

Of course, another option was to follow Travis's suggestion of marrying Anna and raising the kids together. Even though the notion struck me as crazy, I could actually see myself spending the rest of my life with her. It was a preposterous idea as I barely knew her, but in some ways, it felt as if I'd known her my whole life.

Unfortunately, she'd never agree to marry me. *No soldiers* was her dating motto. I didn't blame her for feeling that way. I just wished things were different.

I want to do the right thing, Lord, but I don't know what that means. Give me direction. Show me the way. Amen.

Taking a deep breath, I clicked on the link in Lucy's

e-mail and began scrolling through the list of prospective families for the girls.

IN THE MORNING, I slept through my alarm. Or rather, I'd set the time for p.m., not a.m., so it hadn't even gone off. Frustrated, I scrambled to get ready for church. In hindsight, I should've planned what we were going to wear because it was only in the morning I realized all our clothes were dirty.

Rushing around the house, I found something decent for everyone to wear. Then, I put the dogs in the backyard and loaded the girls into the car. Church started in five minutes, and as long as nothing else went wrong, we could make it. I started the engine and put the car in reverse.

"Um, Uncle Nick?" Hailey called from the backseat.

"Yeah?" Turning around, I saw that Gabby had unscrewed the lid to her sippy cup and dumped milk down her only clean outfit. I closed my eyes and pushed out a deep breath of frustration.

"Does this mean we're not going to church today?" Hailey asked.

I opened my eyes. "I'm afraid not, kiddo."

Anna

AFTER PUTTING TRAVIS to bed Sunday night, I sat at my computer, trying to ignore the churning in the pit of my stomach over my growing feelings for Nick. I was getting too close to him. Becoming too dependent on his smile and touch. This had to end. I needed to change my life and move forward without him.

Determined to take a step in the right direction, I studied the Island Community College website. I'd looked at the site before but had never been motivated to take the next step and schedule an appointment with an advisor.

Was I too old to go back to school and sit in a classroom all day? Intimidated by the prospect of attending college, I clicked on the link that led to the flight school where I'd trained and taught.

My hands trembled as I watched the videos promoting the wonderful world of flying. I desperately missed it. Desperately wanted to fly again despite my fear and guilt.

Was it simply a matter of getting back in the helicopter and trying? I wanted to feel the exhilaration of being in the air, but could I actually find the courage to try again?

The ringing of my phone startled me, and I jumped.

"I'm calling to fix your love life," Jillian declared after I said hello. "Mitch and Bryan are both free

Thursday, so I thought we could double date."

My throat clogged. "This Thursday?"

"Yes. It's seafood night at the country club. Are you available?"

"I am, but . . . I don't know if I'm ready."

Jillian gave a sympathetic sigh. "I was a mess the first time I went out after my divorce, but this isn't a big deal. It's simply four friends having dinner on a Thursday night."

I closed my eyes and remembered Nick laughing at the carnival. Remembered the joy I'd felt, seeing him so happy, knowing I was the reason for his laughter. I had to stop this fascination with him.

"Okay," I told Jillian. "Thursday night."

"That's fabulous. But don't sound so glum. It's going to be fun. Matt and Drew are spending the night with Mom and Dad, so I'm sure they can watch Travis."

I hesitated. "I don't know. Your mom was pretty upset about my friendship with Nick. I can't imagine her being enthusiastic about me going out on a date with Mitch."

"But Nick is leaving. That's why Mom was upset. She's obsessed with Sunday brunch and having the whole family live on the island and attend church together. If you got involved with Nick and left, life would change. Mitch, on the other hand, is safe and stable. He's not going anywhere. My parents already know and like him from church, and so will you. He's perfect."

Was he?

I hung up the phone already knowing how Bianca would react. But what would Nick think about my upcoming date with safe and stable Mitch?

DURING A MID-MORNING break, I rode my bike to the community college for an appointment with a guidance counselor. At the admissions office, I checked in with the receptionist and completed several forms.

Question number eight asked about my reason for attending school. How was I supposed to answer? A desire to complete my degree? Fear of flying? A need to channel my energy away from the gorgeous soldier who occupied my every thought? Nothing seemed appropriate, so I left the space blank.

After a while, a tall woman with a pleasant voice named Nell Reynolds called me into her office. Sitting in a cloth-covered wingback chair, I waited patiently while she read through my paperwork.

On the desk sat a photograph of three men in army uniforms. Nell noticed me looking at the picture and smiled. "My husband is retired military, and both my sons entered the service."

"You must be proud of them," I managed to say.

"I am, but I worry every day."

"You do?"

She nodded. "If I had my way, I'd keep them safe on the island for the rest of their lives, but military service is in their blood. It's what they've always wanted to do, so how can I stand in their way?"

I gave a weak smile, definitely understanding that sentiment.

Nell tapped a finger on one of my forms. "You used to work as a helicopter pilot?"

"Yes."

"But you're not flying anymore?"

I shrugged and looked at the photograph of Nell's family. "I've been thinking about going back," I heard myself say. "I just want to explore all my options before making a decision."

She nodded. "That's understandable."

Was it? Had I honestly admitted I might go back to flying?

"Since you're not quite sure what you want to study, I'm going to suggest you take a career aptitude test. The results might help you figure out what classes to take. Are you interested?"

"Let me think about it," I said, but I already knew what the aptitude test would reveal.

I was meant to fly.

THURSDAY NIGHT, I left Travis with my in-laws and went out to the country club with Jillian, Bryan, and

Dr. Mitch Norman. The four of us sat by the window overlooking the immaculate greens.

"Do you golf?" Mitch asked. He was tall, thin, and good-looking with short brown hair and straight white teeth. He smelled a little like toothpaste, which wasn't necessarily a bad thing for a dentist, but it did remind me of my last cleaning. Not exactly my favorite thing to think about.

"I took a golf lesson in high school," I offered. "But I haven't played since then."

"You really should. It's wonderful exercise and—"

"Very expensive."

"Well, that's true," he conceded with a big toothy smile. "But I don't have children, so I can spend my time and money on the course. If I were to remarry and have children, I'm sure that would change."

From this comment and our brief conversation in the car, I knew Mitch wanted a family. I also knew he'd be an amazing father. I could easily visualize him coaching Little League or having a tea party with his daughter. He'd probably take on the responsibility of brushing his kids' teeth, something I still had to remind Travis to do on a regular basis.

"Jillian told me you moved to the island about three years ago," I said, doing my best to keep the conversation going.

"I did. I love the slow and easy pace here, but my wife—sorry, my ex-wife—grew restless. There wasn't enough high-end shopping for her. Now she's back in Houston, and it's for the best. Without a doubt, her happiness truly is dependent on a mall."

"I hate shopping," I said, blurting out the first thought that popped into my nervous mind.

A huge smile spread across Mitch's face. "I do, too." He lifted his glass and clinked it against mine.

I took a sip of my iced tea. "So, you like living here?"

He sat back in his chair. "I don't ever want to live anywhere else. I think it's the perfect place to settle down and raise a family. My offer to buy an older dentist's practice was just accepted, so I'm excited about my future here."

I studied him carefully, finding nothing wrong with his lean and handsome features. He didn't make my knees buckle or my insides flutter, but I wanted to give him a chance. I wanted to believe with some effort, I could become attracted to him. Maybe even fall in love with him.

"Jillian says you're thinking about going back to school," he said. "What do you want to study?"

"I'm not quite sure. Ultimately, something in accounting or finance, but I might start with an online psychology class."

Jillian reached for a piece of fried calamari. "I loved my freshman psychology class. I still remember learning about the power of positive thinking and how it affects outcome."

Bryan nodded. "They say people who write down their goals are more successful. Even if they never refer to those goals again, writing them down subconsciously triggers their actions."

Mitch pitched in his own thoughts, and the four of us enjoyed a lively discussion about the human brain. After dinner, a country band took the stage, and Mitch led me to the dance floor.

When he took me in his arms, my mind drifted back to all the times Nick had held me. I thought of the thrill I'd felt when he'd kissed me. His smile and the way he'd laughed when I'd won the Jet Ski. How in the world was I going to forget about him?

Later, in the ladies' room, Jillian asked what I thought so far.

I set my purse on the counter and removed a small cosmetic bag. "He's nice."

"I think he really likes you."

"I like him, too." Looking at my reflection in the mirror, I touched up my lipstick. "It's been a wonderful evening, and I'm glad I came."

Afterward, Bryan drove everyone home, stopping at my house first. Mitch walked me to the door even though I told him it wasn't necessary. All night long, he'd been quite the gentleman—opening doors, standing when I left the table, and bringing up interesting topics of conversation.

My sixth grade cotillion instructor would've been pleased by Mitch's impeccable manners. Not that Nick didn't have impeccable manners, and not that I was comparing the two, or even thinking about Nick for that matter.

"I had a lovely time." Quickly, I inserted my key into the lock and opened the front door. Yoda barked wildly, lunging at the baby gate, determined to make his presence known.

"What a cute dog," Mitch said, smiling. "It looks like he has some German Shepherd in him."

"I think so. Do you like dogs?"

"I do. My German Shepherd died recently . . . the same week my wife left me. Not my best week, obviously. But I miss her so much—the dog, not the wife."

I smiled. "I'm sorry."

He shrugged. "Everyone says I just need to get a new dog, but it's not that easy, you know? I found Jezebel when she was a puppy, and she was one of a kind. Not something I can easily replace."

I started to say I knew exactly what he meant, but unexpectedly, he stepped toward me and pressed his lips to mine. I inhaled sharply, shocked he was kissing me.

Then, as though on autopilot, I threaded my arms around his neck and pulled him closer.

Chapter 18

*M*ORE THAN ANYTHING, I was surprised to find myself being kissed by Mitch. As quickly as our kiss began, it ended, with Mitch pulling away first. He grinned at me bashfully. "I hope that was okay."

"Sure," I said, flustered. *Was it okay? I didn't know.*

"I'll call you." He stepped onto the porch and jogged down the stairs, leaving me staring after him, surprised and confused. The kiss hadn't set off any fireworks, but it'd been nice. I'd easily returned his kiss without feeling any of the fear and panic I'd felt every time I'd kissed Nick.

Suddenly, I could see a pleasant future as *the dentist's wife*. I imagined returning to the country club every year to celebrate our first date, raising Travis together, and having more children.

Instead of handing out Halloween candy, we'd offer toothpaste and dental floss. I'd buy Mitch a wooden sign from the Farmer's Market that said *You don't have to brush all your teeth, just the ones you want to keep.* Our Christmas tree would be decorated with dental ornaments; and once a year, I'd accompany him to his annual oral health conference in cities like Chicago and San Francisco.

It'd be a pleasant life, comprised of everything I'd ever wanted. Safety, stability, contentment, fresh breath, and free dental cleanings. So, why wasn't I more excited about a life with Mitch? Why hadn't his kiss left me breathless and touching my lips to relive the passionate moment?

Closing and locking the door, I sighed heavily. Why did life have to be so complex? Why couldn't Mitch be the hot army guy and Nick the safe dentist? And why couldn't I stop thinking about Nick?

Yoda cocked his head to the side and whined.

"You want to go outside, boy?" I found his leash, and we walked up the seashell path to the mailboxes. The moon was only a sliver tonight, and while I'd never been afraid on the island, it was comforting to have Yoda by my side.

Over time, my feelings for the dog had grown. I'd been so angry that first night when he'd destroyed my handbag. Now, I found myself perusing the pet aisle for a special doggie treat every time I went grocery shopping.

As if reading my thoughts, Yoda looked up and wagged his tail.

"Good boy," I said, my voice tender.

Tonight, the house would be excruciatingly quiet. Maybe I should drive over to my in-laws and convince

Travis to come home. He'd probably disown me if I did that because he was looking forward to Grandpa Walter driving him to school in the Corvette. Plus, Luella would ask all about the date, and I didn't want to talk about that tonight.

I slid my key into the mailbox and opened it to find nothing but advertisements. Gone were the days when receiving mail was exciting. Now the majority of my mail went straight into the recycling bin.

On my way home, I glanced up at the Petersons' house and saw Nick standing on the upstairs balcony with Gabby and Hailey. The baby pointed a chubby finger at the moon, and Nick said something, causing both girls to giggle. The sweet sound danced through the quiet night, tugging at my heart.

I stood close enough that I could've called out to them. Instead, I remained silent, not wanting to disrupt their gentle moment. Yoda pulled on the leash, and regretfully, I allowed him to lead me home.

I had a feeling it was going to take several more dates with Mitch before I forgot about Nick and those precious girls.

Like going back to college when you really wanted to fly helicopters, Mitch was second choice.

And when it came to love, second choice was miles behind first.

EVERY FEW MONTHS, the *Morgan Spinsters*—as Bianca had recently taken to calling Jillian, Vicki, me, and herself—convened at The Blue Crab to scrapbook late into the night. Usually, the boys stayed with their grandparents. That Friday night, however, Walter and Luella's salsa dancing club had an event, so the disappointed cousins were stuck hanging out with the women.

Our evening began as it always did by strolling along the beach to the pier for dinner at the Pelican Pub. Matt, Drew, and Travis complained endlessly about walking to dinner.

"You have to understand," Drew said. "For us guys, scrapbooking night is all about drinking soda, eating pizza, and watching John Wayne movies with Grandpa out in the barn. We're just not used to this walking along the beach at sunset stuff."

"Don't forget the burping contest," Travis added.

Jillian sighed. "We don't like this arrangement any more than you do, but there's nothing we can do about it, so let's make the most of it, okay?"

Matt threw the ball down the beach for Yoda. "I don't see why I couldn't stay by myself. I'm fifteen, you know."

"I know," Jillian conceded, "but you're grounded, so think of this as part of your punishment."

He let out a disgusted huff and marched ahead.

"What'd he do to get grounded?" Travis asked once

Matt was out of earshot.

Drew shook his head. "Dude, you do not want to ask that question. Come on. I'll race you."

Drew ran down the beach with Travis following him. They caught up to Matt, who again threw the ball for Yoda, and all three boys raced ahead.

I slipped off my shoes and walked down to the water. The others did the same, and Bianca asked what Matt had done to get grounded.

Jillian shook her head with disgust. "He had his girlfriend over to the house after I specifically said she couldn't be there when I was gone. Then he gave me all kinds of trouble about having to video chat with his father after we arranged a time that would be most convenient for Matt."

"Was Keith mad about that?" Bianca asked.

Pain encompassed Jillian's face as it often did at the mention of her ex-husband. "He wasn't happy, that's for sure."

"So, when will Keith be back?" Bianca asked.

"The unit is supposed to return sometime this spring, but the army is unpredictable, so who knows."

Bianca bent over to pick up a shell. "Did Keith—"

"Can you please stop asking about him?" Jillian said, suddenly irritated. "Last week, I told you I don't want to talk about him, but you're constantly inventing reasons to say his name."

"I can't even ask—"

"No," Jillian snapped. "You can't. Vicki, Anna, and even Mom and Dad finally understand it's over, but you keep pestering me about him."

Tension filled the air, and Bianca, not one to be pushed around by anybody, let alone her older sister, responded sarcastically. "*Sorry,* excuse me for asking about Keith. Excuse me for being interested in your life. I suppose I'm only allowed to ask about *Bryan,* your wonderful new and exciting boyfriend."

Jillian ground her teeth. "Stop talking, okay? Just stop talking!"

Angry silence soured the previously carefree mood. A group of brown pelicans soared overhead, briefly blocking the fading sunlight and casting a dark shadow along the beach.

"Are you okay?" I asked.

Jillian heaved a deep sigh. "Yesterday, Keith's mom sent me a newspaper article for the boys. I shouldn't have read it, but I did, and he sounded like the most amazing, selfless, heroic man in the world."

Her voice cracked, but she cleared her throat and continued. "All that may be true, but he doesn't love me anymore. He doesn't want to be with me, and that hurts. We're divorced, and I don't want to talk about him as if everything is perfectly fine."

I placed a hand on Jillian's shoulder and gave Bianca a pointed look. "We won't talk about him anymore."

Jillian nodded. "I know y'all don't like *Boring Bryan,*

as you call him behind my back—"

"I like him," I insisted, wanting to soothe her pain. "He was very nice when we went out last night, and I enjoyed getting to know him better."

She was quiet as she studied me carefully. "You really like Bryan?"

"I do," I insisted.

"What if I told you Keith called last night, and he wants to get back together? He's sorry for everything he put me through, and he promised to go to counseling and AA. He said he still loves me—"

"Is that true?" Hope exploded inside me. "Did he really call?"

Jillian gave an ironic snort and shook her head. "No, but that's my point. Even you, Anna, won't accept the fact I'm with Bryan now. It's over between Keith and me, so can we just move on?"

Shame settled in the pit of my stomach. Maybe I didn't complain about Boring Bryan like Bianca and Vicki, but deep down, I continued holding out hope for Jillian and Keith. Deep down, I wanted nothing more than to see them back together.

"I'm sorry," I said, regretfully. "You're right."

Bianca skipped a shell across the surface of the ocean. "I'm sorry, too. But just so you know, I don't see you and Bryan staying together forever."

"Well, that's not really your concern, is it?" Jillian shot back.

Bianca shrugged and nobody spoke for awhile as we continued down the beach. I hated when my sisters-in-law fought, but over time, I'd come to realize their arguments never lasted very long. Regardless of the insensitive things they said to one another, they really did love each other and were quick to forgive.

As the Pelican Pub came into view, Jillian broke the strained silence. "Maybe Bryan's not the most exciting person in the world, but he's nice. He treats me well, and he's—"

"He's safe," I said.

She grimaced at first, but then she relaxed as if coming to peace with my observation. "I suppose you're right. Bryan is very safe."

"It's not a bad thing," I insisted. After all, I'd used the same word to describe going to college instead of flying.

And choosing Mitch over Nick.

There was nothing wrong with safe, was there?

AT THE PELICAN Pub, we ate dinner outside on the sandy, wooden deck underneath heat lamps and colorful Christmas lights. As I dipped a chip in salsa, Matt proudly emitted a loud, obnoxious burp. Jillian scolded her oldest son and gave both Drew and Travis a stern look for laughing.

Vicki shook her head. "Boys are so disgusting. I

can't believe neither one of you gave me a sweet—"

She stopped talking and stared directly at her oldest sister. "I'm sorry, Jillian. I didn't mean to say that."

Although Jillian's face paled, she waved a dismissive hand. "Don't worry about it."

A moment of silence followed, and I thought about the unborn baby girl Jillian and Keith had lost. The late-term miscarriage, coming so soon after Marcus's death, had been difficult on Jillian, dragging her into a deep depression that she still struggled with.

"Girls aren't always sweet," Matt mumbled. "Grandma said you three used to fight all the time. And I'm pretty sure you're kind of fighting tonight."

Bianca gave a sly smile. "Did Grandma ever tell you about *The Great Parachute Pants War of 1989?* How your mother borrowed my favorite pants and ruined them with grape soda?"

"That was an accident," Jillian said, pretending to be offended. "I can't believe you're still upset about it."

"I *loved* those pants."

"I guess so." Jillian laughed, and as everyone else joined in, the tension eased. Through the rest of dinner, the Morgan sisters joked and told stories about growing up together. I was a little envious I didn't have siblings, but I'd enjoyed a happy childhood and a close relationship with my parents.

As the Christmas lights above us twinkled in the darkness, a sense of peace enveloped me. I was grateful for the beautiful island, my in-laws, and gorgeous nephews. If I had to be a widow, this wasn't a bad way to do it.

How could I think about jeopardizing my happiness for Nick or any other man with aspirations to leave the island? When Mitch asked me out, I wouldn't hesitate. And I definitely wouldn't think about Nick. No, starting tonight, I'd begin flossing twice a day in preparation for my new relationship.

After dinner, we walked back in the dark, using the flashlights on our phones to spot hermit crabs skittering across the beach. When the boys were little, we used to bring buckets to collect crabs and seashells at night, but nobody wanted to do that anymore.

About halfway home, I saw Nick, Hailey, Gabby, and all three puppies standing near the water. My heart spun at the sight of them. Yoda broke free and raced toward his siblings. I envied the dog's ability to express his emotions without reservation, then I laughed at my pathetic self for envying a dog.

"Hey," Nick said, smiling.

"Hey," I replied, purposely avoiding his gaze.

Bianca gushed over the puppies. "Anna, you should think about getting another dog for Yoda. I bet he'd love to have someone to play with."

I shook my head. "He has Travis and Felix, so no thank you. I'm happy enough with one puppy and one cat."

"Are you?" Nick asked, staring at me intently. "Are you really happy with Yoda?"

I nodded. Although I'd never been a dog person before, the mutt had wiggled his way into my life.

Nick bounced a cranky Gabby in his arms. "I thought she was down for the night, but she woke up crying. Hailey and I hoped looking at the boats on the water would make her feel better, but I don't think it's working. I'm afraid she might have another ear infection."

"Poor angel," Bianca said, reaching for Gabby. The baby batted her away and gave a resounding, "No!"

Bianca laughed. "It doesn't take them very long to learn that word, does it?"

We walked back to the cottage together, pointing out all the Christmas lights and discussing holiday traditions. I'd always enjoyed how the island's residents decorated the wild rose bushes growing along the beach with ornaments and thick garland.

Nick saw us safely to The Blue Crab before taking the dogs and his nieces home. I watched him go, feeling a sense of longing and desire that was downright embarrassing.

Standing behind me, Bianca called out in a singsong voice not quite loud enough for Nick to hear. "Good night, my love!"

"Hush," I told her.

Nick turned around. "What'd you say?"

Bianca started to speak, but I jabbed her. "She said good night. Have a good night, and we'll see you later."

Nick gave a slow, easy smile, making me realize he'd heard exactly what Bianca said. Shuddering, I quickly turned away.

Inside the house, the boys established Video Game Haven in the living room while the women set up our scrapbooking supplies in the kitchen.

Bianca ran her hand over the surface of my table. "Instead of scrapbooking, we should sand down your table and stain it tonight."

Vicki and Jillian groaned, but I gave a pleasant smile. "Not tonight, okay?"

Bianca shrugged. "Sure, but it's a nice table and deserves some love."

I refrained from rolling my eyes. For the next several hours, we worked on preserving our family memories while we talked, laughed, and listened to a radio show where love-sick couples called in to dedicate songs to each other.

Bianca, mischievous as usual, asked me what I'd do if Nick came on the radio to dedicate a song to me.

I gave a nervous laugh. "How old are you, Bianca?"

She giggled. "I'm just having a little fun. Maybe you should be the one to call and dedicate a song to him."

I tossed a package of stickers at her and told her to mind her own business.

Around midnight, Vicki left because she had to be

up in a few hours to open the bakery. Jillian soon followed, but she let Matt and Drew spend the night since they were having so much fun with Travis. Bianca and I continued working until my phone rang around one.

Nothing good ever came from a call at that hour, and my first thoughts went to my parents. I usually heard from them several times a week, but lately, we'd all been busy and hadn't talked for awhile.

Fumbling for my phone, I was surprised, relieved, and confused to see Nick's name on the caller ID. "I wonder why he's calling so late?"

Bianca made immature kissing sounds and spoke in a poor imitation of a male voice. "Oh, baby, I miss you so much. Meet me on the beach for a romantic stroll in the moonlight."

"Be quiet," I scolded. I answered the phone with a cheerful hello, but Nick cut me off.

"Something's wrong with the baby," he said, fear slicing through the line. "She can't breathe!"

Panic raced through me. "I'm on my way."

Chapter 19

Nick

I PACED THE driveway, bouncing Gabby in my arms, cringing every time she gasped for breath. I'd never been more terrified, nor prayed harder in my life. *Please, Lord. Heal her. Don't let anything bad happen to her. Please.*

Anna arrived and I opened the car door to load Gabby into her car seat to take her to the hospital. The baby coughed again, sounding like a seal and sparking a desperation inside me I'd experienced only in battle.

"Will you stay with Hailey while I go to the ER?" I asked.

Anna shook her head and actually gave a little smile of relief. "It's just croup. You don't need to take her in."

I'd never heard of croup. All I knew was the baby couldn't breathe, and she needed medical help.

"I know she sounds horrible, but she's going to be okay," Anna insisted. "Bring her inside, and I'll show you what to do."

I pulled Gabby closer. "You don't think she needs to

go to the hospital?"

Anna's voice was surprisingly calm. "No. If we sit with her in the bathroom and turn on the shower, the hot steam will make her better. Jillian's a nurse, and I can call her if you want, but I'm certain she'll tell you the same thing."

I had a hard time believing steam could heal Gabby's horrible cough, yet, I trusted Anna, especially when it came to parenting issues. Reluctantly, I followed her into the house and down the hall to the bathroom. She turned on the shower and told me to sit on the edge of the tub where Gabby could inhale the steam without getting wet.

I did as instructed, holding Gabby tightly as she coughed and cried. "It's okay, sweetheart," I whispered, hoping my words were true. Again, I silently begged God for help.

A memory from my own childhood came to me. I'd been sick with the stomach flu and had thrown up in the bathroom. Usually, our live-in nanny helped us when we were sick, but that time, my father held my head and rubbed my back. He'd cleaned my face with a wet washcloth and brought me a glass of cold water. Then, he'd helped me back into bed and had stayed with me until I fell asleep.

When I awoke in the morning, Jack had already left for work, but he'd instructed the nanny to let me have anything I wanted to eat. "Your father was worried about you," she'd said.

"He was?"

She'd nodded, giving me a sense of love and security I seldom felt.

Perhaps I'd allowed all the bad memories of my father to crowd out the good ones. After all, my father had provided Ethan and me with a top-rate education, decent nannies, summer camp, and a safe home. Maybe he'd done his best and was simply incapable of doing more.

"She's getting better," Anna said, bringing me back to the present.

I looked down at Gabby and smiled. "Thank goodness."

"I know it was terrifying to hear her struggle for breath, but the steam does wonders. If her cough gets worse, you can take her in for a steroid shot. Although, I worry about giving a baby steroids."

Filled with relief, I closed my eyes and rocked Gabby side to side. The baby's little hand reached up and touched my whiskers. Smiling, I kissed her fingers, and she pulled them away, clenching her hand into a tight fist. She slowly released each finger one by one, daring me to kiss them again. She liked little games like this, and when I tried to kiss her fingers again, she gave a muffled giggle followed by a weak cough.

I patted her back until she stopped coughing. Then I sang her an old Toby Keith song I'd sung to her before. Even though I didn't have the best voice, singing to Gabby always calmed her. As she'd done before, she nestled deeper into my chest.

At one point, I looked up to find Anna gazing down at me, her face tender. A flood of emotions gripped me. Not only did I love this baby in my arms, but I loved this woman before me. Loved this little makeshift family we'd created under such difficult circumstances.

But where did that leave us? What did it mean for the future?

When I finished singing, Anna's eyes were moist. "That's quite the lullaby."

Taken aback by her emotion, I looked down at Gabby, who'd fallen asleep. Her chest rose and fell in a peaceful, steady rhythm. "My singing seems to have this kind of effect on her."

Anna smiled. "You're a good uncle. A good father to these girls."

I sighed, afraid of how that statement made me feel.

"What?" she asked.

I shook my head, not wanting to tell her what I was thinking, but unable to remain silent. "This is going to sound heartless, but . . . I never wanted kids."

"Never?"

"No. Because of how I grew up, I never thought I could be a good parent. I figured the Peterson clan was missing the parent gene."

"*Nick,*" she said, sympathy and kindness in her

voice.

"I just never imagined I was capable of loving a child so much. Now, without a second thought, I'd take a bullet for either one of these girls."

"Of course you would."

"If I wasn't in the army, I think I could do it. I think I could adopt Hailey and Gabby and raise them myself. I still think it would be best if they had two parents, but—"

Her eyes lit up. "What are you saying? Are you thinking about leaving the army to find a different job?"

"No." She recoiled at my direct response, and I stumbled through my reasons. "Even if I wanted to, I couldn't get out of my three-year obligation. But I *want* to stay in the army. It's not a perfect life, but I love it. Even now, I miss it. How many people can say that about their job? I don't want to resign my commission and find myself stuck with a civilian job I hate."

Anna's face fell, but she spoke with a resigned tone. "You sound like my father."

"How so?"

"He's supposed to retire soon, and it's killing him. If he could, he'd stay in the army until the day he died."

I nodded. "It's a calling, you know? Some people have it, and some people don't. I just wish I knew how the girls fit into it."

She pushed off the counter and sat on the edge of the tub next to me. Our thighs touched and water from the shower splashed just enough that it dampened the back of our shirts.

"Not many men could have done what you've done," she said. "The girls are lucky to have you. Regardless of your decision, they're better for having had this time with you."

I reached over and took her hand. "Thanks."

She stared down at our entwined hands and took a deep breath. "When Marcus died, I didn't know how I was going to make it all by myself. I didn't realize I wasn't all by myself. I had my parents, Bianca, Vicki, Jillian, my in-laws, my church family, lots of friends. And I had my faith.

"I also had Travis who gave me a reason to get out of bed every day. What I'm trying to say is, don't underestimate yourself, and don't underestimate what a huge motivator kids are. I wouldn't be the same woman without my son."

I exhaled slowly. "Despite all your fears and unusual quirks, you're a very strong and capable woman, Anna."

"You think so?" She stared right at me. Did she know how deeply I'd come to care for her? How I thought about her all the time?

I let go of her hand and brushed back her hair. My thumb traced a line down her smooth cheek to her chin. And then, I pressed my lips to hers. Everything inside me exploded as we kissed.

"Nick," she whispered.

Hearing her say my name only drew me in more. I shifted the baby in my arms and kept my own eyes closed, afraid if I opened them, Anna would disappear. Running my hand through her silky hair, I deepened the kiss, pressing on the back of her neck to pull her closer.

Gabby stirred, and I pulled away from Anna to check on the baby.

"You can probably put her back in her crib now," Anna said, avoiding my gaze. "You might have to run the shower again, but she should be okay for a few hours. Just leave the humidifier running. It's that funky-looking blue thing on her dresser."

"I know. I looked it up a while ago and watched an online video about it, so I even know how to use it." I stood and turned off the shower, carefully shifting Gabby away from the water. "Don't leave, okay? Let me put the baby down, then we'll talk."

Anna nodded, but the fear in her eyes told me she'd be gone by the time I returned.

Anna

AS SOON AS Nick walked out of the bathroom, I wiped off the mirror with a towel and stared at my reflection. What was I doing? Hadn't Nick just told me he would never leave the army?

"Don't be a fool," I warned the woman in the mirror. Waiting for him now would only complicate the issue, making all rational thought impossible. And I needed to think rationally. I needed to make good decisions in order to protect myself and Travis.

Tapping into every last bit of willpower, I walked down the hallway and out the front door. As soon as my feet hit the seashell path, I sprinted as hard as I could toward the safety of my home.

Running away from Nick was for the best. It was hard now, but eventually, I'd be grateful I'd stopped our relationship before we became too involved.

A little voice inside my head insisted I was already too involved, but I pushed it away and scaled the wooden steps two at a time.

Bianca met me at the front door. "How's Gabby?"

It took me a moment to remember Gabby was the reason I'd gone over to Nick's in the first place. "She's better. It was croup, so we took her into the bathroom, started the shower, and the steam cleared her right up."

Bianca nodded. "I remember you and Jillian doing that when your boys were little."

I blew out a breath and scanned the messy but empty living room. "Did you send the boys to bed?"

Nodding, she let out a huge yawn. "Can I spend the night on your couch? I'm too tired to go home."

I gave a yawn of my own. "Of course. I'll find you a pillow and blanket."

I ran upstairs to the linen closet and returned to help

Bianca make up the couch. When we finished, she sat down and patted the empty space beside her. "So, I know tonight was scary with Gabby, but let's talk about the other scary part. Let's talk about Nick."

My gut knotted. I thought about Nick rocking Gabby back and forth as he sang her to sleep tonight. I thought about all the emotions his kiss had ignited. How much longer could I continue pushing him away?

When I didn't speak, Bianca said, "It's scary for me, too. I don't want you and Travis to leave the island."

I crossed my arms over my chest and stared at my sister-in-law. "I have no intention of leaving Rose Island. Ever."

"You and Nick were meant for each other. I can see the two of you getting married, and you, Travis, and the girls going with Nick to become a family."

Panic seized me. "No. I love it here. Travis and I have built a life here, and your parents would be devastated if we left."

"They would," she conceded. "But a guy like Nick doesn't come along very often."

"He's a soldier," I insisted, despising the hysteria in my voice. "I loved your brother more than anything, but I don't want to fall in love with another soldier. *Ever*. I can't do that to Travis, and I definitely can't do that to myself."

"I know, but you haven't been interested in anybody since Marcus. And don't tell me Thursday night's date with *Boring Bryan's friend* meant anything."

I balled my hands into tight fists, willing them to stop shaking. "Your brother was one of a kind."

"He was," Bianca agreed. "And I know he was the love of your life, but I want to make myself clear. Letting Nick go would be a huge mistake. The way he looks at you and smiles when you enter the room . . . he's in love with you, Anna. He's in love with you, and I know you feel the same way about him."

And that's the problem. That's the huge, no-obvious-solution of a problem.

My stomach wrenched. Despite my best efforts, I'd fallen in love with Nick, and I had absolutely no idea what to do about it.

Chapter 20

IN THE MORNING, Bianca and I sat at the kitchen table, sipping coffee and discussing our plans for the day. Bianca usually opened the salon on Saturdays, but knowing she'd be up late scrapbooking, she'd taken the day off.

When the doorbell rang, I answered it, surprised to find Nick, showered and shaven. Gabby was in his arms while Hailey stood next to him, holding a plate of freshly baked cinnamon rolls.

"We thought we'd bring you breakfast to thank you for helping Gabby last night," he said as Hailey offered the plate.

"Thank you." I kept my gaze on the cinnamon rolls in order to avoid looking at him. "Those smell amazing."

"They taste even better," Hailey said. "I snuck one before we came over."

I gestured toward the groggy boys who'd woken up early to resume their video game. "With this crowd, that was a good idea because once they start eating, you might not get one. You can't imagine the amount of food growing boys consume."

"Nick eats a lot, too," Hailey said, smiling up at her uncle.

I followed her gaze and asked Nick about Gabby.

"As good as ever," he said, bouncing the baby in his arms. "I can't even tell she was sick last night. I called the pediatrician, and she confirmed your diagnosis. She said if her cough gets worse, I can bring Gabby in for a steroid shot, but she'd rather avoid it. She also said not to worry if she was perfectly fine all day and coughed again tonight."

"That's the strangest part about croup," I said. "They seem fine during the day, but scare you to death at night with that barking cough."

Travis rose from the couch and sidled next to me. "Hey, Nick. Hey, Hailey. Hey, munchkin."

Gabby smiled and burrowed into Nick. Travis reached out and tickled the baby under her chin. "What's wrong, muffin head? Don't you remember your ole buddy, Travis?"

To everyone's surprise, Gabby spun around and dove toward Travis. He caught her and held her tight. "Well, hello, shortcake."

"I think she likes you," Nick said.

"She likes all the nicknames I have for her. Especially . . ." he paused for dramatic effect, bounced Gabby on his hip, and shouted, "*Ole Meatball Tutu!*"

Gabby cackled with laughter, but my entire body

stiffened. Travis had given Gabby the name he'd invented for his imaginary sibling. What did that mean?

Standing in the entryway together, I was struck by the vivid image of the five of us forming a family. I imagined vacations, holidays, and everyday meals surrounded by these people I loved so much.

Loved. I'd come to love Hailey and Gabby as though they were my own children. And Nick. I was wildly attracted to him, but more than that, I loved him. Loved him in a way that made me want what was best for him, even if that didn't include a life with Travis and me.

Nick winked at me as if he'd both read my mind and felt the same way. *Did he feel the same way?*

"Bring those cinnamon rolls in here," Bianca hollered from the kitchen.

I motioned for Nick to follow me back, while Travis and Hailey joined the other kids in the living room.

"A soldier who can cook," Bianca said, swiping a cinnamon roll off the plate. "You're a man of many talents, Nick."

He laughed. "Don't get too excited. They're just from a package. I'm sure they don't taste as good as what Vicki makes at the bakery."

"You better hope not," Bianca said. "Vicki wouldn't appreciate the competition."

"Ah, she doesn't have to worry about competition from me. I just mastered macaroni and cheese."

Bianca patted the empty chair beside her. "Come sit down and let me hold the baby while Anna plays hostess and brings us more coffee."

I gestured to the coffeemaker and asked if Nick would like a cup of coffee.

"That'd be great," he said, sitting beside Bianca.

I turned away, grateful for the task that distanced me from Nick. What had he thought when he came downstairs last night to find me gone? And what was he thinking now?

I set a cup of coffee on the table in front of him and refreshed Bianca's mug. Then, I opened the refrigerator to retrieve a carton of eggs and busied myself making scrambled eggs.

"Can you believe this warm weather?" Bianca said, playing patty cake with Gabby. "Last week it was so cold, I turned on the heat. This morning, I made Anna turn on the air conditioning. If it doesn't get cold soon, poor Santa is going to die of heat exhaustion."

"Has the island's Santa ever considered wearing shorts?" Nick asked.

Bianca laughed and lowered her voice. "That's what Anna's father says every year. He plays Santa at church on Christmas Eve, and we always get a heat spell that week."

"Really?" Nick said, surprised.

Bianca nodded. "The pastor gives Santa a blessing on the big night, and it's all very exciting. You should definitely come and sit in the front pew with our family."

"That sounds nice." Nick took a sip of his coffee. "It's been a long time since I attended church on Christmas Eve."

"Well, what are you waiting for?" Bianca asked. "If it's an invitation you need, then here it is. Please come to church with our family tomorrow and the next Sunday and Christmas Eve and every Sunday after that. The door is always open."

Nick smiled. "Thank you, Bianca."

"Of course."

I finished cooking the eggs, then placed them in a Polish Pottery bowl. As I brought them to the table, Nick stared at me as if we were the only two people in the world. My insides went all mushy, and I told myself to look away. I needed to remember why we couldn't be a couple, but his gorgeous eyes made it impossible to remember anything right now.

Clapping her hands together, Bianca winked at Nick. "I've got it! Today is the perfect day for you to help Anna take out the Jet Ski."

Nick looked out the window as if contemplating Bianca's suggestion. Or my dirty windows. "She's right. It's going to be a beautiful day."

Bianca nodded. "You can't let Anna wimp out of the deal she made with you. She did pinky-swear, after all. I'll watch the kids, so you won't have to worry about them."

Frowning, he gestured toward Gabby. "I hate to leave the baby if she's not feeling well."

"She'll be fine," Bianca insisted. "Vicki and I are taking the kids ice skating. If Gabby gets fussy, I'll bring her back to my house while Vicki stays with everyone else."

Nick wrinkled his brow in confusion. "Where are you going ice skating?"

"Downtown near the courthouse. The city installs a synthetic skating rink each Christmas so we can ice skate in our shorts."

Hailey entered the kitchen just in time to hear about the skating rink. "Can I go, Uncle Nick? Please?"

Nick looked at Hailey with concern. "You don't mind me taking Anna out on the Jet Ski?"

She shook her head. "No, I don't mind as long as I get to go skating."

I sat at the table and took a sip of my coffee. "I appreciate everyone's effort to orchestrate my life, but I'm not going out on that dangerous thing."

"Don't be scared," Bianca said. "Nick won't let you drown, right, honey?"

Nick spoke with confidence. "No. I promise I won't let anything bad happen to you."

I remembered how Jillian's ex-husband had promised to bring Marcus back from that last deployment. It'd been unwise for Keith to promise something like that, but hadn't I promised my parents and Marcus I'd be safe flying? Hadn't I promised Travis I'd always come back?

Travis overheard the conversation and ran into the kitchen. "Please, Mom. Please let Nick take you out on the Jet Ski. It's kind of like Yoda. You didn't want to keep him at first, but now you love him. Maybe you'll feel the same way once you get out on the water."

I bent down to pet Yoda who sat at my feet. "I think they're trying to use logic to influence me."

"Is it working?" Travis asked.

I locked eyes with Nick. I knew he couldn't guarantee my absolute safety, but I trusted him. "Will you bring me home if I hate it?"

He grinned. "I will, but you're not going to hate it, Anna. You're going to love it."

LATER THAT MORNING, I stepped onto the wobbly dock and tugged at the tight wet suit I'd borrowed from Vicki. Apparently, the wet suit was supposed to be tight in order to keep me warm, but I felt self-conscious, especially when I caught Nick admiring my figure.

As he backed the trailer down the boat ramp, I held my breath, imagining the whole contraption—trailer, Jet Ski, and Nick—sliding into the water. To my huge relief, that didn't happen.

Jumping out of the Tahoe, he gave a wave. I waved

back and watched him unload the Jet Ski before riding over to me. "I forgot the bumpers and rope to secure it to the dock cleat. Can you hold it while I park the car?"

"Of course." I was nervous, but surely if I could give birth and fly a helicopter, I could complete this simple task without plunging into the water.

Taking hold of the handle, I gripped it tightly as Nick stepped onto the dock. Both the dock and the Jet Ski bobbed up and down, but I held on, determined not to lose my balance.

"Are you okay?" he asked, placing a hand on the back of my life vest.

"Never better."

He laughed at my cynicism. "Okay, I'll be right back."

As he jogged to the car, a pair of roseate spoonbills flew overhead, their pink wings flapping through the air. My sixth grade class had taken a field trip to the aviary preserve where we'd learned that spoonbills did not mate for life. Instead, they chose a partner they kept for that breeding season alone.

Maybe Nick, like the male spoonbill, was only temporary. Maybe these few sweet weeks were all we'd ever have together.

Regardless, I'd never forget him. He'd awoken a part of me I'd assumed was lost forever. A part I'd assumed had died with Marcus.

When he returned from parking the car, he held the

Jet Ski so I could climb aboard. Stepping down, I clung to his forearms with both hands, terrified I'd fall.

"I've got you," he said, griping my arm.

My heart pounded, but I nodded and lowered myself to the seat. With both hands, I grasped the handlebars and held on for dear life. Nick climbed on behind me and hooked the lanyard with the key to my life vest. "This will allow the engine to stop in case . . . never mind. Are you ready?"

Not daring to let go of the handlebars, I twisted around to look at him. "Were you going to say in case we fall in the water?"

"Maybe. But that's not going to happen."

"And if it does?"

He grinned. "Then obviously it would be your fault."

I nudged him with my foot, and he laughed.

"Okay, if we fall in the water," he said, "we'll deal with it. It's not like we're falling from the sky in a helicopter. The water might be a little cold, but we'll be okay."

"You're right. I'm being a big baby. Let's go."

Reaching around me, he showed me how to insert the key to start the engine. Immediately, the Jet Ski rumbled to life and eased forward. A jolt of panic hit me. "Why are we moving? I'm not ready. Where are the brakes?"

"It's okay," he said, squeezing my arms. "Just steer,

and when you are ready, you can pull the gas to make it go faster."

"I don't want to make it go faster. I want to make it stop."

His arm pressed against mine as he showed me how to pull back the brake. *Brake* being used in the loosest sense of the word because, much like a helicopter in the air, the Jet Ski couldn't completely stop, it just hovered in place.

"Should I release the brake?" I asked.

"Sure. And when you're ready, you can pull the gas handle."

"What if I don't want to pull the gas handle?"

His tone was humorous. "Then you don't have to. We can continue this turtle pace all day long. In my opinion, speed is way overrated."

"Are you making fun of me?"

"No."

"Yes, you are."

He laughed. "Maybe just a little."

We putted along for awhile, my confidence growing the farther we traveled. Heat from Nick's hands at my waist singed my body. How did he manage to make me crazy with a simple touch?

"Anna, look!" He pointed to a spot in the near distance where two bottlenose dolphins simultaneously crested the water and leapt into the air. They disappeared below the surface, only to reappear moments later.

Nick directed my attention a little off to the left. "Do you see the other two?"

"Yes, I can't believe they're right here! I've seen them from the air and from the shore, but never like this. It's absolutely incredible."

I continued driving the Jet Ski along the bay at the breakneck speed of half a mile per hour, watching for dolphins. After a while, I grew more courageous. "Okay, I'm ready to go faster. What do I do?"

Nick tightened his grip around my stomach. "When you're ready, squeeze the gas and let her rip."

Taking his words literally, I squeezed the handle tight. The Jet Ski catapulted forward at the speed of light, causing the vehicle to tip one way and then the other. I screamed and lost my balance. Although I tried to compensate by leaning in the opposite direction, the watercraft flipped, plunging us both into the frigid water.

Chapter 21

I GULPED A mouthful of freezing-cold, salty water. Bobbing to the surface, I coughed and frantically searched for Nick.

"I'm right here," he said, wrapping his strong arms around me.

"*Nick.*" I clung to his life vest as my teeth chattered from both the cold and fear. Salt water stung my lips and eyes. Blinking several times, I tried to put things into focus.

"Anna, look at me," he demanded. "It's okay. We're all right. You're wearing your life vest and so am I."

I was wet and cold, and my fear of falling in the water had come true, but I was okay.

"Anna? Are you all right? Say something."

A smile spread across my face, and I broke into laughter. "What happened?"

He grinned. "You squeezed the handle too quickly. You have to ease forward slowly and get used to the speed before you go barreling across the bay like a daredevil."

I laughed again and shook my head, feeling more

alive than I'd felt in years. "Are we going to be able to get back on that thing?"

"Do you want to try again?" he asked, sounding hopeful.

"Definitely. Now that I know falling off is no big deal, I want to figure it out."

"That's my girl."

My spirits lifted at the endearment. *My girl* was probably something that had unconsciously slipped out and didn't mean anything. In fact, he probably said it to Hailey and Gabby all the time, but the gentle way he said it to me made me forget I was cold.

Together, we swam back to the Jet Ski, and Nick pulled down the ladder so we could board. I climbed up first, shivering as the crisp wind swept across my face. Nick followed and folded up the ladder. Because he wore only swim trunks and a T-shirt underneath his life vest and not a wet suit like me, his body was ice cold.

"You're shaking," I said, patting his bare leg.

He scooted closer and pressed his chest to my back. Wrapping his arms around me, he buried his face into my shoulder. His teeth chattered as he spoke. "I'm okay, but how about we drive to Charlie's on the Water and warm up with a burger and fries?"

I agreed and aimed the Jet Ski across the bay, taking his advice of keeping the speed at a slow and steady pace until I felt comfortable going faster. At Charlie's, we docked and made our way to the gift shop where Nick bought a dry T-shirt he changed into before entering the restaurant.

The waitress sat us next to the window and brought each of us a hot cup of coffee. We ordered a cheeseburger to split, so we could save room for Charlie's famous chocolate pecan pie. I had to admit there was something incredibly appealing about a man who based his menu choice on what was for dessert.

Nick looked around the restaurant, taking in the solid wood furniture and large stone fireplace. Finally, he looked back at me. "Well, what do you think about the Jet Ski, so far?"

I smiled and wrapped my hands around the hot mug, absorbing its warmth. "I like it. Seeing the dolphins close-up was amazing. Even falling in the water wasn't as bad as I feared. A little cold, but not scary. And once I figured out how to drive, I had a blast."

"Does that mean you're going to keep it?"

I took a sip of my coffee and exhaled. "I don't know. I've read about so many accidents, I'm still not convinced they're safe. Three years ago, there was a deadly wreck just south of here."

"That's the problem," he said. "You've read about all these accidents, but have you read about all the people who went out and had a good time without any problems?"

I smiled. "That's the same logic I used on my parents when I wanted to get my pilot's license.

Intellectually, I know you're right, but emotionally—"

"It's not so easy," he finished for me. "I get that. But the news is never going to run a story that says, 'Nick Peterson and Anna Morgan went out for a lovely and safe afternoon of Jet Skiing on the bay. They saw four dolphins, fell off their watercraft, and had a nice lunch, but nobody was injured.'"

"I suppose that's true," I reluctantly agreed.

"How many hours did you log in the helicopter without incident?"

"Over two thousand."

He whistled. "Over two thousand. That's the problem with the news. They only report the bad stuff. If you let your life be dictated by all the horrible things that can happen, you'll miss out on so much."

I glanced outside at the sunlight shining on the water. How much had I missed out on because of my own fears? Was I done living like that?

We sat in silence for a moment, then Nick reached across the table and took my hand. "I really appreciate how much you've helped with the girls."

I kept my gaze on him and my thoughts away from his touch. "Of course, that's what friends do," I said, trying to sound casual.

He winced and let go of my hand. Sitting back in his seat, he studied me carefully. "Is that all we are? Friends? Is that why you went out with that dentist?"

"Nick . . ."

"Why did you leave last night?" Before I could respond, he raised his hand. "Sorry, you don't have to answer that. I just wish things could be different. I wish I didn't have to leave, and I wish I could stop thinking about you all the time."

"You think about me?" I asked, unable to hide the smile tugging at my lips.

He made a low growl of frustration. "I probably shouldn't tell you things like that."

I grinned. "If it makes you feel any better, you take up a lot of space in my mind, too."

BEFORE CHURCH ON Sunday morning, my mother called to discuss holiday plans. As usual, we would go with the Morgan family to Christmas Eve service, then enjoy dinner and presents at Luella and Walter's house. Christmas morning would be spent at the beach cottage, but we'd return to the ranch for dinner and our annual cutthroat charades competition.

During a lull in the conversation, I said, "Can I ask you something, Mom?"

"Of course, honey. Anything."

I looked out my bedroom window and watched a family with three little kids walking along the beach. The mom and dad were holding hands and seemed so happy. "Did you ever regret letting Dad stay in the army?"

My mother's voice was tender. "Regret? No."

"Never?"

"Well, of course there were times when it was hard, and I wished he would have stayed with the insurance job, but—"

"Wait, what insurance job?" I was shocked. My father had enlisted in the army immediately after high school, and as far as I knew, he'd never worked anywhere else.

My mom laughed. "After you were born and your father's time was up, he wanted to re-enlist, but I begged him to get out of the military. I hated having him gone all the time, and I worried about his safety. My Uncle Dale gave him a job at the insurance agency. I thought everything was going to be wonderful. I had a beautiful baby girl, a decent apartment, and a husband who came home every night for dinner."

I sighed at the image of domestic utopia. That's exactly what I wanted, too. And that's exactly what I could never have with Nick. "So, what happened?"

"Your father was miserable. After about two weeks, I couldn't stand it anymore, and I made him go back to the army. He put on a good show, pretending he just wanted to make me happy, but I could tell he was bursting to lace up his boots."

I smiled at the thought of my father wearing a suit and tie instead of his uniform. "I can't imagine Dad being anything but a soldier."

"No, neither can I, and I worry about him retiring. He loves the army. Loves the adventure, camaraderie, and patriotism. There have been some rough years, but military service is what he was meant to do. That being said, it's a different army today. Some of these soldiers have deployed several times in the last ten years. That's not good for them nor their families."

"Do you ever worry about Dad getting hurt or not coming home?"

"Honey," my mom said, pausing. "Why are you asking me these questions? What's going on?"

Even though I was close to my mother, I wasn't ready to talk about Nick. "No reason. I was just wondering about your life. So, you don't ever worry about Dad?"

"Of course I do, but I don't let my mind go there. I have faith he'll come back to me."

I swallowed hard. "I had faith Marcus would come back to me."

"Oh, sweetheart. We did, too. We never dreamed anything bad would happen to him. If we could change things, you know we would."

"I know."

Feeling a little down, I finished our conversation and hung up the phone. I wanted to call Nick just to hear his voice. Instead, I spoke to God.

Lord, I don't know what to do about this man. I don't know how we can have a future together. How can I leave the island and the Morgan family? How can I put myself at risk like that again? If it's your will, please find a way to keep Nick here with me. And if I'm not supposed to be with him . . . help me accept that. Amen

I realized all this praying and worrying might be pointless. Nick had never said he *loved* me. He hadn't even hinted at a future together. He'd only said he wished he didn't think about me all the time.

Of course, when I'd admitted the same thing, he'd grinned that ridiculously happy grin of his.

But what that grin meant long term, I didn't know.

Nick

PULLING INTO THE church parking lot, I glanced at the clock and noted I had one minute to spare. Even though I'd chosen our clothes the night before and had woken early this morning, getting the girls and myself out the door had taken longer than anticipated.

I unbuckled Gabby only to realize she was missing one of her shoes. Frantically, I searched the car but couldn't find it anywhere, so I cut my losses by slipping off her other shoe, tossing it on the seat, and heading inside.

We entered the foyer to find the pastor standing off to the side with a few parishioners, their heads bowed. I couldn't hear their prayer, but the sight of this small group preparing for worship hit me hard. I thought about my army chaplain who'd prayed with us on countless occasions, including after the suicide.

"Come on," Hailey said, leading the way into the sanctuary and down the aisle. I followed, and when we reached the Morgan family, Anna stood. She warmly embraced Hailey and smiled at me.

She looked so pretty today in a blue dress that matched her eyes. Eyes that seemed sad. Was something wrong?

"Hi," she said, automatically taking Gabby from me.

My arm brushed against hers as I handed over the baby. "Hi, Anna."

We exchanged a smile, and I found myself wanting to lean over and kiss her good morning. Instead, I quietly greeted the rest of the Morgan family and thanked them for scooting down to make room for us.

Music began, and as we sang the opening hymn, "O Come, O Come, Emmanuel," I glanced at the intricately carved manger scene on the altar steps.

Hailey didn't want to decorate for Christmas this year. While I understood her desire to forget about the holidays, I hoped by coming to church today, she could find comfort in the birth of Christ. Maybe I could buy a little manger scene for her bedroom. I'd seen one at the Christmas store on Main Street near the salon and bakery.

The sermon was about fear and how instead of being afraid, the Virgin Mary had chosen to be the handmaid of the Lord. The pastor went on to explain that people of faith often allowed fear to hold them back from following God's plan for their lives.

"What does God want of you?" he asked, looking directly at me. "And what would you do if you weren't afraid?"

I swallowed hard. *I'd adopt the girls and ask my dad to keep them when I deployed. I'd find a way to help Anna fly again. And if I really wasn't afraid, I'd allow myself to fall deeper in love with this faithful woman beside me. This woman who makes me want to be a better man.*

After church, Travis asked his grandparents if the girls and I could join them for brunch at the ranch. Luella nodded politely, but Walter shook my hand with gusto. "We'd love to have you join us, son. Please come."

"Thank you, sir," I said, warmed by his heartfelt invitation.

Travis and Hailey rode out to the ranch with Vicki while Anna came with Gabby and me. "What'd you think about church?" Anna asked, as we walked across the parking lot to my car.

I bounced Gabby in my arms. "I'm glad I came. I enjoyed singing, listening to the scripture readings, and the message. Of course, sitting next to a pretty girl was nice, too."

She gave me a friendly shoulder bump. "Just one of the many perks of attending church."

BRUNCH AT LUELLA and Walter Morgan's home was amazing. First of all, the view from their property was incredible! I could see the entire island—from the army post on the west, to the church steeple on the east. The ocean seemed even bluer than usual, and using binoculars, I found both The Blue Crab and Ethan's house.

The ranch itself boasted chickens, cows, horses, goats, and a large organic garden surrounded by pecan trees. Most impressive was the love between Anna and her in-laws. It was hard for me to believe they hadn't always gotten along.

Gabby immediately took to Luella, and Bianca pretended to be insulted the baby had a new favorite.

"Of course she adores me, I'm a grandmother," Luella said as we sat around the table enjoying sausage lasagna, garden-fresh salad, and garlic bread from Vicki's Bakery. "I need more grandchildren. When are you girls going to give me more grandchildren?"

In many ways, Luella reminded me of the mother from the movie *My Big Fat Greek Wedding*. She was loud, opinionated, and not afraid to ask for what she wanted. Her question caused Jillian and Anna to fall silent, but Bianca and Vicki groaned, declaring all the good men had been taken and didn't their mother think they should marry *before* having children?

"Of course I want you to have a husband first, but

you have to make more of an effort," Luella said as if finding a spouse was simply a matter of trying harder.

Travis looked right at me with big pleading eyes. "Hey, Nick. What about you and my mom? Couldn't you two have a baby for Grandma?"

Everyone burst out laughing, except for Anna whose entire face turned bright red. She gave me an awkward smile and quickly looked away.

The conversation drifted to the governor's new political agenda, but at some point, Anna reached under the table and clasped my hand. It was a sweet and simple gesture, but her touch caused something inside my chest to ache. I brushed my thumb across the back of her hand and laced my fingers through hers.

Despite knowing the chances of a future together were slim, for that moment, I allowed myself the fantasy of believing I belonged with Anna.

Chapter 22

*O*N MONDAY EVENING, Anna and Travis came over for grilled cheese sandwiches and potato chips. Hailey made a fruit salad, and we ate outside on the picnic table until dark clouds rolled in, and it began to rain.

"This weather is crazy," I said, dragging the food and tablecloth inside. "Hot one moment and cold the next."

Anna gave a sarcastic snort. "Welcome to Rose Island, home of the bipolar weather pattern."

For dessert, we roasted marshmallows in the fireplace. I made the mistake of letting Gabby try a bite of the gooey treat, and her entire face lit up with delight.

Anna laughed. "You're in trouble now. Once they taste sugar, you can forget about green beans and broccoli."

"Is that true?" I asked Gabby.

Anna gestured toward Hailey who stood at the living room window watching the rain fall. "Is she okay? She's been quiet all evening."

"I think I upset her with the nativity crèche I gave

her after school today. I thought it might be nice for her room, but obviously she didn't want it."

Anna patted my arm and stood. "Let me talk to her, okay?"

I nodded. "Sure."

Anna walked over to Hailey and placed a gentle hand on her shoulder. "Are you okay, sweetheart?"

Hailey nodded and turned to look first at Anna, then at me. "I was just thinking we should set up the Christmas tree tonight. I know I said I didn't want to, but I think it's important for Gabby. This is her first Christmas, and I don't want her to miss it just because I'm not in the mood to celebrate."

I treaded carefully. "Are you sure?"

"Yes. After all, Gabby's too young to understand what happened to our parents."

Travis gave a rowdy whoop that excited the puppies and caused them to jump up, tails wagging. "Okay, let's get this party started."

Hailey smiled. "Yeah, let's get this party started."

Travis and I climbed into the attic and brought down the artificial tree and boxes of ornaments. I allowed Hailey to dictate which decorations went on the tree and which remained packed.

Travis brought down a sturdy box containing several Waterford Crystal ornaments. "What about these?" he asked Hailey.

Her voice wavered. "Those belonged to my mom.

She began collecting them when she was a little girl. Each year, my dad and I buy her a new ornament. Well, we used to, anyway."

"They're beautiful," Anna said.

Hailey squatted beside the box and pulled out a crystal train. She held the ornament by its ribbon, allowing it to spin one way, then the other. "When you were in the attic, Uncle Nick, did you see a little pink tree in a clear plastic bag?"

"I did."

"That's the tree my mom always set up in my bedroom. Do you think I could put her ornaments on it this year?"

I imagined the ornaments had to be worth hundreds of dollars, but I didn't hesitate. They were worthless sitting in a box, and if Hailey accidentally broke one, what difference would it make? "I think that would be a great idea, honey."

She smiled and I was pleased I'd said the right thing.

Anna

AFTER THE TREES had been decorated and Gabby put to bed, Nick turned on the movie *McFarland, USA*. Hailey and Travis lounged on the floor while Nick sat next to me on the couch. Almost immediately, I could tell something was bothering him because he didn't laugh at any of the funny parts.

"Are you okay?" I whispered.

He forced a smile. "Yeah."

I studied him, wondering what had suddenly upset him. Wanting to comfort him, I clasped his large hand with both of mine and gave it a squeeze. He squeezed back but continued to keep his distance.

After several minutes, I stood and motioned for him to follow me outside. We went onto the back porch and sat on the same bench where we'd kissed nearly a year ago. "What's wrong, Nick?"

He stared straight ahead and rubbed a hand over his rough jaw. Apprehension filled me. Had I been too pushy, forcing him to come outside with me?

"Sorry," I said. "It's none of my business, but—"

"It just seems wrong that I'm here instead of my brother. Why in the world did God spare me? Why?"

I squeezed his arm, wanting to take away some of his anger, but not knowing what else to say except sorry.

"I wish we'd had more time together as adults. I should've spent more of my leave time here on the island. You can't imagine how difficult it is to be in the house without him and Ivana. Every time I turn around, I see something that reminds me they're gone."

"I know," I said, feeling my words didn't even come close to the sympathy I felt for him.

"Yesterday, I read the inscription in my brother's Bible. Did you know Ivana gave it to him when they first started dating?"

I shook my head and he continued. "They had this whole life together, and now it's over. I just don't understand why it happened."

I scooted close and wrapped my arms around his big broad shoulders. He leaned into me, rigid at first. But then he turned, pulling me toward him and engulfing me with his embrace.

We didn't speak but simply held each other. After a long time, he let me go.

"Sorry." His eyes shot downward as if he were embarrassed for being so emotional.

"Nick, it's okay." I took a deep breath and formed my next words carefully. "Look, I want to say something profound and encouraging about being grateful for the time you had with your brother, but sometimes all the time in the world isn't enough, you know?"

"Yeah."

"And sometimes we can't see God's greater plan, but I promise you, it gets easier. It really does."

He nodded. "Thanks."

A melancholy silence fell between us, then Nick took my hand and stared down at it. He turned it over and pressed his palm to mine. A shiver worked its way up my arm to my neck. "I don't want you to leave, Anna."

"Leave? What do you mean?"

He gave a sly grin and met my gaze. "Every time I kiss you, you run away. When I kiss you this time, I want you to stay."

I laughed nervously, but when he reached up and brushed back my hair, my throat went dry. His eyes locked on my mouth, and he caressed my lower lip with his thumb. Everything inside me turned to hot liquid. More than anything in the world, I wanted Nick to kiss me.

"Don't run away," he said.

"I won't."

He nodded as if the matter were settled. Then he lowered his lips to mine, kissing me like I'd never been kissed before.

THE NEXT NIGHT, Travis and I went with Nick and the girls to the Pelican Pub. Nick was in a good mood and gave the kids lots of change for the video games so he and I could talk without interruption. Gabby cooperated by sitting in the high chair, occupying herself with a bowl of chocolate pudding.

"I have great news," Nick began, scooting closer to me. "I asked my dad about taking care of the girls if I deploy, and he said yes."

"What?"

"I'm going to adopt Hailey and Gabby, and my dad has agreed to be on my Family Care Plan."

"Seriously?"

He nodded. "I haven't told Hailey yet, but when

Gina and my dad come down for Christmas, we're going to tell her together."

My heart filled with joy. "I'm so happy for you. And for the girls." I ran a hand over his strong jaw. He'd recently shaved and smelled deliciously clean like soap and shaving lotion. "How do you feel about your father taking care of the girls?"

"It'll be tough, but we'll hire the best nanny money can buy. Plus, he promised to cut back on his hours at work so he can spend more time with them. I'm not going to hold my breath on that one, but at least he's trying."

"That's wonderful."

Nick took my hand. "I never would've asked my dad had I not seen you with your in-laws at brunch on Sunday. I'm amazed at the relationship you have with Luella, especially given your past. I've heard other people talk about forgiveness, but you really live it."

I hugged Nick. Time was moving fast, and I didn't want to think about him and the girls leaving. I had no idea what would happen between us, and I was still scared, but I couldn't stop the feelings I had for Nick. All I knew was I didn't want to stay away from him. I wanted to embrace each moment we had left together no matter what that meant.

"Look," he said, pulling back so he could see my face. "I don't want what we have between us to end just because I'm leaving."

"I don't either," I agreed.

"I know a long distance relationship isn't ideal, but I don't want to give you up, Anna."

I nodded and we discussed staying in touch through phone calls, e-mails, and video chats. Maybe it wouldn't be so bad.

ON THE DRIVE home, the kids, hyped-up from too much sugar and video games, told silly knock-knock jokes and laughed hysterically. An old Randy Travis song came on the radio, and Nick cranked up the volume.

"This is such a lame song," Hailey said, giggling.

Nick took the challenge and began singing at the top of his lungs. He didn't know all the lyrics, so he made up his own silly version.

"Stop," Hailey yelled, covering her ears with her hands.

Nick sang louder and Hailey laughed. "Look, even Gabby wants you to stop."

I turned to see the baby imitating her big sister by covering her own ears and shaking her head from side to side, saying, "No, no, no."

All the kids cracked up, and I laughed so hard my stomach ached.

For a brief moment, I had faith everything was going to be okay. Somehow, Nick and I would find a way to grow closer despite the distance. Somehow, it would work out.

Then, we drove around the bend, and everything changed.

Chapter 23

*A*S THE CAR rounded the bend, a deer jumped into the middle of the road. Nick slammed on the brakes. The car skidded forward with a shrieking sound, crashing into the unsuspecting animal and flinging its body over the Tahoe.

The seatbelt tightened against my shoulder, pressing hard as it saved me from flying through the windshield. In slow motion, we screeched to a halt. My heart thudded and my hands shook, but when the car finally stopped moving, I was okay.

Frantic, I scanned the car and breathed a sigh of relief that nobody had been hurt.

"Was that a deer?" Travis asked.

Before I could answer, Gabby let out an ear-piercing scream as if just now comprehending what had happened.

Nick pulled the car to the side of the road and flipped on the hazard lights. He turned around and unbuckled Gabby, who continued screaming. Lifting her into his arms, he held her tight. "It's all right, baby girl. You're okay." She gulped massive amounts of air and shivered as she clung to him.

He rubbed her back. "I think she's fine, just scared. Is everybody else okay?"

"I'm fine," Travis said.

"But the deer isn't fine, is he?" Hailey asked in an angry voice. "I told you to turn the music down, Uncle Nick. You shouldn't have been playing that horrible song so loud."

"I know," he said, his tone regretful.

Gabby's screams softened, but her little jaw trembled. Nick wiped her cheeks with his fingertips. "Will you go to Anna so I can check on things outside?"

"Come here," I said, taking the baby.

Nick stepped out of the car and walked down the road to the fallen deer. I stared out the back window, hoping the animal had just been stunned and not fatally wounded. We frequently saw dead deer along this part of the road. Nobody knew what compelled the creatures to jump into the traffic, but they did it all the time.

When Nick reached the animal, he looked back at the car and shook his head.

"It's dead!" Hailey pounded her clenched fist on the seat.

Travis opened the car door. "I'll be back."

"Shut that door," I said, more sharply than intended.

"This is a man's job, Mom. I need to help Nick. You can stay in the car with the girls, but Nick needs me."

I softened at the seriousness in my son's voice. How could I argue with his desire to be a man and support Nick? "Okay, but be careful and stay to the side of the road."

"Yes, ma'am."

"And watch for cars."

He nodded. "I will."

Hailey let out a furious puff of air. "I can't believe he killed that deer."

I met her gaze. "It was an accident, honey. There was nothing Nick could have done."

"*Whatever*." She folded her arms across her chest and glared out the window. I wanted to say something to ease her anger, but what?

Gabby settled against my shoulder and sucked her thumb. Rocking back and forth, I smoothed down the baby's hair, which felt like straw from the dried chocolate pudding.

Nick and Travis dragged the dead deer to the side of the road, then Nick placed a hand on Travis's shoulder and said a few words before returning to the car. Opening the passenger side door, he took the baby and strapped her into the car seat.

"You killed it," Hailey said, glaring at Nick.

"I know." His voice was sad and weary.

"You were driving too fast."

"You're right," he conceded. "But even if I'd been

going slower, I still would've hit him. He came out of nowhere."

"Can we make him one of those roadside crosses?" Travis asked, buckling his seat belt.

I nodded. "That's a good idea. Maybe you can nail it together and Hailey can paint it."

Hailey exploded, kicking the back of my seat. "Like that's going to help."

I blinked, shocked by her outburst. I'd seen people express sadness through anger, so I tried not to take her contempt personally. Still, it hurt to have her so cross with me.

Nick, on the other hand, wasn't so understanding. "Don't be rude. Apologize to Miss Anna. Now."

"*Sorry, Miss Anna.* But even if I build the cross and Travis paints it, it's not going to help. You can make a million crosses and that deer is still going to be dead. He's dead, and he's never coming back."

We drove the rest of the way home in silence. When we parked in the driveway, Hailey shot out of the car, slamming the door behind her. Nick went upstairs with the baby while Travis ran home to check on Yoda. I took the puppies outside before making myself at home in the kitchen.

While I waited for Nick, I looked through Ivana's generous collection of cookbooks. Next to the recipe for caramel turtle cheesecake, she'd drawn a star and written the words *A Peterson Brothers' favorite.* Seeing the deceased woman's handwriting in the margins was devastating. Although I hadn't been close to Ivana, we'd been friendly with each other, often talking about kids and events at school.

Using my phone, I took a picture of the recipe, vowing to make it for Nick before he left.

A few minutes later, Nick strode through the kitchen, his eyes weary and brow furrowed. Holding a freshly bathed Gabby with one hand, he made a bottle with the other before joining me at the table. "Hailey's never going to forgive me for hitting that deer. I tried talking to her, but she wouldn't listen."

I reached out and took hold of Gabby's little hand. "She's mad now, but she'll be okay in a little bit."

He gave a defeated sigh. "I hope so. I hate seeing her like this."

I closed the cookbook and changed the subject, wanting to lift his mood. "It was pretty cute how Travis manned up to help you. He told me to stay in the car with the girls."

Nick shrugged. "It's instinct. Men are built to protect and take care of things. When we were kids, Ethan and I often played war. It wasn't that we were violent; we just wanted to defend our home. We'd strategize for hours about how to fight off the bad guys if they attacked."

"That's kind of sad, but I guess it makes sense. All my childhood games revolved around ice skating in the

Olympics or . . ." my voice trailed off.

"Were you going to say flying?"

I nodded. "When I was ten, I saw a documentary on female helicopter pilots. That film had a major impact on me, and I begged my parents for a ride. When they finally relented and took me for my birthday, I was hooked."

Nick wet his lips and stared at me. "I'm going to say something, and I don't want you to be mad."

An uneasy feeling rolled through me. "Okay . . ."

"You need to get back in that helicopter. You're selling yourself short by not flying, and you need to try again."

I shook my head. "I've tried, but I can't do it."

"You have to try again." He shifted Gabby and reached into his wallet to pull out something that resembled a gift certificate. "This is a voucher I bought last week. I was going to give it to you for Christmas, but I want you to have it now. It's for a helicopter tour of the island. For both of us. I thought we could go together. Maybe it will be the first step in getting you back in the pilot's seat."

I stared in disbelief at the gift certificate. A tingle of annoyance worked its way through me. Did he think he was capable of fixing me? If conquering my fear of flying was so easy, wouldn't I have done it by now?

"You're not excited about going to college," he continued, completely oblivious to my irritation. "You want to fly. Everything you say and do points to that fact, but you're letting an irrational fear hold you back."

An irrational fear? I gritted my teeth. "I've been to therapy. I've prayed about this, and I've even taken medicine, but nothing has helped. I can't believe you think you can miraculously cure me with a gift certificate."

"I'm not trying to *cure* you. I'm just trying to help."

"By curing me. You're trying to help by fixing something that can't be fixed."

I started to say something else but was interrupted by a loud crashing sound which shook the ceiling. We both looked up and heard the sound again.

"What's that?" Travis asked, coming into the kitchen.

Nick jumped to his feet and handed me the baby. "It's Hailey!" He tore through the living room and raced upstairs. Travis and I followed, my heart pounding.

Nick threw open the door to Hailey's bedroom just as she smashed another one of her mother's crystal ornaments against the wall. Clenching her fists, she glared at Nick and yelled, "You killed that deer. He died because of you, and I hate you. I hate you, Uncle Nick!"

Shattered glass covered the floor, and the pink Christmas tree lay next to her feet. Her face was red and tear-stained, and her body shook.

Nick put his hands up and walked toward her. "Hailey, honey, calm down."

She took a step back, her bare foot almost landing on a piece of glass. "No. Don't tell me what to do. You're not my dad. You don't even want to be here. You're going to give us away and make us move. And then, you'll probably die, like that deer and everyone else in my life!"

"I'm not," Nick insisted, shaking his head. "I want to adopt you and Gabby. I want to take you with me when I leave."

She took another step back, closer to the glass. "You're lying."

"Stop," he shouted. "You can yell at me all you want, but don't you dare move another inch and step on that glass. Let me help you. I'm not going to allow anything bad happen to you or me. I promise."

"You can't promise that. Could you promise you weren't going to hit that deer and kill it? Could you promise my parents wouldn't die? Can you promise *you're* not going to die?"

Nick hung his head in silence for a moment. "No. You're right. I can't make promises like that."

Hailey looked down at the last crystal ornament in her hand, a depiction of the baby Jesus with Mary and Joseph. Her voice softened. "Go away, Uncle Nick. I don't want you here."

"I know you don't mean that."

She shook her head and began to cry. My heart split in two, and I hugged Gabby tight. Travis tucked his hand in the crook of my elbow and pressed his head against my arm.

"Hailey, let your Uncle Nick help you," I urged. "You don't want to end up going to the emergency room for stitches."

Her shoulders slumped in defeat. Nick lifted her into his strong arms as tears silently streamed down her cheeks.

"I've got you, honey," Nick said.

Saying nothing, she clutched her mother's only remaining ornament and allowed Nick to carry her over the broken glass and out the door.

Nick

IT WAS PAST midnight by the time Hailey finally settled down. She'd cried so hard that I called the pediatrician and counselor. During it all, Anna remained calm, encouraging Hailey to take deep breaths and relax. If Anna hadn't been there, things could have easily spiraled out of control.

Now, Travis was sleeping in front of the TV, and Hailey was curled up with Gabby on their parents' bed sound asleep. As Anna and I cleaned up the mess in Hailey's room, I wondered how things had gone so horribly wrong. Could I have done something differently to prevent the explosion?

What kind of father would I be if I couldn't even

handle a temper tantrum? I was tired, frustrated, and full of self-doubt.

"We might be able to save this one," Anna said, holding up an angel with only a chip missing from the wing.

Feelings of failure pressed down on me, and I gave a non-committal shrug. "Sure."

Anna bit her bottom lip. "Look, I know tonight was horrible, but Hailey's going to be okay."

"Is she?" I didn't know how Anna thought this wasn't a big deal. I should've tried harder to talk to Hailey after we hit the deer. I should've stopped her from storming off and locking herself in her bedroom. I should've prevented this disaster.

Instead, I'd gone downstairs to talk to Anna while I fed Gabby.

Careful not to cut myself, I threw a piece of glass into the garbage can. "Look, Anna. You don't have to help me. It's late and I can clean this mess up without you. Why don't you and Travis head home?"

"I don't mind," she replied.

Something about her cheerful optimism caused me to snap. "But I mind. So please, just take Travis and go home."

The edge in my voice sliced through the air, and I apologized immediately, ashamed I'd spoken to Anna like that.

"What is it?" she asked, her tone compassionate.

I shook my head. "Hailey was completely out of control tonight, and there was nothing I could do. If you hadn't been here—"

"But I was."

"But you're not always going to be around to help me, are you? When I leave for Germany, you'll be here on the island with your family."

She flinched, and I regretted hurting her feelings, but I couldn't continue my dependence on her. The sooner I learned how to handle the girls on my own, the better. I'd thought Anna and I could date long distance, but now I understood what a ridiculous idea that'd been. I wasn't capable of taking care of the girls and having a relationship with a woman.

"It'll be okay in the morning," she assured me.

Would it? I couldn't imagine this mess magically disappearing by the morning, so I said nothing as she gathered her things and left.

Chapter 24

Anna

I AWOKE THE next morning with a knot in my stomach. Things hadn't ended well last night with Nick. He'd basically told me to go home and leave him alone. Oh, he hadn't used those exact words, but it was pretty obvious he was irritated with me.

Glancing at my phone on the nightstand, I discovered he'd sent a short text. "Keeping Hailey home from school today."

"How's she doing?" I texted back, hoping they'd both slept well and were feeling better this morning. Seeing them so distraught last night had been tough.

"Better," he replied.

I waited for more and was disappointed when he didn't text back. After a few minutes, I asked, "What about you?"

He didn't answer me, and his silence scared me. I desperately wanted to call but thought it best to give him space.

All day at the salon, I checked my messages. He's just upset, I told myself. It was a rough night, and he just needs some time.

Determined not to obsess about Nick, I poured myself into every client who walked through the door. During my down time, I swept, mopped, dusted, and folded the laundry. Bianca asked what my problem was, but I brushed her off, insisting I was just tired. Truthfully, I was afraid to tell her what had happened for fear of how she'd interpret the events.

After work, I took Travis out for pasta. "Why didn't Nick and Hailey come with us?" he asked, swirling his straw through his ice water.

I forced a smile and tried to keep the sadness out of my voice. "I think they're busy doing something else."

His eyes narrowed. "Is it because Hailey is grounded for breaking her mother's ornaments?"

"No, honey. She was just having a really tough time yesterday. I don't think Nick punished her."

In bed that night, I stared at my phone, willing it to ring. Finally, I took matters into my own hands and texted Nick. "Hey, how's Hailey?"

After several minutes, he texted back a one-word response. "Fine."

I waited, frantic for a call, a text, or something. I didn't want to scare him away by aggressively pestering him, but I didn't want this tension between us to continue either. Plus, I was sincerely worried about

Hailey. "Did you take Hailey to the therapist today?" I texted.

Five minutes passed, then ten, fifteen, and twenty. I fought the urge to run next door and demand that he tell me why he was avoiding me. Tell me if we were going to be okay.

After what seemed like ages, my phone pinged with his answer. "Yes."

My disappointment turned to anger, and I jumped out of bed to pace the floor. Was Nick the kind of guy that only cared about the chase? Had he pursued me only until I stopped running away? I honestly didn't believe he was like that, but why was he shutting me out of his life?

Consumed with anger and frustration, I yanked his ridiculous gift certificate out of my purse, and before I could change my mind, I ran it through the paper shredder. The high-pitched whirl cut through the silence, destroying his gift.

Then I stared at all the pieces of paper and panicked. Was it possible to tape the voucher back together?

THE NEXT MORNING, my parents arrived. Having them back on the island was usually wonderful, but I had a hard time staying in the moment as my thoughts kept circling back to Nick.

Everything had changed after we'd hit the deer, and

there was nothing I could do about it. I continued rationalizing his detached behavior by telling myself he was simply worried about Hailey, but I feared I was losing him.

And yet, wasn't losing him *now* better than losing him in the future? He was still in the army. Still a soldier. The only thing that had changed was my heart and my desire to be with him regardless of the circumstances.

Not wanting my parents to worry, I pretended everything was fine as we drove home from the airport and introduced Grams and Pop to Yoda. Travis, ignorant of my pain, continued touting Nick's incredible accomplishments.

"And who is this Nick Peterson?" my father asked.

I explained he was Hailey and Gabby's uncle, but I left out the fact that he'd become much more important than just a neighbor.

Down at the pier, we ate lunch and watched the fishing boats unload their morning catch. Afterward, we wandered over to the bakery for a treat and to say hello to Vicki. My parents loved Vicki, and the three of them spoke for several minutes about the benefits of flax and hemp seed in the bakery's whole wheat bread.

"If you don't mind," Vicki said when the conversation turned to the new Christmas decorations on Main Street, "I'm going to let Piper take your order while I steal Anna away for a minute. I want her opinion about something in my apartment upstairs."

"Of course," my mother said, peering into the display case. "You girls go right ahead. I see a piece of pecan pie with my name on it."

I followed Vicki through the kitchen, up the stairs to her living quarters above the bakery. She gestured toward the couch in front of the large window overlooking Main Street. "Sit down and tell me what's wrong. You look horrible."

"I'm fine." I insisted, sinking onto the couch. Then, without warning, I burst into tears.

"Oh, Anna." Vicki sat next to me. "It's Nick, isn't it? I saw him on the bike trail with the girls this morning, and he looked miserable."

"He did?" My heart filled with hope. I didn't want Nick to hurt, but maybe if he was brokenhearted, too, we still had a chance. "What did he say?"

"Nothing, but I could tell something was wrong. What happened between you two?"

In slow, painful detail, I explained everything that'd happened—Nick deciding to adopt the girls, the two of us talking about dating long distance, hitting the deer on the way home, and Hailey's horrible breakdown. "Ever since then, he's pushed me away like he no longer cares."

The reality of my dismal situation prompted fresh tears. "I love him so much, but I'm afraid he doesn't want me in his life anymore."

"You love him?" Vicki asked.

I nodded, realizing I'd just admitted my feelings aloud for the first time. Yes, I truly loved Nick. Loved him more than I loved my safe and stable life on the island. Loved him more than my fear of being involved with another soldier. "What am I going to do? I love him so much. I don't want to lose him."

"Have you talked to him about it?"

I shook my head. "No, I'm afraid to talk to him. What if it's really over? What if he doesn't want me anymore?"

"He does. He's just scared."

I blew my nose again. "I'm scared, too."

"Then talk to him. You were so adamant about not dating another soldier, maybe he believes you're not interested in anything long term. Maybe Hailey's breakdown disturbed him more than you realize, and he doesn't want to distract himself with something that's only temporary."

"You think?"

"Nick loves you," Vicki declared. "I can tell by the way he looks at you. You need to make sure he knows you feel the same way about him."

My heart lurched. Nick had never said he loved me, but surely he did. Didn't he? What if his feelings didn't run as deep as mine?

Then again, what if they did?

I felt as if I'd climbed the ladder to the top of the

high dive and was standing on the edge of the board, too petrified to jump, yet unable to climb back down to safety.

What if I told Nick I loved him, but he didn't feel that way about me? What if he'd changed his mind about staying together? I clenched my fists tight, afraid of the answer to that question.

Afraid of everything.

But most of all . . . afraid of losing Nick.

THE REST OF the day dragged on endlessly. My father took Travis fishing, while my mom and I Christmas shopped. I thought I was doing a good job pretending to be happy, but every time my phone rang or buzzed with a text from someone other than Nick, I became a little more depressed.

A gentle mist fell as we slipped into the Christmas Store on Main Street. My mom held up one of the handmade, wooden ornaments the boutique was known for. "This would be adorable for Vicki."

I glanced at the little baker dangling from her fingertips. "It's cute."

My mother loved professionally themed ornaments, and for a while, I was the recipient of either a pilot or a helicopter. Those ornaments were currently boxed up in the attic, as I hadn't been able to place them on the tree since I had stopped flying.

Lifting one of the little soldiers and spinning him around, my mother asked, "Does your mood have anything to do with our phone conversation about your father and the army?"

I bit my bottom lip and nodded.

"Oh, honey. Tell me about him."

With a deep sigh, I told my mom the story of how despite not wanting to, I'd fallen in love with another soldier, and now I was afraid I'd lost him.

WHEN WE RETURNED to the cottage later that day, I excused myself and went to my bedroom. Curling up in the reading chair beside the large bookshelf, I called Nick. Like Vicki, my mother had encouraged me to confront Nick and tell him how I felt. My heart raced when he answered the phone.

"How's Hailey doing?" I asked, trying to sound cheerful.

"Better." His voice was distant, and I immediately regretted calling. I tried telling him I'd phone later, but the words got caught in my throat.

A commotion in the background broke our tense silence, and Nick addressed Hailey before turning back to me. "Hey, I'd better go. I promised I'd help her wrap a few presents and—"

"I'm really good at wrapping," I said, unable to help myself. "Maybe I could—"

"Anna . . ."

"I'm sorry." I spoke quickly, afraid my words would only push him further away. "I know I'm not saying the right thing, but I want to help."

"I know." He hesitated and released a slow breath. "This morning, Hailey wrote me a sweet note apologizing for her tantrum. I think she just snapped, you know. Some sort of PTSD. We had a long session with the therapist and it helped."

"She's been through a lot."

"She has."

I held my breath, waiting for more. How could I keep Nick from pulling away? Desperate to hold onto him, I invited him and the girls to dinner for tomorrow night. "My parents are here, and I'm making my famous sour cream enchiladas. My dad promised to make guacamole if he can find some decent avocados at the Farmer's Market."

"Look, Anna," he began.

I squeezed my eyes tight, bracing myself for what was about to come. The beginning of our end. Nick was preparing to leave and start his new life as a father, and he didn't want me to be part of it. What he'd said in the Pelican Pub about staying together no longer mattered.

My stomach plummeted and a vise clamped on to my heart, squeezing it tighter and tighter and tighter. "I understand if you can't make it. It's okay. Maybe I can send over a plate, and you can reheat the enchiladas later. I just want to help. How can I help?"

I was blathering, and even though I hated the anxiety in my voice, I couldn't stop talking. At the same time, I couldn't find the nerve to tell him what was really in my heart. To tell him how much I needed and loved him. How I didn't want to live my life without him.

He sighed before speaking in an apologetic, but self-assured voice. "I know you're trying to help, but right now Hailey needs to be my main focus. Hailey and Gabby."

"Of course. I don't want to interfere with that. With them." I needed to tell him good night and hang up the phone before he told me our relationship was completely over, but I was out of my mind. "What about lunch on Monday? Do you want to try out that new taco trailer down by the surf shop? I'm working in the morning, but we could have a late lunch."

"I can't. I need to go on post and run some errands. I have to see about expediting the girls' passports and collecting their medical records. Plus, I have to sort out what the dogs need to travel and talk to the realtor about putting the house on the market."

Bile burned my throat. I couldn't tolerate this game of pretend any longer. "What's going on, Nick? Why are you pushing me away?"

He gave a prophetic sigh. "I'm leaving the Monday after Christmas, Anna. So . . . I think it would be best if you and I stopped seeing each other. I care about you a lot, but it's going to be hard enough when I leave, and right now, I need to concentrate on Hailey and Gabby."

The lump in my throat throbbed, pressing against my windpipe, blocking off my oxygen supply. I tried to breathe. Tried to hold back the tears. Tried to wrap my mind around what he was saying. "I thought you wanted to continue seeing me, even after you left."

"I know I said that, but . . ."

Gabby started crying and Nick mumbled something about a new tooth coming in and needing to give her more baby Tylenol.

My heart was breaking, but he'd already moved on. He didn't want me anymore, and my pride and self-worth prevented me from staying on the phone, begging him to love me.

"Are you okay?" he asked.

"Of course. I understand." I lifted my chin and nodded into the phone. "I'll be starting college classes in January, so I need to figure some things out with my schedule and transcripts. And my parents are here. I'll be busy with them through the holidays. My dad—"

"I'm sorry, Anna."

I sucked in a sharp breath. "I know. It's fine. I'm fine. Honestly, I understand."

He said something to Hailey, and I must've told him good-bye, but when the dial tone sounded in my ear, I was still clinging to the phone, wondering what I'd done to lose him.

And what I was supposed to do to get over him?

Chapter 25

*T*HAT NIGHT, I cried quietly into my pillow, not wanting Travis or my parents to hear my grief. Several times, I thought about running next door and begging Nick to take me and Travis with him to Germany. But then I'd think about all I'd have to give up, and I knew I could never leave the island.

Plus, Nick hadn't even asked me to come. In fact, he'd done the exact opposite by breaking up with me. I needed to accept that it was over and move on with my life.

In the morning, a headache kept me home from church and family brunch at the ranch. I took an ibuprofen and slept for several hours. When I awoke, I listened to the voice mail my parents had left, saying they were taking Travis and his cousins hiking near the Rose Mansion.

I showered, grateful my headache was gone. I dried my hair, put on makeup, and biked to the supermarket, determined to put Nick and my broken heart behind me. At the store, I gathered ingredients for tonight's dinner. Travis and my parents might return with no appetite, but I could save the dish for tomorrow.

As I stood in the checkout line, I thought about Ivana's caramel turtle cheesecake. I pulled my phone out of my purse and looked at the picture of the recipe. It would be easy to collect the ingredients while still at the store.

Maybe I could make the cake for Nick and the girls and leave it on their front porch. Would Nick think I was some kind of deranged stalker if I did that? Or would he accept the gift for what it was ... a simple token of my affection.

Before I could change my mind, I raced up and down the aisles, gathering the ingredients. Just because I bought everything to make the dessert, didn't mean I had to follow through. Besides, maybe I'd let Travis and my parents enjoy it.

On the ride home, I fought off depression by going through my gratitude list. I had so much to be grateful for—my health, my family, the island, my job.

What about flying? a voice deep inside me asked.

"I can't do it," I whispered.

Have courage.

Standing up to pedal, I rode as fast as I could, resolute on escaping the truth that not only had God given me the gift to fly, but the means to do it.

On their own accord, my lips began to chant a Bible verse I'd learned as a child. *The Lord is with me, I will not be afraid. The Lord is with me, I will not be afraid.*

As my house came into view, the wind kicked up, making the last leg of the journey nearly impossible. I pushed hard on the pedals, trying to out race the storm, but the sky opened and hard raindrops pinged my helmet and the back of my neck.

Hunched over, I flew down the seashell path, mud and bits of shells splattering my legs. I quickly stowed my bike, grabbed the groceries, and headed toward the steps.

"Let me help you," Nick said, coming up behind me.

I whirled around, surprised to see him. He took the groceries out of my hands and led the way. His wet jeans clung to his strong thighs as he took the stairs two at a time.

Inside the house, Yoda barked relentlessly at the sight of us. "I'll take him outside," Nick said, brushing past me and setting the groceries on the kitchen counter.

"You don't have to do that."

Ignoring me, he scooped up the puppy and went outside. I stood still, too shocked to move. What was Nick doing here? Why had he come?

Smoothing down my soaked T-shirt, I went into the kitchen and threw the perishables into the refrigerator. Moments later, Nick returned with Yoda, both of them drenched.

The wet dog scampered across the kitchen floor, elated to see me. Leaning over, I petted Yoda, grateful for his enthusiasm and unconditional love.

"*Anna,*" Nick said.

My heart in my throat, I stood and met his gaze. "What are you doing here, Nick?"

He shoved his hands into his pockets and stared out the window. I held my breath waiting for him to tell me why he was standing in my kitchen. Did he regret what he'd said on the phone last night? Did he still care about me?

"I wanted to make sure you were okay," he finally said. "You weren't at church today and—"

"You went to church this morning?"

He gave a half-hearted grin. "Two Sundays in a row, can you believe it? But more than that . . . I've asked God to come back into my life again. I realize I can't be a father without His help. I have to rely on His strength, because I'm not strong enough on my own anymore."

"Nick, that's wonderful."

He nodded but made no mention of asking God's hand in our relationship. "So, you're okay?"

My throat felt raw, and I swallowed hard before answering. "I had a headache this morning, but I'm fine now." My voice broke on the last word, revealing how *not* fine I actually was. Tears followed and I swiped them away, not wanting to cry in front of him.

Without a word, he stepped toward me and took me in his arms. I collapsed against him, pressing my cheek to his chest. Breathing in his spicy scent, I savored the moment, wanting to believe our love could overcome any obstacle, including a long-distance separation.

But I had no right to place those kinds of demands on him. He didn't owe me anything. He'd never made promises of quitting the army or finding a way for us to be together. He'd never even said he loved me.

"What is it?" he asked, the question scraping my soul.

Didn't he know he was breaking my heart? I wet my lips and took a deep breath. "I love you, Nick. I do. I can't imagine not seeing you and the girls every day. You've become part of my life, and I'm terrified of losing you."

"Come with me," he said, his voice husky and urgent.

My heart lifted. "What?"

"I want you and Travis to come with me."

I didn't understand. "You want to get married?"

Sheer panic marred his face, revealing that marriage was the last thing on his mind. He wasn't ready to make that kind of commitment, and I didn't blame him. We hardly knew each other. You couldn't pledge to love, honor, and cherish someone you'd just met.

He surprised me by nodding emphatically. "Yes. If you want to get married, then let's get married."

My blood ran cold. "If *I* want to get married?"

He shook his head. "I'm sorry. That didn't come out right. I know we haven't spent a lot of time together, but I don't want to lose you. So, let's get married."

Resentment filled me. "Not wanting to lose me isn't a reason to get married."

He cringed. "I know."

"And that's not even the right way to propose to someone," I said, my indignation building. "Do you know how degrading you sound?"

"You're right, I'm sorry. Will you marry me, Anna?"

"No," I said, not quite understanding my anger, but feeling it nevertheless.

"Why not?"

"Because you're not really asking me. This is not a *real* marriage proposal."

He flinched, and then without warning, he pulled me close and covered my mouth with his. I wanted to resist, afraid of masking our issues with physical intimacy. But as he deepened the kiss, I leaned into him and kissed him back.

Images of Marcus's coffin marched through my head. I remembered receiving the flag, folded into a tight triangle. Remembered the sound of taps, the rifle salute, and Travis's little hand, clinging to mine. I also remembered the devastating loneliness of that first night and the nights that followed.

How was I supposed to do this again? How was I supposed to risk it? I'd been stupid to fall in love with another soldier. Did he expect me to give up everything I wanted and follow him around as he pursued his dreams? What about my dreams?

"Anna, I'm an idiot," he moaned against my mouth. "Come with me. Marry me."

I pulled away and shook my head. "I can't. I don't want to be married to a soldier. I've served my time. I made the sacrifice for my country, and I won't do it again."

All the color drained from his face as he stared openmouthed at me. Stepping back, he shoved a hand through his hair. "You're asking me to give up my livelihood. To quit the army and be a different person. Is that what you really want from me?"

"I don't know." I blinked several times.

What did I want from him? Was I really asking him to resign his commission? To give up his dreams and principles for me?

Or was that simply an excuse to protect my heart from someone who'd only proposed because I'd burst into tears? Not because he truly loved me.

I BEGAN THE next morning with a gut-wrenching cry in the shower. Later, I looked at my red, puffy eyes in the bathroom mirror and knew there was no hiding my pain today. Christmas was two days away, then Nick and the girls would leave and things would get easier.

Before I knew it, a new family would move next door, and memories of the Peterson family would fade.

At least, that's what I told myself.

Unable to sleep last night, I'd made Ivana's cheese-cake but hadn't decided what to do with it. Maybe this morning, I'd crawl back into bed with a large pot of coffee, a fork, and the entire cheesecake, eating until I made myself sick.

Walking into the kitchen, I found Travis at the table wearing a stocking cap, winter coat, and cargo shorts. "Grams and Pop went for a walk along the beach," he announced. "Pop said if he didn't keep exercising, he wouldn't be able to fit into his Santa costume."

I studied my son carefully. "His Santa costume? What are you talking about?"

Travis rolled his eyes. "Come on, Mom. Stop pre-tending. I figured out a long time ago that Pop plays Santa at church."

"You did?"

"Yeah. I'm not a little kid anymore."

"That kind of makes me sad. Does this mean you no longer believe in Santa?"

He snickered and took a sip of his orange juice. "No, I still believe. I'm not stupid. I know what hap-pens when kids stop believing."

I smiled sadly and ruffled his hair. Peering out the window at the Petersons' house, I waited for Nick to come outside and lean against the porch railing as he drank his morning coffee.

"Nick took Hailey and Gabby to Dallas for Christmas," Travis announced. "Pop and I talked to them this morning when we went fishing."

My stomach twisted as I stared at the vacant house. The rolling shutters had been lowered and the patio furniture covered. "They're not staying on the island for Christmas?"

"Nope. They want to go ice skating on real ice at the Galleria and see a show downtown. Plus, Hailey wants to see her new bedroom at Grandpa Jack's house. And this time, the puppies are staying at the vet's."

I turned my attention to the gray ocean where a single boat rocked on the waves. The sky above was dark and eerie. Sometime during the middle of the night, the heat had kicked on, but it was still cold inside our house. Shivering, I crossed the kitchen and turned up the thermostat.

It hurt to learn that Nick would not be spending Christmas on the island. Had I angered him so much, I'd forced him to leave? Blinking back tears, I turned on the coffeemaker and watched my son run his spoon through one of the rough gouges in the kitchen table.

Could Travis and I drag the table onto the back porch, sand it down, and re-stain it this morning without my parents thinking I'd lost my mind?

"Can we bake Christmas cookies?" Travis asked, interrupting my thoughts.

I pressed a hand to my chest. If I'd known how painful losing Nick would feel, would I have been more careful?

Probably not because the truth was you couldn't always help who you fell in love with, and I'd definitely fallen in love with Nick Peterson.

But that was over, and now it was time to move forward with my life. Indulging in a high carb, high sugar pity party sounded a lot more fun and practical than disrupting my kitchen with a major refurbishing project.

"How about a piece of caramel turtle cheesecake," I said, opening the refrigerator.

"Umm . . . I thought you made that for Nick."

I stared at the empty shelf where I'd placed the cheesecake last night. "Travis?"

"Sorry, Mom. You told me not to eat it because you were making it for Nick."

"Where is it?"

"I gave it to him before he left."

I closed my eyes. "What'd he say?"

Travis shrugged. "Not much. Just 'thanks' and 'it looks good.' I'm sorry, Mom. I didn't realize you wanted to eat it yourself. I thought—"

"It's okay," I said.

Travis's eyes gleamed with mischief. "Does that mean we can bake cookies now?"

I smiled. "Definitely. Let's bake the cutout kind, smother them with frosting, and eat until we get a bellyache."

Travis grinned and gave a thumbs up. "Sounds like a good plan, Mom!"

TWO HOURS LATER, the kitchen was a mess from baking cookies, and I was worried about my parents. I'd called both their cell phones only to hear them ringing in Travis's room. My father must be taking his vacation seriously if he left his phone at home because his job required that he be available day and night.

"Maybe Grams and Pop got lost," Travis offered.

I looked out the window expecting to see my parents walking along the beach toward the cottage. "It's not like them to be gone so long. Should we take our bikes and try to find them?"

Travis agreed, but before we left the house, my cell phone rang. Even though I didn't recognize the number, I picked it up to hear my mother's frightened voice.

"Your father's having chest pains. We're at the hospital right now."

My stomach plunged. "Is he okay?"

"I don't know. He passed out and the doctors won't let me see him."

"We'll be right there."

"Hurry."

"I will, Mom."

Travis and I jumped in the car and raced to the hospital where we found my mother in the chapel, sitting on one of the wooden pews, shredding a tissue. "They just took him back to surgery," she explained.

I hugged her. "He's going to be okay. You know that, right?"

Travis nodded. "That's right. Pop is the toughest. Besides, he has a job to do on Christmas Eve, and he's not going to let those kids down."

Chapter 26

Nick

*A*FTER THE TERRIBLE marriage proposal, I couldn't stay on the island for Christmas. I rationalized my decision to go to Dallas by telling myself it would be better for Hailey.

Fortunately, my father was thrilled we'd be at his house for the holiday. "The decorator hasn't finished the girls' bedrooms yet, but Hailey can at least check on the progress."

"The decorator?" I had asked, somewhat skeptical.

"She's Gina's aunt, but she's wonderful and I've been pleased with her vision so far. It's not that I want you to deploy, son, but when you do, I'll be ready for the girls."

I'd hung up the phone, completely shocked by my father's transformation. Maybe like Paul, people really could change.

Around noon, we reached Dallas, and I pulled into my father's driveway. I glanced again at the cheesecake on the passenger seat beside me, embarrassed by how emotional I felt over a dessert. What had compelled Anna to make me Ivana's cheesecake?

"There's Grandpa Jack," Hailey said, opening the car door.

My father helped Hailey out of the car and gave her a big hug. "I thought you'd never get here. Wait until you see the Christmas tree Gina and I bought. It's so tall, it almost touches the ceiling."

"Have you decorated it yet?" Hailey asked.

Jack shook his head. "No, Gina thought it would be more fun if we waited for you."

Gina, Gina, Gina. Who was this woman capable of changing my grouchy father into a man excited about decorating a Christmas tree? It was like she was the cocktail waitress version of Maria from *The Sound of Music.*

Most of my childhood holidays had been spent skiing in Colorado. Not necessarily a bad thing, but it had meant we'd seldom decorated a tree, hung stockings, or engaged in the conventional Norman Rockwell activities of the season.

"How are you doing, son?" Jack asked.

"I'm fine." I pulled Gabby out of her car seat. "I appreciate you letting us change plans at the last minute."

"No problem."

"Gina didn't mind?"

Jack completely missed the sarcasm in my voice.

"Not at all. You'll finally get to meet her tonight."

"I'm looking forward to it," I said.

Inside the house, we were greeted by the smell of fresh paint and an enormous Christmas tree in the foyer.

Hailey gushed over the tree, then asked if she could see her new room.

"It's the last door on the right," Jack said, gesturing upstairs. "The paint should be dry, but be careful, okay?"

"Okay!" She raced up the stairs and disappeared down the hallway.

Jack noticed Gabby wiggling to get out of my arms. "Come into the family room. Gina helped me buy some toys from her cousin's store."

I'm sure she did. I followed my father into the other room where Gabby squealed when she saw the brightly colored baby toys. I set her on the ground, and she speed crawled across the room.

"I knew she'd like that toy," Jack said triumphantly.

Instead of being pleased by my father's transformation, I resented the fact it'd taken a combination of Ethan's death and the remarkable Gina to make my father care about his granddaughters.

As if reading my mind, he placed a hand on my shoulder. "I know I haven't always been there for you, son. I want you to know that when your mother left me . . . well, it was devastating. It changed me. I'm afraid that in the end, it was you and Ethan who suffered the most. I deeply regret that, and I'm sorry."

I stared in disbelief at this stranger before me. My father never spoke of anything more emotional than the fluctuations in the stock market or the Cowboys' inability to go to the Super Bowl.

"Don't look so shocked," he said with a good-natured laugh. "Gina suggested I go to therapy."

"Let me guess. Her uncle is a therapist."

My father's face hardened. "I know you disapprove of my fiancée, but until you meet her, don't be judgmental. She's a good woman, and believe it or not, a good woman can change everything."

I believed it all right, especially given how much Anna had changed me without even trying. "Okay, so Gina sent you to therapy and—"

"I sent myself," Jack corrected. "She encouraged it, but I made the decision to go. She told me I needed some help dealing with my problems. Until then, I'd always be running. Always be trying to replace your mother with a new woman to prove her leaving hadn't shattered me."

My pulse pounded hard as it always did at the mention of my elusive mother. I'd always wanted to know about her, but my father had forbidden us to talk about her.

"So, you've been paying to talk about your emotional problems with a counselor?" I asked, trying to keep the skepticism out of my voice.

"I have."

My phone rang with a call from a number I didn't recognize.

"Do you need to get that?"

Although half tempted to answer the call in order to escape the intense conversation with my father, I shook my head and let it go to voice mail. "So, has therapy helped?"

His face broke into a genuine smile. "Yes. It's helped tremendously. I was skeptical at first, but I'm glad I did it."

I studied my father carefully, wanting to ask the question Ethan and the nannies always said was best left unanswered. Before I could find the words, however, Hailey raced into the living room.

"Oh, Grandpa! I love my new room. Thank you, thank you, thank you!" She leapt into Jack's arms and squeezed him tight.

My father's eyes grew moist as he gave Hailey a huge hug. "I'm so happy you like it. Wait until your new canopy bed arrives."

Anna

DURING MY FATHER'S surgery, Travis and I prayed with my mom. *He's in your hands, Lord. We know nothing can happen that isn't in your divine will, but please protect my father. Please let him make it.*

Marcus's parents and sisters came to the hospital to pray, offer support, and wait. My mother and I took comfort in Jillian's explanation that the surgery to insert a stent in my father was minor compared to open-heart surgery. Still, I yearned to call Nick and be comforted by his voice. I resisted, however, knowing reaching out to him would only delay the pain of our ultimate breakup.

At one point, Luella made a coffee run. I tried to drink the latte she brought back for me, but I couldn't stomach the bitter taste. I felt nauseous from a combination of worry, too much cookie dough, and heartbreak.

After several hours, the surgeon finally came into the waiting room to announce everything had gone well. My father was expected to make a full recovery. Travis asked if Pop would be able to play Santa on Christmas Eve, but the surgeon shook his head.

I placed a hand on my son's shoulder. "What's important is he'll be able to do it next year."

Luella and Walter took Travis to their house, telling me he could stay for as long as needed. Both my mom and I stayed at the hospital as my father slept off and on all day. In the evening, I convinced my mom to go home, take a shower, and lie down for a few minutes.

As I sat in the chair next to my father's bed, I thanked God for sparing his life. I wasn't ready to let him go, not that I'd been ready to let Marcus go. Still, I was grateful for God's mercy today.

My father's eyes flickered. "I need some water," he said, his voice rough and gravelly.

"Of course." I stood and poured a glass of water from the pitcher on the table beside the bed. Holding his head, I helped him take several sips. "Are you okay, Dad? Can I get you anything?"

He flopped against the pillows and heaved a great sigh. "I'm fine, honey, but ... did I die? Am I in heaven?"

"No." Dread coursed through my veins. Had the anesthesia affected his brain? "You're at the hospital on Rose Island. Don't you remember? Mom just left, but you woke up and talked to her after the surgery. You told her not to worry."

My father captured my hand and gave a mischievous smile. "Calm down. I thought I was in heaven because of this angel at my bedside."

I laughed with relief, and had it not been for the IV in his arm, I would've given him a playful punch. "You're so corny."

He smiled. "How's your mother doing?"

"Good. She ran to the house, but she'll be back soon. She's worried sick about you."

"She worries about me too much."

"Well, why are you giving her something to worry about?"

"Touché." He closed his eyes and rested for a minute. I hated how old and frail he looked. Did the nurses and doctors realize he wasn't some random man off the street? Did they understand he was a highly decorated soldier who could run faster and do more push-ups than most men half his age?

"I need you to do me a favor," he said, his voice wobbly.

"Of course. Anything."

He shifted in the bed uncomfortably. For a man who thrived on physical activity, the hospital stay and recovery would challenge him. "I have something for your mom at the jewelry store on Market Street. It'll be ready Christmas Eve. Will you pick it up for me? Have it gift wrapped so I can give it to her Christmas morning?"

I stared at my father incredulously. "Mom's Christmas gift is the first thing you're worried about after surgery?"

He smiled. "Your mother's put up with a lot. There's nothing more important than making sure she's taken care of on Christmas morning."

I agreed to my father's request, thinking he had to be the most romantic and honorable man in the world.

"Good. Now, all I have to do is find Santa's replacement."

"Don't worry about that, Dad. Just get better, okay?"

"Okay." He closed his eyes for a moment, and I thought he was going back to sleep, but he surprised me by speaking. "I finally met this Captain Nick Peterson my grandson is obsessed with."

I nodded. "Travis told me you spoke to him and the girls this morning."

"We did. What's the status of your relationship with this man?"

I shook my head and gave a sad smile. My father may have been recovering from major surgery, but his army speak was still in place. "My relationship status with this man is classified."

He placed an unsteady hand on his chest. "My daughter, the comedian."

"I care about him," I admitted, "but it's not going to work out. We're too different. We don't want the same things out of life, and he's—"

"He's a soldier like your old man, and you hated being an army brat. You pouted every time we moved and—"

"He's a soldier like Marcus. I was an army wife for almost four years, Dad, remember? I don't want to do that again."

My father winced. "Of course. Forgive me, sweetheart. I wasn't thinking."

I clasped his calloused and knobby hand. "It's okay."

"Marcus was a good boy. Your mother and I think about him every day."

"I do, too." I blinked hard and sighed. "Nick asked me to marry him and move to Germany, but I don't know."

My father's brow lifted. "You don't love him like that?"

I shook my head, wanting to deny my feelings for Nick. Wanting to tell my father I didn't love him at all, but that wasn't true. "After Marcus died, it took me a long time to feel safe. How can I give up life on the island for Nick?"

"You gave up flying for Marcus," my dad said flatly.

"What? That's not true."

"No? After he died, you stopped living your dream."

My father didn't know what he was talking about. "I gave up flying for Travis. I didn't think it was responsible to fly when I had a son to raise."

"No," he said, shaking his head. "Those girls, Halle and Berry—"

"Hailey and Gabby," I corrected.

"Yes, Hailey and Gabby. They lost their parents because of a car accident. Have you stopped driving because it's too dangerous?"

"No."

He scooted up in bed. "Each year, people die in bicycle accidents. You haven't stopped riding your bike, have you?"

"No, but I always wear my helmet."

"I know you do. My point is you stopped flying to punish Marcus . . . or yourself. Either way, you stopped flying, not because of Travis, but because of you.

Whether it was fear or guilt, it doesn't matter. You let Marcus's death define you."

"*His death did define me*! Losing him shook my confidence and changed me." Wounded, I stood and walked across the room to the window. Night had darkened the sky, but moonlight lit the ocean in the distance. "Nick bought me a gift certificate for a helicopter tour. He thought he could fix me with a gift certificate, can you believe that?"

My father huffed. "What kind of monster would try to fix any woman, most of all you?"

I gave a little smile and turned back around to face him. "I was pretty angry."

"I imagine so. Is that why you refused his marriage proposal?"

I shrugged. "No. He's not ready to get married, and neither am I. We've barely spent any time together."

"I married your mom two weeks after we met. When you know, you know."

"But you proposed to Mom on top of the Sears Tower in Chicago with flowers, a diamond, and a prepared speech. Nick's proposal was truly awful. He didn't have a ring, and you always told me a guy wasn't serious unless he had a ring."

"Did I?"

"Yes. Don't you remember?"

"No, I only remember forbidding you to date until you were thirty-five."

We exchanged a smile, and I walked back to the chair beside his bed. "If I'd waited until thirty-five, you wouldn't have Travis."

"True. But look, honey. You're a good pilot. This idea that you have to stay grounded on the island is ridiculous. You need to have faith in yourself and your abilities. And God. If God wants you dead, there isn't anything you can do about it, flying or not flying."

"Well, that's comforting," I said sarcastically.

"It's the truth, and I actually do find it comforting. You can't outrun God. You can't outthink Him or hide from Him. He's in charge of your life whether you want Him to be or not."

I sighed. I knew I couldn't change the fact my husband had died, but I wished I could change how it affected every aspect of my life. I wished I didn't worry so much and could just let go and trust that everything was going to work out for the best. Mostly, I wished I could get back in the helicopter and prove to myself I still had what it took.

"I don't want to upset you further," my father continued, "but I told Travis I'd try to keep you and Nick together. I'm no matchmaker, but here goes. You deserve a good man, and according to Travis, Nick is perfect."

I rolled my eyes. "According to Travis, Nick walks on water."

My father grunted. "I'd think you of all people

would agree that a man who can walk on water isn't a bad thing."

I grinned and studied my father closely. "Dad, tell me the truth. Did you run a background check on Nick?"

Surprise, then resolve, flashed across his face. "Did you?"

"Of course, but my access isn't as detailed as yours."

He gave a curt nod. "Then you know you can trust me when I say Nick Peterson is a good man. Whether or not you want to marry him and create a life as a military family is a whole other issue. But all my sources, including the look on my daughter's face, tell me Nick is one of the good guys."

Chapter 27

Nick

IN THE EVENING, Gina arrived to decorate the tree and eat dinner. I instantly liked her and regretted any bad thoughts I'd had about her. She was young—only a few years older than me—but she was nothing like my father's previous girlfriends or wives. I could see she really cared about him, and he cared for her in a way I hadn't seen before.

Gina offered to put the girls to bed, and Hailey willingly accepted.

Feeling a little lost, I wandered downstairs where I found my father sitting on the couch in the study. "Do you mind if I join you?" I asked, hesitating at the door.

He beckoned me forward, and that's when I saw the old photo box on his lap. I'd been about Hailey's age when I'd found the box in my father's closet while playing hide-and-seek with Ethan and one of our nannies.

The pictures of my mother had mesmerized me so

much that I hadn't heard my father enter the room. Jack had strictly forbidden us from playing in the master bedroom, but I was tired of being *it*, so I'd broken the rule to hide in my father's closet.

"You're not supposed to be in here," he'd said.

I'd apologized and tried not to be afraid as my father silently took the box and placed it in the nightstand. I thought he'd be angry, but he was calm as he spoke. "She's no longer part of our lives. Do you understand that, son?"

He'd stared at me for a long time with something that resembled compassion. I was confused by the emotion and wondered what my punishment would be. Instead, he'd given me an uncharacteristic wink. "If you look behind the laundry room door, I think you'll find your brother."

"Yes, sir." I ran out of the room, pleased and shocked by my father's help. Later, when I returned to look at the pictures, the box was gone. I'd spent weeks searching for it but had never seen it again until this moment.

"Do you remember?" My father gestured toward the box, bringing me back to the present.

I nodded. "I thought you threw it away."

"No. I hid it from you because I convinced myself it was best if you didn't know about your mother."

My pulse raced. "Why'd she leave, sir? You never told me, and I always wanted to know."

He looked at one of the photographs and took several deep breaths. "I was dirt poor when she married me. I want to believe she loved me, but I suspect she simply needed a father for Ethan."

My stomach dropped. "What?"

He nodded. "I never wanted anyone to know, but it's true. Ethan wasn't mine. Not biologically, anyway. I thought I could change your mother. Tame her. We married the day Ethan turned one, and you were born a year later. I honestly thought we were happy."

He leafed through several photos before continuing. "I never guessed she was seeing someone else until the day she left. I told her she could leave me, but she wasn't taking you or your brother. I threatened to take her to court and prove her an unfit mother if she tried."

"But why?" I asked. "Why did you want us?"

He put the lid back on the box. "I thought she'd come back for you."

My gut churned to learn my father had kept Ethan and me for revenge. We'd been unwanted by our mother and simply used by our father.

"I loved you and your brother," he said, as if reading my thoughts. "I know it didn't always seem like it, but I did. I just wasn't prepared to be the kind of father you needed. And, according to the therapist, I was obsessed with getting your mother back."

"But she left you," I stated, my voice angry. I hated how the wound of abandonment was still raw after all these years. "She left us."

He gave a resigned nod. "It wasn't your fault. I want you to know that she didn't leave because of anything you and Ethan did or didn't do. Something was wrong with her. Something is still wrong with her. You can tell when she's on TV. Her eyes are shifty, and she does this thing with her mouth that you used to do."

My heart thudded. "Dad, who are you talking about?"

He locked eyes with me and took a deep breath. "Mary Williams. The governor's wife. That's your mom, son."

"What?"

"It's true."

I allowed the implication of that to wash over me. I couldn't believe it.

"I did the best I could with you and your brother," Jack said, his eyes pleading with me for understanding and forgiveness. "I want you to know that I deeply cared about you two. But I admit, I wanted revenge. I wanted to work so hard and be so rich she'd regret leaving us. I dated and married those women to make her jealous. It wasn't fair to them, nor to you boys. And for that, I'm truly sorry."

Something inside me broke. I'd wondered about my mother my whole life. Wondered if I'd done something wrong. Now, I knew.

"I just hope," Jack continued, his breath ragged, "I

hope you can find a way to forgive me."

Anna

ON CHRISTMAS EVE morning, Travis and I rode our bikes downtown to collect the present my father had ordered from the jewelry store. While the clerk gift wrapped the beautiful bracelet, Travis pointed to a gold necklace with an inscription written in cursive lettering. "What's that say?" he asked. "I can't read that fancy writing."

"It says, 'Take a chance.'"

He pushed up his glasses. "Take a chance? On what? Gambling?"

Both the clerk and I smiled.

"I think it means take a chance on life," I explained. "On love. On happiness. On following your dreams."

"Oh," he said, unimpressed.

The jeweler handed me the gift and nodded at the necklace. "I just received it from a local artist. What do you think?"

I didn't know what to think. Was this some sort of sign I was supposed to take a chance, throw caution to the wind, and jump in a helicopter to chase after Nick? "It's lovely," I said. "I'm sure you'll sell it right away."

Afterward, Travis and I walked over to the clothing store to buy him dress pants and a button-down shirt with a clip-on tie for church tonight. He came out of the dressing room, tugging at the long pants. "I miss my shorts. These clothes itch and make me feel like I'm in a straightjacket."

"I know you'd rather wear shorts, but it's supposed to be cold tonight. Plus, don't you want to dress up for Christmas?"

He shook his head. "No, not really."

Before going home, we stopped at Vicki's Bakery for coffee and ran into Jillian and her boys. "How's your father?" Drew asked.

"Better," I replied, touched by my nephew's considerate question. I'd always had a soft spot for Jillian's kindhearted youngest son. "My dad is anxious to get out of the hospital, but he has to stay a little longer."

"What about Santa?" Matt asked.

"*Matt,*" Jillian warned, giving her fifteen-year-old a pointed glance before motioning to Travis.

Travis swung the shopping bag in his hand. "It's okay, Aunt Jillian. I know Pop is Santa."

Realizing his mistake, Matt tried to rectify it by acting shocked anyone would insinuate the Santa who stopped by church on Christmas Eve was not the *real* Santa. "What? How can you say that?"

Travis groaned. "Stop messing around, Matt. I'm almost eleven, you know."

I smiled. "Hopefully, someone else will step up and play the role of Santa this evening, but it won't be my dad."

Jillian squeezed my arm. "I'm headed out to Mom and Dad's right now. Why don't I take Travis with me, and we'll meet you at church this evening?"

"Can I go, Mom? Please?" Travis asked.

I hesitated. "I wanted to give you a haircut."

"I'll get Bianca to do it," Jillian said. "She's going to cut Matt and Drew's hair, so I'm sure she won't mind. That would give you a break or a chance to visit your dad."

The word *chance* knocked around my head, and I thought about the *Take a Chance* necklace from the jewelry store. "Actually, there is something I'd like to do, so if you don't mind taking Travis, that would be wonderful."

"What do you have to do?" Travis asked. "Buy a present for me?"

I winked at him. "Something like that."

Nick

I SLEPT IN Christmas Eve morning because I'd stayed up late, looking through the pictures of my mother. I knew from my birth certificate her maiden name was Mary Smith, a name so common there were over thirty-seven thousand in the United States. My father explained she'd simply taken on the history of another Mary Smith.

She hadn't needed to change her name, only the story that she'd never been married nor had given birth to two little boys.

I didn't know what to do with this new information. I couldn't exactly drive down to the governor's mansion in Austin and say, "Hey, Mom. It's Nick, the kid you abandoned. How've you been?"

If only I could talk to Anna. But now wasn't the time. Maybe later, after we'd both healed from our breakup. Yet, I didn't want to break up with her. I loved her. Truly loved her. I'd just messed things up.

While shaving, I remembered the call from the unfamiliar number on Rose Island. I turned up the volume and tapped the message to listen.

"Nick, this is Luella Morgan. Anna's father had a heart attack and is in surgery right now. I know how close the two of you've become . . .

"I know I haven't been very encouraging of your relationship with her, and I'm sorry. She loves you. I think she's scared to tell you how she feels, but if you care about her, please don't give up."

My pulse raced. I wiped my face with a towel and immediately called the Rose Island hospital, hoping to learn that Anna's father had made it through surgery.

Why hadn't I checked my messages last night? Should I just call Anna directly? What if the news wasn't good, would she want to talk to me?

A woman at the hospital answered, and I explained the situation.

"One moment," she said.

I held my breath, never expecting to be connected directly to Anna's father's room.

"This is Tom Chamberlain," Anna's father said in a rough voice.

I hesitated. Even though, technically, I was Tom's superior officer, I felt nervous and unsure of myself. "This is Nick Peterson. I just heard about your surgery. How are you doing?"

Tom's voice was strong. "I'm fine, sir, but what's this about you asking my daughter to marry you without a ring or speaking to me first?"

Chapter 28

Anna

WITH TREMBLING HANDS, I drove out to the airfield, knowing if I didn't go now, I might never do it. My heart pounded, but instead of feeling afraid, I felt empowered. Enough of this anxiety. Enough of focusing on the worst-case scenario. Today, I was going to fly.

I passed through the airport entrance and headed to the last hangar where Patricia ran the flight academy. My hands shook as I parked the car and marched to the office, only to find the door locked. Was everyone already gone for the holidays? Would I have to wait until after Christmas to conquer my fear of flying?

Slowly, my pulse returned to normal as it sank in that today would not be the day I flew. Nevertheless, I walked around the side of the hangar and stared at the R-44. As though pulled by an invisible cord, I moved toward the aircraft. How many times in the past had I made this journey?

Reaching the helicopter, I ran my hand over the metal, down to the cowl door. Muscle memory kicked in, and I opened the door to begin my pre-flight safety inspection.

"It's been a long time," said Patricia, walking toward me.

I smiled at the older woman. "Hey."

"Hey, yourself. Do you have your voucher?"

"No," I said, surprised and a little bit guilty. "I ran it through the shredder."

Patricia threw her head back and laughed. "I told that man you wouldn't appreciate a gift certificate. I told him to buy you a sweater or perfume, but he was adamant, so he left me no choice but to take his money."

"Serves him right."

"No kidding," she said. "But you don't need a voucher to fly with me. I'll just charge you for gas. You know that."

"Thanks. Do you think I can still do it?"

"It's like riding a bike, honey. I'll be with you every step of the way."

I looked from Patricia to the helicopter. "You'll take over if I can't do it?"

"Yes, but that's not going to happen."

I nodded and continued the preflight. Climbing into the pilot's seat, I put on the safety belt and headset. I ran my hands over the instruments, amazed it felt like yesterday instead of seven years since I'd last sat here.

You can do this. Trust in yourself and your skills. Know that I am with you.

"Let's fly over your in-laws' ranch and out to Camp Windham," Patricia suggested.

"Sounds good." The summer camp was located about ten minutes away and abutted a large practice field the flight academy often used. Marcus and his sisters had all gone to the summer camp as little kids and worked there during high school.

Turning on the master switch, I exhaled deeply and reminded myself I'd done this plenty of times. I took my time running the system checks and cleared the area. Then it was show time.

Taking a deep breath, I gently lifted the aircraft into a hover, holding it there longer than necessary. A jolt of excitement rushed through me, and I beamed with pride. Pilots compared the skill of hovering to balancing a marble on top of a beach ball, but I'd never had any trouble.

"Okay, hot shot, you've proved your point," Patricia growled. "Let's see what else you remember."

I grinned and pushed forward on the cyclic to gain speed. When the machine reached forty-five knots, I pulled back slightly, allowing the helicopter to climb and accelerate.

I followed the river out to the camp, amazed by the spectacular view. To my relief, flying really was like riding a bicycle, and I had no problem keeping my altitude and speed. I'd missed the adventurous woman I used to be and regretted all the years I'd stayed on the ground.

Below, I saw the white caps of the ocean, green fields, deer, and a pair of roseate spoonbills. I thought of Nick and wondered what he would say if he could see me now.

Walter and Luella's homestead came into view as well as Jillian's car in the driveway. I waved as I flew over the ranch and continued past the summer camp until we reached the helipad. A hint of fear rushed through me as I thought about landing, but I pushed the anxiety away, determined to be brave even if I didn't feel like it.

"You've got this," Patricia said. "Keep it into the wind, and you'll be fine."

I aligned the helicopter with the pad and reduced the power by slowly lowering the collective. I pulled back on the cyclic to descend, maintaining the heading with the pedals.

Wind from the blades scattered rocks and dirt surrounding the helipad. The tall grass swayed like waves in the ocean. When the skids hit the ground, I let out the breath I'd been holding as a rush of exhilaration washed over me.

I'd been so mad that Nick had tried to fix me with that stupid gift certificate, but getting back in the helicopter was exactly what I'd needed. Regret sank in as I realized he'd been right about flying again. I simply had to try, despite my fear.

What was I supposed to do now? I couldn't call him back and accept his half-hearted marriage proposal. If he'd been serious, he would've proposed properly. He would've knelt down on one knee, confessed his undying love, and offered me a ring.

But he hadn't, and telling him no was the right thing to do.

Still, I couldn't let this moment pass without sharing it with him. Pulling out my phone, I stared at it, wondering what to say.

"Texting lover boy?" Patricia asked.

I smiled. "Maybe."

"I remember you always called Marcus after you landed safely."

Sadness filled me, but it didn't hurt as much. Even though I would never forget my husband, it was time to move on. Time to kick fear to the curb and take a chance.

Smiling, I fired off a quick text to Nick. "I'm in a helicopter right now. I just flew, and it felt amazing."

His reply came immediately. "Texting while flying is not safe!"

I laughed. "We're on the ground."

"Good. Proud of you."

I waited for more, and when he didn't text back, I

returned the phone to my pocket. *If we're supposed to be together, Lord, I know you'll make it happen. Otherwise, I'll have faith that this is how things are supposed to be for us right now.*

BEFORE WALKING INTO church, I checked my phone messages. Still nothing from Nick. Resisting the urge to text him a *Merry Christmas*, I turned off my phone and stuck it in my purse.

I'd flown today, and if that was all that came out of my relationship with him, I was going to be okay.

"Do you think Santa will show up this year?" Travis asked with a wink.

I smiled. "When I talked to Grams this afternoon, she said the church found a replacement."

"Who is it?"

"I don't know," I answered honestly. "She wouldn't tell me. Maybe it's the real Santa."

Travis laughed. "Good one, Mom."

We entered the church, decorated with green garland and sparkly gold stars. A tall Christmas tree lit with thousands of soft yellow lights stood near the altar.

Travis and I took our usual seats in the front pew with the rest of the Morgan family. Luella gave me a big hug and wished me Merry Christmas.

Across the aisle sat the Woodalls with their new son Colton and a baby girl about the same age as Gabby.

"It's Christmas Eve!" Colton said in a voice loud enough for the entire congregation to hear.

Carrie smiled at her newly adopted son and gently explained he needed to be quiet in church. But nobody minded. The entire assembly buzzed with anticipation only Scrooge could disapprove of.

The service began with the hymn, "O Come All Ye Faithful." As I sang, I became very emotional, missing Nick, the girls, Marcus, and my parents. My mother had opted to stay at the hospital with my father, and even though I had the Morgan family beside me, it didn't seem like Christmas without my own parents.

As for Marcus, I would always miss him, but I was willing to trust that God had a plan.

I had no idea what would happen between Nick and me. He'd returned my text this afternoon, but he'd been silent since then. Maybe our relationship was over.

Or maybe having an entire ocean between us would provide the time and distance we needed to grow our friendship. And maybe in the end, our friendship would develop into something more.

I loved Nick, and I loved those girls. I already missed them and I didn't want to lose them, but like I'd told Nick after his impromptu proposal, losing someone wasn't a reason to get married.

Wanting to make a lifelong commitment was, and that's what I wanted. That's what I was ready for, but until he was ready, I'd have to wait. I'd have to live without him and embrace the life God had given me. I'd go back to flying. Back to living my dream.

And through it all, I wouldn't be afraid. I'd hold my head high and have the courage to overcome my fears and anxiety.

Taking hold of Travis's hand, I gave it a firm squeeze.

"Ouch, Mom," he hissed.

"Sorry. I just wanted you to know I love you."

He rolled his eyes. "I know that already, so you don't have to break off my hand."

"Do you love me?"

He gave my hand a fierce squeeze. "How's that for an answer?"

I smiled, my heart bursting with love for this kid I hadn't planned. He'd been such a joy, especially during the worst time of my life.

Glancing down the pew, I took in the Morgan family. My family. The family that had loved and supported me all these years. I was so fortunate to have them in my life.

The service was beautiful, and right before the last hymn, the pastor asked the congregation to remain seated for a special announcement. "As you know, we're fortunate to have an important visitor every Christmas Eve."

"Santa!" Colton shouted, jumping up and down. "It's Santa!"

The pastor smiled "That's right. I can see someone has been paying attention. This very special visitor asked us all to pray for Tom Chamberlain, who's in the hospital tonight, but God-willing, will go home soon."

I smiled, confident my dad would make a full recovery. The pastor continued. "We all know Santa is very busy tonight. In fact, this is his busiest night of the entire year. But despite his hectic schedule, he still made time to come to church, and I'd like to give him a blessing. Would that be okay?"

All the children, even Travis, shouted a resounding yes. A wave of excitement swept through the congregation, and heads turned to watch Santa make his way down the aisle.

I was almost thirty-years-old, but every year I became swept up in the magic of this moment, and tonight was no exception.

"It's Santa!" Colton said, bursting with elation. "It's really him!"

"That's right," the pastor said. "Santa has come to church on this most holy night because he understands that being busy is no excuse to stay away from God."

As Santa came closer, I became highly aware of my pulse.

Something about the way he carried himself seemed familiar. When I saw those beautiful, mesmerizing gray-blue eyes, I had no doubt as to his identity.

Chapter 29

*V*ICKI LEANED OVER and whispered, "Good-looking Santa."

"It's Nick," I said, my voice squeaking.

"Really?"

I nodded. What was Nick doing here at the church playing Santa? Had my father coerced him into coming back? Or had Nick returned on his own?

And more importantly, was he here only to play Santa, or had he come back for another reason as well?

When Nick reached the front of the church, the pastor placed a hand on his head.

Heavenly Father, we ask you to bless this man and his endeavors. Help him to always seek your guidance and rely on your benevolence to do Your Will. Protect him tonight and give him the strength to accomplish his mission. Amen.

"Amen!" Colton shouted, causing the gentle sound of laughter to echo through the church.

"Okay," the pastor continued, "we can't keep Santa any longer. As you know, he has a lot of work ahead of him tonight, so let's all stay in our seats and sing our closing hymn as he leaves."

Colton Woodall rebelled by flying out of his pew and flinging himself at Santa. Nick embraced the child, then bent down and whispered something in his ear.

"Yes, sir," Colton said, running back to his mother.

Nick turned to leave, but before he did, he looked directly at me and winked. My heart leapt out of my chest, and it took every ounce of self-control not to follow Colton's example by throwing myself at Nick.

The music began, and as the congregation sang "Joy to the World," I had visions of grabbing Colton's hand and sprinting through the church to find Santa.

When the song finally ended, Vicki squeezed my arm. "Don't trample any little kids, okay?"

I smiled and pulled free. I had to reach Nick. Had to find him before . . . before what? Before he hopped on his sleigh and flew off into the night?

I laughed at myself but kept my head low and focused on getting to Nick. Several people stopped me to ask about my father. I smiled and quickly addressed their concerns while continuing to move up the aisle, hoping I didn't appear rude.

"Anna." Dr. Mitch Norman smiled as he stepped from one of the back pews to stand before me. "Merry Christmas. Let me introduce you to my mother."

My stomach clenched, but I forced a smile and exchanged pleasantries with the dentist's mom. Like her son, Rita Norman was also a dentist with impeccably straight, white teeth and a friendly personality.

My mind raced for a way to politely excuse myself from the conversation, but before I could figure out what to say, Mitch leaned forward, gripped my arm, and winked. "We don't want to hold you up. I know you're anxious to talk to Santa."

"To Santa?"

He nodded. "I met your mother and him in the jewelry shop this afternoon."

My heart jumped. "What do you mean?"

He grinned. "It's okay. Nick Peterson is a lucky man, but if you ever change your mind or find yourself looking for someone to take you golfing . . ."

Both stunned and confused, I thanked Mitch for being so understanding. I said good-bye to his mother and hustled out of the sanctuary. Frantically, I scanned the crowded narthex, but Nick was nowhere in sight. Had he already left?

"Mom, there's Hailey and her Grandpa Jack!" Travis shouted, pointing outside.

I hadn't realized Travis had caught up with me, but I followed his gaze. On the church steps outside stood Hailey, Grandpa Jack, and a young woman holding Gabby.

I dashed through the doors toward them. Gabby gave a squeal of delight and hurled herself into my arms.

"What are you doing here?" I asked.

"Grandpa's watching us while Nick does an important job," Hailey explained. "This is Gina. My new grandma."

I gave Hailey a hug and said hello to Jack and Gina. "I thought you were spending Christmas in Dallas."

Hailey smiled. "We came back."

"I'm glad you did."

"Are you?" asked a deep voice behind me.

I spun around to see Nick. He wore a blue button-down shirt open at the collar, and his gaze was so intense, it reminded me of the first time we met. Exhilaration swept through me. "*Nick*. What are you doing here?"

He removed a small, velvet jewelry box, just the right size for an engagement ring. "I wanted to give you this Christmas present to make up for the horrible gift certificate I gave you."

I stared down at the box. Did it contain a ring? And if it did, was this his idea of a proper proposal?

I was torn between being elated that perhaps he'd bought me a ring and frustrated he'd shoved it at me without any preamble.

"Open it," Hailey urged.

"Here, I'll take the baby." Nick's father reached for Gabby. "The kids and I will go introduce Gina to the Morgan clan."

"But I want to see Miss Anna open her gift," Hailey protested.

Travis gave an enthusiastic nod. "Yeah, me, too!"

"She'll show it to you later," Jack said, leading the

way back inside the church.

Gina and Travis followed, but Hailey stood rooted in place. Nick squatted so he was eye level with his niece. "Let me talk to Miss Anna alone for a minute, okay? Then you can see her gift."

Hailey jumped into his arms. "Okay, but I'm coming back."

"Of course." Nick set her on the ground, and she left with the others.

Taking my hand, he led me down the church steps, away from all the commotion. Although the air was crisp, his strong hand in mine and the anticipation racing through my body warmed me.

Underneath an oak tree on the sidewalk, he gestured toward the box in my hands. "Okay, open it."

I gripped the box tightly before handing it back to him. "You don't have to do this. Not now. We can wait."

He grinned. "Your parents said you were stubborn. Just open it, okay?"

"I can't believe you spoke to my parents."

"I was in your father's hospital room when you texted about flying. Your parents are so proud of you. And so am I."

A wonderful tingly feeling zoomed through me. I'd flown the helicopter for myself, but having the support of my parents and Nick meant the world to me. "How did you know about my dad?"

"Luella called me."

"She did?"

He nodded. "She told me you loved me. That was one of the things your father and I discussed this afternoon."

"One of the things?"

He chuckled. "Well, he wanted me to play Santa, and I wanted to ask his opinion on what's in the box."

"What is in the box?"

He laughed and shook his head. "Open it, you stubborn woman."

I stared down at the box, afraid of what it contained. I'd vowed to no longer be afraid, but at that moment, I was scared out of my mind. "Before I open this, I have to tell you something."

"Okay."

My throat throbbed, and I swallowed hard. "I've been a fool. I've held back from flying and living my life and loving you because of fear. I thought living a full life would be a dishonor to Marcus, and I was afraid of letting him go. I loved my husband, Nick. I really loved him."

"I know you did. And I know you still do."

"I'll always love him. But you've come into my life, and . . . I'm in love with you, Nick. I never meant to fall in love with you, and I don't want you to go, but I want what's best for you, even if that doesn't include me." My voice broke and I blinked back tears. This was so hard.

Nick remained silent, patiently waiting for me to finish. Suddenly, I was afraid. Maybe the contents of the box had nothing to do with love and commitment. Maybe he'd simply found an empty box and had stuffed it with jelly beans.

"Open it," he said.

Terrified, I lifted the lid. Inside, I found not an engagement ring but a neatly folded piece of paper. Confusion and disappointment swept over me. "What is this? Another gift certificate?"

He smiled and shook his head. "Such a cynic. Just read it."

I slipped the velvet box into my coat pocket and unfolded the piece of paper to discover it was a formal letter dated three years in the future.

Dear Commander,

I, Nicholas Peterson, Captain, Infantry, hereby tender my resignation as an officer of the Army.

I stopped reading. "Nick, what is this?"

He stepped closer and pointed to the date. "I have to finish my obligation, but as soon as my time is up, I'll resign my commission. I'll go anywhere you want to go. If you want to come back to the island and raise our family, I will."

"*Our family?*"

He nodded. "I want to marry you, Anna. Not because I'm afraid of losing you, but because I love you more than anything in the world. I want to build a life with you, have more children with you. I want to do everything in my power to give you the life and love you deserve."

I blinked back tears and stared down at the note. "But what about your career?"

He shook his head and placed both hands on my shoulders. "We'll figure it out together. I love you. And just so there's no mistake . . ."

He pulled a diamond engagement ring from his pocket and knelt to the ground. "Anna Morgan, there is nothing more I want in this world than to be your husband. Would you do me the honor of marrying me?"

Tears flowed freely down my face. I swiped at them and somehow managed to speak. Deliberately, I folded the letter and gave it back to him.

His face dropped, but he took the note and came to his feet. "Anna . . . I—"

I squeezed his hand. "I love you for who you are, Nick. I don't need you to change for me. When the time comes, we'll make the decision about your career based on what's best for our family."

"Does this mean—"

"Yes, Nick. Yes, I'll marry you."

He gave a shout of joy and pulled me against his chest. I lifted my face, and when his lips met mine, fire consumed me. Why had I ever been afraid of this man?

Why had I ever pushed him away?

"Did she say yes?" Hailey called from the church steps.

I turned around to see not just Hailey, but Nick's father, Gina, Gabby, Travis, Walter, Luella, Jillian, Matt, Drew, Bianca, and Vicki waiting with eager anticipation. Bianca held up an iPad, showing my parents waving from the hospital room.

"Have you given him your answer?" my mother asked.

I smiled at everyone and turned toward Nick. "Yes. I said without a doubt, yes!"

The crowd burst into cheers and loud applause as Nick took me in his arms and kissed me.

THE END

Thank you so much for reading *Anna's Courage, Rose Island Book #1*! I hope you enjoyed it. If you did...

1. Help others discover my books by leaving a review on Goodreads or wherever you purchased this book. The review doesn't have to be long. Just one or two sentences giving your honest opinion would really help me out.

2. Sign up for my New Books Newsletter on my website to be notified when my next book is available. I promise never to spam you, and you can unsubscribe anytime.

3. Come like my Facebook page. This is where I'm most active on social media. You can also email me directly at Kristin@KristinNoel.com.

Thank you so much for your support! I really appreciate it! Being a writer is a dream come true for me, and I couldn't do it without my readers, so thank you!

Turn the page for a sneak peak at Jillian's Promise, Rose Island Book #2, available now!

Jillian's Promise

Rose Island Book #2

By Kristin Noel Fischer

Chapter 1

Keith

Seven years ago

BEFORE I DEPLOYED to Iraq for the third time, my wife and I threw a barbecue for our friends and family on Rose Island. The evening was perfect as I manned the grill and watched the kids race through the sprinklers, laughing.

Despite the fact our rental house didn't have a view of the ocean, my wife Jillian loved our tree-lined street and close proximity to the boys' school and the assisted living facility where she worked as a nurse. Her parents owned a small hobby ranch a short, ten-minute drive up the mountain, and both her sisters lived within walking distance.

In other words, Jillian couldn't have been happier when I received orders to return to Fort Xavier on the island where she'd grown up. Finding out I was immediately deploying hadn't pleased her, but at least this time she'd be close to family.

Taking a sip of my Dr. Pepper, I flipped the burgers and admired my wife working the crowd. The fading sun shone on her long, honey-brown hair as she offered our guests drinks, appetizers, and encouragement. When she looked up and smiled at me, I knew I was the luckiest man in the world.

After ten years of marriage, two healthy kids, several deployments, and five moves, I could honestly say I loved Jillian and our life together more today than the day we married.

Later that evening, after the barbecue ended and the boys were tucked into bed, I found Jillian in the kitchen washing dishes. Walking up behind her, I wrapped my arms around her waist and held her tight. "Come on, baby, let's go to bed."

She leaned against me, and I inhaled her sweet scent of vanilla and strawberries. Sweeping back her hair, I trailed kisses down her neck. Without warning, her shoulders began to shake, followed by tears streaming down her face. She thrust a hand to her mouth to stifle a cry, but it managed to escape.

My stomach dropped. "Jills, what's wrong?"

She swiped at her eyes. "I don't want you to go."

"Oh, baby." I pulled her close, rocking her against me. She was such a strong, independent woman that her vulnerability caught me off guard. "This is just a short trip. I'll be back before you know it."

"You're going to be gone six months," she protested. "You'll miss Matty's birthday and Drew's first baseball game."

"I know." Guilt swept through me as if I'd been personally responsible for my orders. Most deployments these days were eighteen months, so relatively speaking, this mission was short. Still, being separated was never easy.

I turned her in my arms so I could see her face. "I love you, Jills."

She smiled sadly. "I know you do, and I love you, too. I'm proud of what you do, but it's really hard sometimes."

I cupped her face with my hands. "When I return, I'll take you anywhere you want to go. Just you and me. Or we can bring the boys if you want. We'll get away, spend a ton of money, and just be together."

She swallowed and shook her head. "I just want you here on the island with me."

"Okay. Whatever you want."

My words calmed her, and she rubbed a hand over my whiskers. "What about Marcus? Is he going to be okay?"

Jillian's younger brother, Marcus, was deploying with my unit for the first time in his army career. Tonight, I'd promised his wife, Anna, that I'd keep him safe. Making a promise like that wasn't the smartest thing to do, but I'd wanted to ease Anna's fears. I wanted to give her the strength to be strong so she could take care of their son as she waited for her husband's return.

Of course, I couldn't make that same vow of Marcus's safety to Jillian. As a long-time army wife, she knew there were no guarantees in the military.

"Jills." I brushed my thumb across her bottom lip. "Your brother has a family who loves and prays for him. He's smart and has been well trained. He's prepared for this."

"I know." The sadness in her eyes grew so deep I couldn't stand it.

Clueless as to what else to do, I drew her toward me and kissed her. Although she returned my kiss, I sensed her hesitation. She pulled away and looked at me intensely.

"What?" I asked.

Looking down, she placed a hand on her flat belly. "I wasn't going to say anything, but I'm pregnant."

"Seriously?" A mixture of confusion, joy, and fear filled me. We'd always wanted more children, but Jillian had suffered several miscarriages, and she'd struggled with both boys' pregnancies. The idea of another child—completely unplanned and unexpected— shocked me.

"I haven't been to the doctor yet, but I took a test this morning and it was positive."

My throat tightened, and I covered her stomach with my hands, wanting to protect both her and our unborn child. I started to speak, but my voice caught and I swallowed hard.

Jillian smiled. "I thought I was just late and gaining weight from stress, but I guess not."

"I'm speechless."

"Just be happy."

I pulled her into my arms. "I am happy. Thrilled. But I won't be here to help you. I'm going to miss your entire pregnancy—the first time he kicks, your sonogram—"

"How do you know it's a boy?" she teased.

My chest clenched. We both longed for a daughter. "If you find out it's a girl on the sonogram, and I'm not here—"

She placed her fingertips on my mouth to silence me. "It'll be okay. You'll be home in time for the birth, right?"

Suddenly, the months stretched out like miles before me. What initially seemed like a short mission, felt interminable. "When I return, Matty and Drew will be done with baseball season and you'll be as big as a house."

Her eyes gleamed with mischief. "So, Captain Foster, you better take advantage of me now before I get all fat and grumpy."

Laughing, I scooped her up and carried her down

the hall to our bedroom. "I'll love you forever, Jills."

She wrapped her arms around my neck. "I'm counting on it."

THE MOOD WAS somber as we passed through security and drove onto post the day of deployment. Jillian amazed me by looking past her own fears, sadness, and morning sickness to comfort everyone else.

I was eager to say my good-byes and begin the deployment. The sooner we left, the sooner we could return.

I hugged Jillian's parents and her sisters. Then, I faced my mom, who'd struggled with some health issues this past year. Tears filled her eyes as she pressed a hand to my cheek. "Be safe, Son. I'll pray for you every day."

"I'll pray for you, too, Mom."

I turned to my oldest son, seven-year-old Matty. "You're the man of the house while I'm gone. Take care of your mom and little brother."

"Yes, sir," Matty said, always eager to please.

My youngest son Drew jutted out his chin. "I don't want Matty in charge of me."

I knelt so we were eye level. "Will you take care of Bella while I'm gone?" I asked, referring to our yellow Lab. "Will you walk her, feed her, and make sure she doesn't forget all the tricks I taught her?"

Drew's eyes brightened and he jumped into my

arms, wrapping all four limbs around me like the baby orangutan at the zoo. "Yes, sir, Daddy!"

We were called to order, so I pried Drew off me and stood to face Jillian. "I forgot to tell you the lawnmower is almost out of oil. There's a new container on the workbench, but—"

"Just come home to me. And take care of my brother. Make sure he doesn't do anything stupid, okay?"

"Hey, I heard that," Marcus said, nudging Jillian's shoulder.

She nudged him back and gave him one last hug. Then, she focused her attention on me as if we were the only two people in the world. "Just promise me you'll be safe, Keith."

"You got it, babe." The crack in my voice betrayed my true feelings, but I forced a smile and turned my focus to the job at hand.

Marcus and I boarded the plane with the other soldiers. Once our flight was in the air, I did what I always did—I looked one last time at my family picture before tucking it away and shutting the door on my domestic life.

With those first deployments, I'd made the mistake of thinking about my family too much. Now, I believed it was best to focus on work and avoid obsessing about home.

I'd encouraged Jillian to do the same by engaging in her own life during our separation. I purposely limited our letters and phone calls, knowing sometimes communication made things more difficult. Not all military families handled deployment this way, but it worked for us.

Looking out the airplane window, I prayed for Jillian, the pregnancy, my mother's health, my children's safety, and the success of our mission.

Watch out for Marcus, Lord. Send your army of angels to protect that kid, his wife, and their little boy, Travis. Use me for your will and return me home safely.

I'd had very little rest over the past month, and overcome by exhaustion, I leaned my head back and fell asleep.

Almost immediately, a searing pain ripped through my body, jerking me awake. I looked down at my leg, certain it was on fire, but I couldn't see anything due to the blinding lights around me. *What in the world?*

"Hold still, Mr. Foster," said a woman with a thick Slavic accent.

I stared at her, disturbed by the fact we didn't have anybody in our unit who spoke like that. "Who are you, and what's going on?"

She didn't answer me right away, but as my eyes adjusted to the light, I realized I was lying in a hospital bed. The room was filled with machines and medical staff. Someone spoke of the bullet they'd removed from my leg.

I'd been shot? Where? How?

Get Jillian's Promise, Rose Island Book #2 now!

CPSIA information can be obtained
at www.ICGtesting.com
Printed in the USA
LVHW111628170519
618255LV00001B/171/P